THE LOST SISTER

A DETECTIVE ARLA BAKER MYSTERY
ARLA BAKER SERIES 1

M.L ROSE

CHAPTER 1

February 1997

Nicole ran. She didn't know where she was going. It didn't matter. Breath rasped inside her chest, air clawing out of her lungs in painful gasps.

The thick grass rose to her knees, and she splashed into a frozen puddle. She muffled her shriek and clambered out, her shoes now blocks of ice. Her tights were soaked up to her knees.

Fear burned inside her, making her legs move as fast as she could. The pain in her abdomen was like a spear, lancing into her hips. She muted her scream and bit her lips. Hot, saline drops forced their way out of her eyes. Her hands flew down to her abdomen, holding it, feeling it move. Her breath came in desperate gasps. She felt blood, warm and thick trickling down her thighs. Tall plants brushed against her legs. But she didn't stop running.

The moon slipped out from between clouds, a useless, deep yellow sickle. She saw little and heard nothing but the panting from her lips.

Lights. In the distance, like fireflies dancing in the dark. Anywhere was better than the hell she had just left. A sob escaped her lips as she felt something twist inside her abdomen. The pain was now unbearable, almost forcing her to stop.

A voice. Behind her, shouting her name. She stopped for a second, fetid air hot around her lips. She recognised the voice, and a cold slither of panic ran down her spine. If he caught up with her, she was as good as dead.

Nicole shuddered, and ran faster. When she got closer to the lights, she realised it was a church. There was no one outside, only the lights glimmered faintly in the dark. She kept moving somehow. She got closer to the fence separating the grass from the church and collapsed against it.

She heard the voice again, and saw a shape moving out from the darkness. Panic bulged inside her heart. She gripped her heavy abdomen, and heaved herself up, leaning against the fence. She turned, crashing through the fence gates, almost

1

falling. She straightened and lurched towards the door. She pushed the door open and stood there, blood pouring down her head and pooling down her legs onto the floor. She heard the voice again, louder this time. He was right behind her.

She wanted to keep running, but there was no escape. She was exhausted.

Her knees crumpled, and she fainted.

CHAPTER 2

Charlene Atkins breathed in and out rapidly, trying to calm the incessant thudding of her heart. Her panicked breaths became vapour in the freezing night air, dissipating as rapidly as the warmth in her body. She shivered and stared at The Holy Communion Church.

Why had she come? It was too late to beg for forgiveness. Her heart had hardened into a slab of stone long ago.

No one could judge her, not even a God she didn't believe in anymore. No one but herself – and that was the hardest part. The part she had to live with.

The church stood shrouded in darkness, a tepid yellow light in the front illuminating the stone pillars outside the main door, and the empty, silent stone patio. A gust of wind blew gnarled yellow leaves onto the patio. They made a sound like bones being dragged across the hard ground. A round white moon rose behind the church steeple, its orb suspended in the clutches of a skeleton tree.

It was time for him to speak. She walked forward, leaves crunching underneath her feet. She stopped short when she saw a shape separate itself from a large tree in front of her. Fear grabbed her throat in a vice-like grip, and she could barely breathe. Mesmerised, she watched the dark figure walk towards her in slow, measured steps. The heels of his boots made no sound on the ground.

"Hello, Charlene." The Keeper's voice was low and measured.

She stood her ground, resisting the impulse to turn and run as he came closer. He stopped three feet away.

"Where is it?" he asked. His voice was harder, like steel. She recoiled at the question.

"Not here."

She could see him smile in the dark, his lopsided grin like a psychotic joker. "Is it back in the house?"

"First you need to tell me…" The words died in her mouth as he lunged for her. She pivoted on her feet and turned away. She went to run, but stumbled on her ankles, dropping to her knees. In a flash, the Keeper was above her, a black mass blanking out the cold light of the moon. He grabbed her hair and pulled it back viciously, making her cry out. He brought his lips closer to her face.

"Tell me," he whispered. She shook her head.

The stinging blow to the side of her head rocked her vision. Red and yellow globules of pain burst inside her eyes. She cried out and slumped forward.

"One last chance," he whispered, his breathing calm and easy.

"No."

A blow to the nose almost felled her, and she only stayed kneeling as he held her hair. Warm, metallic liquid poured down her nose, and she could taste it on her tongue. Her breath came in gasps, and she retched, spitting out a cracked tooth. She screamed in pain as he stood up suddenly, pulling her to standing by the hair. He dragged her with him, stepping off the narrow road into the softness of the grass.

She fell to her knees again and scratched his hands at her hair. The blow that landed on her stomach made her double up and gag. Mucus trailed from her open mouth, seeping into the hoary winter grass. He dragged her deeper into the darkness of Clapham Common.

The trees seemed to hunch closer, hushed in silent witness. The moon broke free from the bony barnacles of branches, and rose up into the black, muted sky.

CHAPTER 3

Detective Chief Inspector Arla Baker thanked the Uber cab driver and jumped out of the Toyota Prius. She hurried up the steps of the brown-brick building of Clapham Police Station. The building was four floors high, wide and squat. Grilled, white-framed windows lined the ground floor. A blue sign above the main door said "London Met" in white letters.

She swung the double doors open, checking her watch. She was more than half an hour late, damn it.

She recognised the desk sergeant on duty. John Sandford was a tall, wide-shouldered black man with closely cropped, wiry hair. His eyebrows rose when he saw Arla. She noticed his eyes run over her. She was glad she had worn her regular office clothes – black trousers, flat, black shoes, white blouse shirt and long, black jacket. Her shoulder-length chestnut hair was tied back in a ponytail. Her boss had mentioned this to be an informal meeting, but she had a feeling it would be anything but.

"Hi, John," she read from his name badge.

"Hello, guvnor. You back now?"

Arla cringed at the question. Did everyone know about her? She decided to take it in her stride and shrugged casually.

"Not sure yet. Is the boss waiting for me?"

"Yup, he phoned five minutes ago." John reached down and pressed the buzzer below his desk. Arla walked around the desk, and pushed the blacked-out, bulletproof, glass-panelled steel door that led inside the station. She thanked John and disappeared inside.

She strode down the busy corridor, nodding at a few colleagues. She noticed the uneasy look on their faces, hidden behind the blank greeting. A sense of foreboding rose inside her like black exhaust fumes. She fought it down with an effort.

Outside Detective Chief Superintendent Wayne Johnson's room, she knocked and heard the gruff voice calling her in immediately.

"You're late," he said, as soon as she stepped inside.

"Good morning to you, too, sir," Arla said in a steady voice.

They stared at each other for a few seconds. Johnson's hair was going white at the edges. He was tall, with a sharp nose and sculpted jawlines that still preserved a handsome face in his early fifties. His flat, dark eyes bore into Arla's with frank irritation, then looked away.

The glass cover on the table reflected the dull daylight spilling in from the windows at the back. A glass cabinet behind him held the DCS's framed achievement awards, a couple of photos of him shaking hands with the Commissioner and other dignitaries. They were flanked by photos of his wife and teenage daughter.

Johnson was wearing his uniform. His black and white cap, peaked edge shining, lay on the desk.

"I have to give a statement," he said tersely. That explained the uniform. She remained standing, not having been asked to sit down.

"Sorry for being late, sir. Bloody police van held up the traffic."

Johnson snorted at her joke, and the tension dissipated from his shoulders somewhat.

"Can't keep blaming others for our mistakes, DCI Baker," he said.

Arla clamped her jaws at the reprimand. She knew what he meant, and it hurt deeper for all the right reasons. "No, sir," she said.

"Are you all sorted now?" Johnson asked.

Arla bristled but kept her face impassive. "If by that you mean it's not going to happen again, then yes. Sir."

Jonson sighed, and his shoulders sagged a little. Lethargy lined the corners of his eyes. "Come on, Arla. I can't keep standing up for you. You assaulted a man."

"A man with a criminal record and known child abuser. Yes, I did. He didn't get a conviction because there wasn't evidence, but we all know what the truth is. Don't we, sir?"

Johnson jabbed a finger in her direction. "You're a damn good cop, Arla, but you're on thin ice. You punched him outside the court, in front of multiple witnesses. What do you think the press made of *that*?"

Arla flapped her hands and grimaced. "Jeez, sir. I said I'm sorry."

"And are you?"

Their eyes locked on each other, neither giving an inch. Arla looked away. "Yes I am, sir."

"Then act like you meant it." Johnson grunted. His face lost its hostility for a few seconds.

"Look, Arla, I know after what you've been through, hating these guys come naturally. But…"

Arla stepped backwards and raised her voice. "Will that be all, sir?" She wouldn't look Johnson in the eye.

He put his large, bear-like paws on the table and lifted himself up to his imposing height of six feet four. "Come with me," he said brusquely. He clamped the cap on his head, positioning it correctly, and walked out of the door. He spoke as he walked, expecting Arla to keep up.

"A body was found on the Common last night. On the blooming bandstand, of all places. Throat sliced."

Arla walked quickly to match his step as he thundered down the corridor. His voice remained soft.

"Media haven't got to it yet. But it won't remain secret for long, given the prominent location. We need an ID, and a quick investigation." Johnson got to the Incident Room and paused, resting his hands on the door handle.

"Ready?" he asked Arla. She looked at him, flabbergasted. *Ready for what?*

"Who's the Senior Investigating Officer in the case, sir?" Arla asked, aware of her heart's staccato beat against her ribs.

"You are, DCI Baker," Johnson said and walked into the hubbub of the room, leaving the door open. Arla stood at the entrance, her mouth open.

CHAPTER 4

Arla let out a long sigh and squared her shoulders. She tried to rub off the shocked expression on her face, but her insides were tangled up in a tight knot. It didn't help that the voices died down as she walked in.

She took in their eyes, unflinching. They felt like darts on her body, but she didn't care. She had done nothing wrong. They could judge her all they liked. Her eyes fell on the blonde curls of Detective Constable Lisa Moran. The chubby-faced twenty-eight-year-old smiled at her, and Arla nodded back, her face impassive. Towering above Lisa was the lanky, well-dressed frame of Detective Inspector Harry Mehta. His eyes burned with inquisitiveness, then his lips twitched. She twitched hers back, feeling a little life flow into her veins. Harry would have a joke for this occasion, later on. She really didn't want to hear it.

Around thirty faces looked expectantly as DCS Johnson walked in front of the blank screen.

He raised his voice and told them what he had just said to Arla.

"Now, like you, I can see the headlines already. Make no mistake, this will sell inches on tabloid columns. Everyone likes a murder mystery with their morning coffee. But we don't need any more headlines."

Johnson continued hurriedly. "DCI Baker will be the SIO. Give her all your support." All eyes turned to her again, and she stared back. This time, she saw grudging acceptance, mixed with the blank stares of the career detectives.

Johnson nodded to the crowd curtly and walked over to her. "I want a progress report by this evening. ID and list of suspects. Got it?"

"This evening, sir?" Arla asked, matching his low whisper. She hoped her voice conveyed the incredulity she felt.

"Yes."

He turned and left the room. Arla strode to the top of the room, struggling for composure. She didn't know what was eating Johnson. He was known to be a hard taskmaster, but he had never had ants in his pants this big.

She faced the detectives and uniformed officers with her back to the screen.

"Right, I want DI Harry and DC Lisa to come with me to the crime scene. We'll be back in three to four hours." She glanced at the clock on the wall. "So we meet here at 14.00 for a full debrief, hopefully with SOCO in attendance." Arla knew from previous experience that scene of crime officers would probably be at the site already, gathering evidence.

The gathering broke up and filtered out through the gaps in the partition wall into their offices. Arla saw the conspicuous, gangly frame of Harry ambling in her direction. His brown cheeks were smooth-shaven, and black hair was gelled back from his forehead. The stench of aftershave assaulted her nostrils. His well-pressed navy-blue suit and tie went well with the white shirt. Smooth Harry, they called him. Girly Harry, she called him, because he paid more attention to his clothes than a woman did.

"Well, well," Harry said, his chestnut-brown eyes dancing. "The prodigal daughter returns."

She ignored him and turned to Lisa, saying hello.

"Let's get going, then," Arla said. She glanced at Harry. "You got the car?"

He stretched out a long arm. "Your carriage awaits, guv."

"Save it for later, Harry," she said, walking away from him. As soon as they came outside the rear entrance of the station, the cold wind knifed through them. Late-November leaves skittered along the ground, and desolate trees creaked in the wind.

They watched as Harry drove the unmarked BMW CID car over. Arla got in the front, Lisa in the back.

The first drops of rain arrived as the car left the station barriers. Arla could feel Harry's eyes on her. She looked out of the window.

"How's it going?" he asked eventually.

"Fine." He said nothing for a while. She didn't mean to be rude, but she wasn't in the mood.

"Did the DCS drop you in it?" Harry was referring to her sudden appointment as the SIO for this case.

She sighed. "Looked like that, did it?"

She could feel him smile without looking at him. They had never been an item, and probably never would be. But Harry came the closest to understanding her out of everyone she worked with.

"It did, but you did well to recover."

After a pause, Harry said, "You know where he's going with his posh uniform on, don't you?"

She turned to him this time. "A press conference, he said. Is there another homicide in the SCU?" The Serious Crime Unit was the overarching department they belonged to, rife with silos and paper-pushers.

"No. He's being plumped for the big job. Going to meet the Deputy Commissioners today in London Bridge. The press might well be there."

Light dawned at the back of Arla's mind. His urgent attitude now made more sense. "What job?"

"Deputy Assistant Commissioner." The DAC was two roles down from the highest authority in the London Metropolitan Police Force.

Lisa said from behind, "Commander Johnson. We might have to start calling him that."

Harry snorted, and Arla rolled her eyes, but she also felt a sense of dread at the way she had suddenly been shunted into this case. Johnson wanted a fast result, and Arla would be hung out to dry if she couldn't get one.

The rain turned into a downpour as they arrived at the road that led inside the green expanse to a parking lot. From there, they had to walk. Arla got out, flinching in the rain. Harry opened the trunk and took out two umbrellas. He handed one to Lisa and unfurled one above Arla and himself. Rain drummed above their heads and spat on the tarmac as they hurried down.

The bandstand was circled by a paved area with a gentle slope. A blue and white police crime scene tape surrounded the paved area.

Arla lifted her badge up as they approached the uniformed sergeant. Harry closed the brolly and they ducked underneath the tape. White-suited SOC officers were walking around. Sterile stepping mats had been laid on the floor leading up to the bandstand. They paused to put green shoe covers on their feet. Shoe prints disturbed evidence, especially on a wet day like this.

Arla could see three SOC men inside the bandstand. One was bending over with a knee on the ground, over what must be the body. The other two were taking photos from opposite ends, digital cameras balanced on tripods. She went up the steps, and took a few steps inside, taking care not to step outside the mats.

The SOC man looked up, and their eyes met. He stood up gingerly, wincing as his knees clicked. Jeremy Lyons was the Area Manager for the South London Met SOC team. The fact that he was here with three of his team meant there was a scarcity of dead bodies in their area today. Wonders would never cease.

As Jeremy stood up, Arla got her first look at the body.

CHAPTER 5

The skin was a mottled grey. A Caucasian woman in her fifties seemed about right. Her throat had been sliced open, exposing internal organs. Blood was caked at puncture wounds on her ribs. The jagged marks looked like stab wounds from a kitchen knife, to Arla's eyes. She was stripped naked, her white skin marbling in the cold. Flat on her back, her dead eyes were open, staring at the domed roof of the bandstand. It was an implacable, insulting sight, a lifeless human being left lying there without a shred of dignity. Arla looked around and felt a pang of anger at the lack of any protective covering around the bandstand to shield it from prying eyes.

She tore her eyes off the victim as Jeremy approached her.

"Anything?" she asked.

He bent his lips and shook his head. Jeremy was in his forties and had been at the game longer than her. A lab scientist in a former life, his days were now spent collecting minutiae at a crime scene.

"Body's been scrubbed clean. I can smell the iodine. No fibre, no hairs around her."

Arla looked around her. Below the bandstand, the light yellow paved area was clean. *Damned rain,* she thought to herself. *Washed away crucial evidence.*

She asked, "Any evidence the body was dragged here after death?"

He shrugged. "We haven't looked around yet."

"Any other wounds apart from the visible ones?"

"No."

"Can I take a closer look?"

"Sure, as long as you don't touch anything." He smiled.

Arla walked down the last of the duck planks and leaned near the head. Coppery hair was swept back from her forehead, probably by the killer when he cleaned the body. The eyes were a nondescript greyish brown colour, and the black pupils dilated and fixed. As always, Arla resisted the urge to reach out and close the eyes. Bring an end to the horrors inflicted upon her before she died.

She noticed the golden cross hanging from a gold chain at the neck. The pendant was long, but the chain was short, stopping well above the cleavage. She leaned closer without breathing over the body. There was a sculpture on the cross, a relief of Jesus.

She looked around the hair, noting the matted, dark blood at the base of the neck. Blood had pooled there, so she had her throat cut here, it seemed. She gazed at the stab wounds. Deep, wide gashes in multiple locations on the ribs, both sides. They seemed to have been done in a frenzy, butchering her chest.

Arla stood up. The two types of wounds were very different in character. At the neck, it was a thin, deep and straight line, almost like a surgical incision. The chest was a different matter. It seemed the work of a madman.

She walked down to the feet and looked up the naked body towards the head. The body lay flat, legs together. No obvious signs of sexual assault, but she hadn't seen the underside.

She heard Harry's voice at the steps and look to her side. The forensic pathologist had arrived. Dr Bandy was in his late-fifties. He wore his usual shabby suit and shuffled as he walked up the steps, hunched forward slightly. Arla watched as he took off his coat and shoes and shrugged into a white jumpsuit. She stood to one side as he approached.

His eyes lit up when he saw her. "You're back, Arla!" She was getting used to the common refrain. But she couldn't help smiling back. Dr Bandy was slow, ponderous, humble. He reminded her of a bear who slouched around, looking for titbits on the ground. More Columbo than Quincy. A stalwart of the Met, they had worked numerous cases together.

"Back to work," she said.

"Work keeps us alive, even when we deal with the dead."

"A bit early for the preaching, Doc."

Bandy chuckled. He looked down at the body, and the mirth died in his face. Arla walked past him and let him get on. Bandy squatted near the head as Arla had done and went down the body. With the help of an SOC officer, they raised the body to its side. Bandy peered underneath, then examined with gloved hands. Satisfied there was no anal sexual assault, he inserted the rectal thermometer.

Bandy held the thermometer aloft, squinting at it. She walked over carefully.

"Time of death?" she enquired.

"Rectal temperature is nine degrees, same as ambient. Given that the body's been left in the open, I would say normal time to get to ambient. And there's rigor mortis in the large muscles."

"So?"

"12 to 13 hours I would say, as a rough guess. Need to look at her properly."

"What's the bruise marks?" Arla pointed at the angry purple welts on the elbows, shoulders and knees.

"Well spotted. What do you think?"

"She bled to death here," Arla said, "but she might have been knocked unconscious elsewhere. Could the marks be a result of the body being carried here?"

"Probably, but I think something worse."

The look on Bandy's face gave Arla a chill. The old veteran wasn't given to dramatics, but his countenance was troubled.

"What?" she asked.

"Seasoned killers bend and stretch limbs on a body. It delays onset of rigor mortis and confuses the hell out of pathologists." He rubbed his chin, looking at the bruise marks.

Light dawned over the canyon in Arla's mind. "So we have trouble getting a time of death?"

"Exactly."

"So you're not sure of twelve to thirteen hours ago?"

Bandy smiled sheepishly. "I am kind of. Her body weight is average, so she loses heat like a normal person."

"Thin bodies lose heat quicker."

"Correct. So the rectal temp must be worth something. But I have to open

14

her up and take other measurements, you know."

Arla nodded. "I need a report by tomorrow morning."

Bandy raised his eyebrows. "I got a drowning and an RTA lying in the morgue. This…"

Arla cut him off. "This takes priority." She pointed outside, where the crowd of onlookers had grown as the rain had relented. "We need answers. Especially as we might be dealing with a pro." The words stuck in her throat, and a shiver worked down her spine.

In her experience, killers such as these never struck in isolation. She hoped she was wrong this time. But everything, from the cleaned body and surroundings, right down to the MO, reeked of someone who had done this before.

CHAPTER 6

The Keeper watched from behind the crowd. Across the blue and white tape cordoned crime scene, he could see the dark-red-haired woman speaking to the older man in glasses, then issue orders. He had seen her alight from the black tinted car with blue light on top. From her mannerisms, and the suit she wore, he knew she was a cop, and the one in charge.

Excitement mounted inside him. She would be a challenge for him, and one that he would welcome with open arms. He liked her, too. The hair, swept back in a ponytail, showed the sharp angles of her face. The jaw juttng out, the nose small and pretty, large eyes moving around restlessly. The Keeper could feel the tension in her body. He was like that last night, when he killed Charlene Atkins. He didn't regret it. The bitch had it coming. She should have done what the Keeper had asked her to, then her death would have been painless. But she chose to fight and paid the price.

The policewoman looked around, and for a moment, the Keeper felt her stare at him. Their eyes met for a second or two, and a thrill passed through him. From the look on her face, he was sure she felt it too. But she looked away, searching for something in the crowd, then the trees. It didn't matter. The connection had been made, and the Keeper knew it.

"You're mine," the Keeper whispered softly.

He was irritated as a tourist bumped into his back. The man apologised and tried to snap a photo with his phone. A uniformed officer turned towards them and stretched his hands out.

"No photos, please. This is a crime scene, and you are requested to leave the area. Now."

A woman asked, "Are we in danger?"

The Keeper snorted. The woman was pushing a pram, and he could only see the back of her head. People were so stupid. He felt the familiar distaste when he thought of everyday, normal human beings. Stuck in their way, never able to open their minds and actually see for themselves. Fed fake news by the media, garbage on television, content to have their children taught lies in mediocre schools.

Mediocre. That's what the world was like. Everyone just plodded along, marching to the same drum beat. No one thought for themselves or wanted to leave their mark behind.

He did. When this was over, everyone would remember his name. They would think of him with reverence, and yes, some would be scared. That didn't bother him. It would be clear very soon that he was only making space, clearing out the bodies that didn't belong in this world.

But the game had now started. The body of Charlene was just the beginning. Anticipation tingled inside his spine again, and he took a deep breath. The air smelled fresh, cold, damp. Wet earth mingled with the mush of dead leaves on the ground.

A thought struck him. He went forward, pushing past some people. His pulse quickened as he approached the broad back of the uniformed officer. If he only knew how close...the Keeper loved these games. After all, he would declare himself to the cops one day. Already, he had left his mark on the bodies. The black triangles. They simply had to discover them, and he had no doubt they would.

The Keeper edged forward till he could touch the officer. The man sensed him and glanced behind.

The Keeper kept a straight face and smiled amicably. "Excuse me, officer, what's happened here?"

"It's a crime scene, that's all I can say at the moment."

"Who is the woman wearing the suit?" A daring question, but the Keeper wasn't afraid to play a few games. After all, he had played with the police in the past, and had the morons found him?

Hell no. Bunch of idiots, like the majority of the human race.

The officer turned and gave the Keeper a look. The Keeper smiled as nicely as he could, almost fluttering his eyelashes.

"Police officers. If you want any more information, please look at our website."

The officer turned his back to the Keeper again. Respectfully, the Keeper stepped back. But he didn't go away. He watched the woman speak to the men in the white space suits, then to a smaller, older man in a suit and glasses, who the Keeper thought looked like a doctor. This man stepped down from the bandstand and walked down the path. He was about to duck under the blue and white tape when he pulled up.

He turned around and called, "Detective Baker?"

The Keeper looked sharply at the bandstand. No one moved, and the man called out that name again. This time, the woman turned and came down the stairs of the bandstand.

The Keeper smiled. Now he had a name.

Detective Baker.

CHAPTER 7

Harry parked the car in a space near the rear double doors. The rain had started up again, this time with a wind that blew sharp drops like shards into Arla's face as she came out of the car. Her hair blew back in the bluster, and she rushed for the door. Lisa had gotten there already and ran through the double gates.

Arla went to get a cup of coffee, while Harry and Lisa fiddled about with the projector in the incident room. When Arla arrived with a hot mug, the room was full. A photo of the body was up on the blank wall. A white board and writing pencils stood next to a desk. Arla walked over and perched her bum on the table and looked at the faces. Most were staring at the photo, but some had inquisitive looks on their faces as they watched her.

Wondering what happened to her behind the scenes. Nothing she could do about the wagging tongues.

"OK, listen up," Arla said in a loud voice. A hush fell across the room.

"Victim is mid-fifties, white female, killed from severe blood loss as a result of throat and chest sharp knife trauma. We don't know that for definite and have to wait for the pathologist to confirm." She paused and saw that all eyes were trained on her.

"First things first. We need an ID. SOC have dusted fingerprints for us. Harry?"

Harry spoke up from the side, laptop remote on his hand to manage the projector slideshow.

"Prints will go through IDENT1 as soon as we finish up here." IDENT1 was the national criminal database of fingerprints. Arla doubted she would get anything of value.

"Good. We need to send off DNA to see if there's a match with the missing persons database." She looked at her watch. It was 13.45 and Friday. The National DNA Database was shut half of Saturday and Sunday. She didn't have high hopes of getting a result back till next week.

"A mobile phone wasn't recovered from the area, but we need to keep looking. As soon as we get an ID, we can start asking phone companies for call data. Ditto with social media."

She paused. "I need dental records and any recognisable body features like the necklace photographed and shown to potential witnesses. Till we hear more from SOC and the pathologist, that's it for the body."

Arla took a sip of the coffee, and Harry changed the photo to a wide view of the bandstand.

She put the mug down with a thunk. "This is Clapham Common, people. The worse place to have as a murder scene. Joggers and strollers trampling evidence everywhere. So we need to get to it. Put on your muddy wellies, and let's join the uniforms for a two-mile radius search."

She turned to Lisa. "I want a door-to-door on that two-mile radius as well. The Common tube station is within that distance, so I need a poster outside and inside the station, and uniforms present to question witnesses. We need a TV appeal on Crimewatch and a radio bulletin on the London news channels." She lifted up a hand as voices murmured.

"Yes, I know that's giving it to the media on a plate, but let me assure you, *News of the World* and *Sun* scavengers are there already, clicking away. We might as well get any help they can give us. On the Common, I want photos on tree trunks, street lights, everywhere. I need uniforms asking questions of everyone they can see on the Common. The murder probably happened at night in darkness, but someone could have seen something. That's enough to get you busy. Let's get cracking."

The crowd broke up. Harry stood up and said under his voice, "Until the next body shows up."

Arla ignored him, the best way to deal with Harry. Lack of attention riled him, and it was amusing to watch. She said, "CCTV?"

Lisa spoke up from her side. "I called the tech office while you were getting coffee. They're checking cameras as we speak."

"Good work, Detective Constable."

She went to her office, turned the computer on, and started pounding on the keyboard. Harry poked his head in.

"Nada on IDENT1. She's clean."

Arla spoke while looking at the screen. "Missing persons?"

"Arla Baker. Detective Chief Inspector, turned into a robot who gives orders. Last seen..."

"Shut up, Harry." She glanced at him and saw the corners of his lips twitch. She frowned, letting him know that he was getting to her. It made his grin broader.

Harry said, "Nothing."

"Damn." Arla's fingers hovered over the keyboard. She hated not having an ID. A name to the face. Until then it was just a face. Harry seemed to read her thoughts.

"Something familiar about her, you know."

She squinted at him. "What do you mean?"

His arms were folded, and he rested his lanky shoulder against the door frame, feet crossed. She could smell his aftershave again. He shrugged.

Arla leaned back in her chair. She had been thinking the same thing. Something about the woman's face. Intuition could be a funny thing. It needed time to develop, and having seen scores of dead bodies, she had learnt to trust that sixth sense inside. But it was too early to follow her gut.

She said, "Call Bandy and find out how far he's got. If nothing else, we need those dental records."

Harry strode off. The cold November wind howled outside, lashing rain against her open window pane. She got up to shut it and turned the radiator on full blast.

There was a rap against the window facing the open-plan office, and she saw Harry beckoning her. He mouthed something, and she recognised it as CCTV. She walked over to his desk, where Lisa and a couple of others stood around the screen.

Lisa clicked to enlarge the frame, and the dim view of a figure in the penumbra of a street light filled up the screen. She clicked play, and the figure started to walk. They had her back view. She turned inside the dark expanse of the Common and disappeared from sight.

"Do we have a frontal image?" Arla asked. "How do we know it's her?"

"Matches her height, weight and gender. About 22.32 hours on the screen, which keeps us in the twelve- to fourteen-hour time window."

"That still doesn't prove it's her."

They waited while Lisa scanned the files sent over to her. She clicked on another two and got nothing. The last file gave them a frontal view. They got her profile, but it was well lit. The image was black and white, but Arla could tell she wore a scarf, and her coat had a hoodie, which was thankfully down.

"It's her," Lisa said. Four heads craned to the photos stuck on the display board, then turned back to the screen. Lisa had closed up on the face. Arla walked over to the board, picked over a photo and brought it over. The photo showed a bloated, grey face, but the similarities were clear.

"OK, we have a visual. Good work. Now, get more images, Lisa, and see if you can work out where she came from."

Lisa said, "Done that already. She crosses a road further back and then walks up the A3." She brought up Google Maps, and showed them the street. "No cameras there."

Arla said, "Well, at least that shows she didn't come off the tube train. If she walked from a side road, unlikely she came off the bus either. Which means she might live locally. What's the name of the side street?"

"Elmhurst Drive."

Arla glanced at her watch. 16.45. Mums at home with schoolkids, dads still at work. It was normally the mums who were vigilant about goings-on in their street.

"Start a door-to-door on Elmhurst Drive and the surrounding streets. Call me if anything happens. Harry, take the photo to the artists and get an image drawn by the photofit guys. Uniforms can use that."

Before they could move, Lisa stopped them with a frown on her face.

"Something weird just came up, boss." The tone of her voice matched the confused look on her face. "We did a face recognition search based on the images that we have. And guess what?"

Lisa answered her own question as Arla and Harry stared at her. "A woman matching her facial image was found on CCTV of the station."

Arla frowned at her. "You mean, she was here?"

"Yes."

They followed Lisa back to her computer. She clicked on the keyboard and downloaded a file. A crop of images came across the screen, all of them video shots. Four at the top and four at the bottom, photos of the reception area of their police station. Lisa pointed to a photo in the middle, on the bottom row. She zoomed in. The image was not the best, but the face was clear enough. Arla leaned closer to the screen.

"Yes, that's her." She noted the shoulder-length dark hair, the shapeless, back coat, white hands folded on the lap. "Why was she here?"

"That's the odd thing," Lisa said. Both of them looked at her.

"She wanted to see you."

A jolt hit the back of Arla's mind, and she was suddenly at a loss for words. She could only stare at Lisa. Lisa shrugged.

"The desk files state she knew your name. She specifically asked for Detecitve Chief Inspector Arla Baker."

Words were frozen inside Arla's mind. With an effort, she asked, "What name did she leave for herself?"

Lisa shrugged. "She didn't. She would only speak to you."

CHAPTER 8

Arla got off at the Tooting Broadway tube stop. Flower stalls lined the railing opposite the station. A drunk slouched against the wall, drinking from a bottle. An old man in torn jeans and ripped coat pushed an empty trolley, talking to himself.

She turned left into her street, Coverton Road. Terraced houses ran all along the street on both sides. The stuck-together look was deceptive, as the buildings were large inside. Most of them had been converted to two or three apartments. She lived alone in a ground-floor, two-bed apartment. The rent was expensive, but cheaper than Clapham, and the proximity to the tube station more than made up for it.

She opened the door to her apartment and groped the wall to turn the light on. The hallway was narrow and led to the lounge and kitchen area at the rear. Two bedrooms, one only large enough for a single bed, led off the main corridor.

She flicked on the lights of the lounge and checked the fridge. Not much, apart from a half-eaten pizza. That would have to do. She turned the oven on and stuck the pizza in.

She went to get changed in her bedroom. On the mantelpiece of the fireplace there was an old photo. Her father and sister, with Arla in between them. Arla had never known her mother. She died when Arla was a baby, and she was raised by her grandma, Nana Moon. Nana Moon died when Arla was fourteen, then it was her father. He did the best he could, she supposed. She had taken herself to university and got a degree. She hardly saw him now, and she knew that was the way he liked it.

What she liked, or wanted, didn't come into the equation. Her father acted like he was relieved to get rid of her.

Arla picked up the photo and held it closer to her eyes. Nicole, her sister, stared back at the camera with innocent, teenage wonder, impish smile on her

24

face. She was darker, with more wavy hair, taller by a few inches. Nicole. The chasm opened inside her, that blinding, limitless fall into her recurrent nightmare.

She had been good with the drink lately. In her two-week suspension, she had hit the gym every day. Only drank at the weekend. As the headache got worse, the bottle of rum seemed more enticing. *To hell with it,* she thought and poured herself a drink. She went to the bathroom to splash water on her face. She stared at herself in the mirror.

Two weeks ago, a serial child abuser, a predator who preyed on teenage girls, had walked free due to lack of evidence in court. The child's evidence was unreliable, and there were no witnesses. Arla had caught the bastard having a smoke outside the station, and he passed a sarcastic comment. Arla's temper had gotten the better of her. She had swung at him and connected. The rest was, as Johnson had said, a disaster. And it was time to admit to herself as well, it was the last in a line of events.

She knew what she was looking for, and maybe it was time to admit she would never find it. *Justice for Nicole.*

She took out the pizza and chucked it in the bin, her appetite suddenly gone. She drained the glass then took herself to bed before she had another one.

*****

Rain lashed against the window. A furious wind howled in the sky, moaned in the alleys between the houses. Arla could hear the screams in the other room, and she pulled the blanket over her head, trying to shut the sounds out. They were muffled but didn't drown out completely. She heard a door slam and then a loud male voice. It faded.

Arla stiffened as she heard the footsteps coming up the stairs. Her bedroom door creaked open. She sat up in bed, heart beating fast, breath coming in gasps.

"Who is it?"

A black shadow moved closer into the room. Terror struck Arla, and she moved back into her bed, hitting the wall.

"Shh. It's me, silly," Nicole whispered. Arla squinted in the darkness but couldn't see anything.

"Nicole? Is that you?" Arla whispered back.

Nicole perched on the bed. She was older than Arla by three years, sixteen to her thirteen years. She lay down and put her arm around Arla's shoulders.

"Did Dad wake you up?"

Arla didn't reply. Nicole pulled her closer into an embrace, and they hugged, comforted in each other's warmth.

"Did you try to stop him?" Arla whispered.

"Yes. But he's going out again to waste his money." Arla could feel Nicole shake her head in the darkness. "There's no food in the fridge, and he's gone to waste his money on drink."

Arla's throat constricted, and her tummy grumbled. Since Nana Moon died, her Dad had gone off the rails. He was always drunk and barely spoke to them. Slept in the day and went out at night. Nicole bought food when she stole money from his wallet, and he had caught her once and slapped her. That led to another round of screaming, and Arla had watched, cowering behind a sofa.

"I swear to you, he's never going to hit me again," Nicole's voice was determined. They were lying down now, side by side. Arla gripped Nicole's hands tightly. She didn't know what to say. Dad had never been like this. She could remember happier times, but now, every day was a nightmare.

"I wish Dad would go away, and you and I could live together," Arla sniffed. The wind blasted in through the cracks of the single glazed window, buffing up the curtains.

"We need money for that, and a new house." Nicole paused. "I've been thinking."

"Of what?"

"Of ways to get money."

Arla felt her spirits rise, but in truth, she was conflicted. "You have a job?"

Nicole patted Arla's shoulder. "Something like that. Listen, you need to do something for me."

Arla waited for her sister to elaborate. Nicole said, "I've contacted social services. Told them about Dad. They'll come soon."

"OK." Arla had heard vaguely about the social services.

"When they come, tell them I've gone to live with a friend for a few days."

Alarm gripped Arla. Her hands became claws on her sister's arm. "Where are you going?"

"Shh," Nicole said, stroking her hair. "Don't worry. I have to see someone to get some money, OK? And then I'll be back, I promise."

A heavy weight was lodged at the back of Arla's throat, and she couldn't swallow. "No, Nicole. You can't leave me here. Not with Dad, no, please."

"That's why I've called the social services, silly. They will come tomorrow, trust me." Nicole's voice was gentle.

Tears prickled the back of Arla's eyes. "But I want to go with you. Social services will take me away." She remembered now. She had heard rumours of this happening to other girls. But she never thought it would happen to her.

Nicole paused. "That might happen. But I will come and get you, I promise."

Arla sat up in bed, tears running down her cheeks. "No. I want to come with you."

Nicole hugged her tight. Arla could hear her sister's heart beating. Nicole said, "I'll only be gone two days, that's it. Then we'll be together again. OK?"

"No."

"Arla!" Nicole's voice now had steel in it. "Listen to me. I can't do this with you, alright? I can't look after you. I have to be myself."

"But why? I don't understand." Arla hugged Nicole tight and wouldn't let go.

"You will one day. I'll tell you everything." Nicole's voice broke as her arms wrapped around Arla's shoulders. Then she removed them slowly.

Arla fought, sobbing, holding onto Nicole.

"Now listen, listen." Nicole held Arla's hands down. "Don't cry. Stay here and go to sleep. I'll be back before you know it."

Nicole embraced Arla, and they both clung to each other fiercely, one last time. Arla wouldn't let go again, and she wet Nicole's shoulders with floods of tears.

"I need you to stay here, sis. I need to know you're safe." Nicole fought her hands down again, and kissed Arla. This time Arla felt her sister's wet cheeks and knew that she had been crying too.

She went out the bedroom and stole down the stairs. Arla went after her and stood by the doorway.

Nicole went out quickly, and slammed the door shut. Arla tried to open it, but her sister had locked it from the outside.

"Nicole," Arla screamed, scared and lonely, sob heaving her body. "Nicole."

Arla ran up to the window as lightning flashed. For a moment, Nicole's dark raincoat was lit up as she crossed the road. Then the rainy night swallowed her up. Arla felt a strange pull inside her, like she should stop her sister, or at least go with her.

"Nicole!"

"Nicole!"

Arla sat up straight in bed, heart hammering in her chest, forehead drenched in sweat. Her mouth was open, tongue dry and stuck to the roof of her mouth. She licked her lip and blinked. The alarm was beeping loudly.

She groaned and slapped the bedside clock. 0600. She swung her legs to the floor, and the dizziness almost made her topple over. She couldn't shake off the nightmares. Were they nightmares?

All of it had happened in real life. She suppressed it the best she could, but the dreams came back with depressing regularity.

The dreams came back, but Nicole never did.

CHAPTER 9

The Keeper could see the clotted darkness of the Common opposite, and the lights glimmering outside the Holy Communion Church. Across the parkland, street lights were strung like a halogen garland. They fell on the handsome row of imposing Victorian houses facing the Common. He counted them until he got to the one he wanted. It was the only house with lights off on all four floors. Black and desolate. A toothless cavity in a row of expensive real estate incisors.

He crossed the road and stood in front of the seething darkness of the Common. Like he was facing a giant beast, observing him in silence. The distant lights of the church were its glittering eyes. Only the railing separated him from the grass. There was a gate, and he pushed it, the rain-soaked wrought iron wet on his fingers.

His right hand delved into his pocket and felt the warm butt of the hunting knife. The weapon was still in its scabbard, and he loosened it till the blade was free. He thought of the man who had written to him. Vincent Bruhn. The fact that Vincent had found his phone number, after all these years, was alarming enough. All of this was happening because that woman had died. One by one, they were coming out of the woodwork.

The Keeper snarled, his breath becoming vapour in the freezing air. *Let them come,* he thought. All of them would meet with the same end.

The Keeper didn't remember Vincent that well. The faces seemed to merge in his mind. But what Vincent had mentiond in the text was enough cause for concern. The Keeper smiled. The idiot had signed his death warrant by saying he was coming to pay the woman his respects.

The Keeper had used his contacts to trace the call Vincent had made to his phone. Now he walked quickly across the common, breaking into a jog. He liked that, the exercise warmed up his body. He traversed a couple of miles quickly and came out on the other side. Across the street, on the corner, stood the large detached Victorian building which was the hotel.

The Keeper got closer but didn't go inside. He settled down to wait, hidden in the overhanging shadows of the trees. Half an hour passed, and the Keeper was patient. He enjoyed lying in wait for his prey.

When the man appeared at the gates of the hotel, lit up in the light, the Keeper caught his breath. Yes, of course. He remembered Vincent. His first taste of a young buck. He closed his eyes in ecstasy. The heady feeling of power he had now was making him delirious. His hand was tight on the butt of the knife.

He had found Vincent once, and now he would destroy him. It had come full circle. Surely there was poetic justice in that? The Keeper was a well-read man. He murmured a few lines from TS Eliot's Wasteland in his mind. It amused him.

November was the cruellest month, surely. Not April.

Vincent was crossing the road. The Keeper lay low and vaulted over the fence of the common. The granite blackness engulfed him, and he melted into the night, rushing across the wet earth with barely a sound, a nocturnal predator.

Vincent was walking along the path, heading for the lights of the church. The Keeper followed. He knew Vincent would go there to pay his last respects. The bandstand was close by, where Charlene had been found.

Vincent stopped when he was fifty yards from the church. Silent as a ghost, the Keeper stepped into the path and got closer.

A noise. A scurry in the bushes. He stopped and so did the noise. Probaby an animal. His heart thudded against his ribs, the sound pulsing in his ears.

Vincent turned and looked behind him. The Keeper got closer, and saw the young man's wide, fear-crazed eyes.

"Vincent."

Goose pimples broke out on the Keeper's skin like hoary frost, chilling him to the bone. His pupils dilated and hands clenched. His hands were still in the dark, but the knife was now out, and held by his side.

A few feet away, the Keeper stopped.

Vincent found his voice. "You're finished."

After a silence, the Keeper spoke again softly. "You shouldn't have come."

"It's too late for that."

"Is it really?"

"Yes."

"You should forget it, Vincent. Go back. This is your last chance."

Vincent smirked and stepped forward. His lips were bent in a snarl. "Now, everyone will know. The whole world. There will be no escape for you."

"Guess I should crave your forgiveness, in that case." The Keeper laughed. Then he got serious. "You are a dead man, Vincent."

"Threats will not work anymore…"

The Keeper moved with an alacrity that surprised Vincent. An arm shot out, the serrated blade of the knife flashed. The stroke caught Vincent in the exposed neck, and blood arched up as the jugular vein was sliced in half. He clutched his neck and sank to his knees. Jaw clenched tight in concentration, the Keeper stepped forward to finish his kill.

CHAPTER 10

Arla could hear sounds. The ticking of the round clock on the wall, black arms moving on a white dial. Her own soft, regular breaths, almost inaudible. Almost not there, like she didn't want to exist in this moment in time. Like she could turn into a desert storm and disintegrate, involute into herself, disappear.

"DCI Barker, do you know what I mean?" The steady voice spoke from opposite her. It snapped her out of her reverie.

Arla looked into the grey eyes of Dr Mark Seddon. A pair of glasses nestled on the bridge of his nose. His gaze was fixed firmly on her face, with eyes that were friendly but vigilant.

Arla cleared her throat. "Yes, I do."

Dr Seddon clasped his hands together on the desk. "Then tell me."

She chose her words carefully. "I am projecting suppressed emotions. It's the only way I can make sense of them. But I shouldn't be doing it to harm others."

Dr Seddon's head nodded, his chin almost touching his chest. She detected a look of relief when he raised his head. "Very good."

"Thank you."

Dr Seddon was the last in a line of psychiatrists arranged by the London Met's Occupation Health Department. To be fair, he was the easiest one to get along with.

His gelled-back black hair was parted neatly in the middle. He adjusted the tie on his pinstripe suit before continuing. "We still haven't delved properly into the suppressed emotions."

Arla's throat constricted. "Right now, I don't want to go there."

"You know that sooner or later we have to."

And I have to climb that wall. Why? What will change? She was aware the doctor was watching her. She shifted her back against the soft armchair, sitting further up.

32

"Guilt is a terrible thing," Dr Seddon said, his smoothly shaven face impassive. His cheeks tapered into a strong jaw and chin. At any other time, Arla would have found the face attractive. He still *was* attractive, and she wondered if that was why she was more receptive to his probing.

"In your case, it is the main suppressed emotion. You have lived with it for so long, you can't even see it. When you hurt others, you are hurting that part of you that feels guilty."

She winced visibly. "I am not hurting others. That man got what he deserved."

His voice was calm, but warm and apologetic. "I didn't mean to imply you are hurting anyone innocent. Of course, your job is to dispense justice. But you cannot act impulsively."

She studied her nails, then turned to the window to see drops of rain silently sliding down the pane. Like tears down a cheek.

"I know," she said, staring out of the window.

"Anger and guilt go hand in hand, Arla. You are using your anger against that guilt."

She turned back to look at him. His words hung in the air, a thick presence between them. She knew it, but to hear someone speak it out loud made a difference. But what could she do about it?

He seemed to read her mind. Their eyes met, and she saw understanding in them. He was so damn good-looking. Her heart skipped a beat, but she didn't move her eyes away.

"When anger surfaces, it's for a righteous cause. Right? That's why we get angry, after all."

She nodded. He said, "But for you, there is also a switch that turns on, and you can't tolerate what happens after. You lose control. Am I right?"

She nodded again, unable to speak. He held up two fingers. "So, there we are. Anger, then the loss of control. Both driven by the deep sense of guilt. You can't let go of it, even though you might not feel it consciously."

Her eyebrows creased, and a dark emotion swept over her. "Oh, I feel it alright."

"You feel it right now because you are aware of it. But subconsciously, you are not aware of how much it drives your everyday decisions. None of us are, actually. What we do and say every day is due to what is deep inside us, but unfelt, unheard, on a day-to-day basis."

Arla let out a breath. Bloody hell. This shit was getting deep. But she understood.

"Are you with me?"

She nodded. He was helping to untangle the tortuous, entwined fibres of her soul. And for that, she felt grateful.

"So, what do you do with it?" he asked, eyes fixed on her.

"What?"

"As hard as it might be at that point in time, you take a step back. You let go. It's not worth it. Don't let it run your life."

She shook her head, feeling something move inside her, like a glacier fragmenting. "But I can't forget," she whispered.

"Exactly." He was sitting forward, a light in his eyes.

There was an urgency in his voice. "You can't forget. That is why it's so powerful. All sad emotions are. But you recognise that now. Step back. Turn off when you feel the anger. The frustration."

"Let it go," her voice was still a whisper, and she looked down at the lines on her palms, like they bore a map she could navigate her life with.

"Good." He had settled back in his chair, his handsome face half lit by the light from the window, the other half in darkness. "I feel we are making progress."

Arla sighed again. He shuffled papers on the desk. "I will report back to your Detective Chief Superintendent. You will receive a copy as well."

Arla nodded. They murmured goodbyes, then she got up and left the room. The Occu Health, as it was known, was based in a building next to Charing Cross Hospital. She walked out into the brown carpeted corridor and followed the signs back to outside. The November chill had spread like an iron cloak, the rusty, freezing sky covered in clouds. Arla wrapped her burgundy jacket close and adjusted her scarf. Her breath made fumes in front of her face. Clicking heels on the pavement, she navigated the traffic and pedestrians to Fulham Broadway tube station.

As she walked, she couldn't get rid of Nicole's face from her mind.

Then she thought of the woman lying dead in the bandstand, and she shivered.

CHAPTER 11

Arla hated the fat, grubby Maths teacher, Mr Symonds. He droned in a nasal voice and stared at the girls while he picked his nose. But most of all, she hated Phily, the tallest girl in her class who sat behind her. Phily, short for Philomena, was the schoolyard bully. She and her two fat chums got homework out of the nerds, and Arla was one of them. Although Arla hated Mr Symonds, Maths made sense to her, and her grades were good. Phily sat behind her for a reason. Every time an exam was on, she poked Arla in the back with her pencil. The pokes became progressively painful if Arla didn't show Phily her paper.

The one time that she refused, the bullies surrounded her, tore her books to shreds and ate her lunch. Arla didn't dare complain. Things would only get worse.

An exam was on, and Arla was having trouble with these questions. Concentrating was difficult as Phily kept poking her, but Arla didn't have the answers to give her. She rushed the last few questions, and before she could turn back to Phily, the bell went. Mr. Symonds waddled down the aisle, a patch of soup on his protruding belly. He smiled at Arla, showing yellow teeth. It made her gag.

The class broke up, and Arla went to the loo. She came out and a pair of hands grabbed her shirt and threw her across the sink. Phily was waiting, and she held Arla's neck and bent it down to the open tap. Arla fought silently, but Phily was taller and stronger. Her neck felt like it was going to snap off, and she could feel the water splashing on her scalp. She could see the three girls smirking, blocking the door.

Phily pulled on her hair, and Arla cried out. Now her hair was all wet.

"If you pull a stunt like that again, I'll cut your hair off next time," Phily snarled. She said something else, but it was lost in the sudden bang that came from the door. It slammed open, and the three bullies who were guarding it went flying.

Nicole, tall for her sixteen years, came striding in, face ablaze with fury. One of the bullies came up to her, then fell back as Nicole kicked her in the shins. Arla felt the pressure on her neck suddeny ease, and she fell to her knees, massaging her neck.

Nicole was over to her in two strides. Arla looked up to see her sister's right arm flash out and slap Phily across the face. The thirteen-year-old reeled back and Nicole stepped in, grabbing the back of her neck.

"Get up, Arla," Nicole shouted.

Arla scrambled to her feet as Nicole bundled Phily inside the loo. Phily fought, but Nicole was much stronger. She pushed Phily's head into the commode and held it there.

"Flush it," Nicole said. Arla obeyed gleefully. The brackish water cascaded over Phily's blonde locks, and she choked and coughed.

"Do it again," Nicole commanded. Arla was less sure this time, as Phily was showing signs of weakness.

"You sure?"

"Arla, do you want her to start bullying you again?"

"No."

"Then flush the loo now."

Arla did as she was told. Nicole pulled up the water soaked Phily and leaned her against the wall. Phily was crying, but she was almost drowning in water anyway.

Nicole pointed at her. "Will you ever bother my sister again?"

Phily shook her head from side to side. "No," she whimpered.

Nciole took her face closer till it was inches from Phily's. "If you do, the whole lot of us will come down and do this to you, and your stupid friends, every day. Understood?"

"Ye…yes."

Nicole looked up at Arla. "Let's go."

CHAPTER 12

Arla flopped back in her chair, shattered. She had just dropped off the report at Johnson's desk. He liked a hard copy. She finished emailing him as well then gathered her stuff. She craned her neck. Most of the cubicles and desks were empty, but she spotted Harry staring at his screen. She got into her jacket and turned the lights off. She stopped by Harry's desk.

"What are you doing?"

"Got a list of witnesses from the uniforms at the station. Seeing if any of them have a record."

Arla looked at her watch. 20.15. She yawned. Second day back and she was already feeling like she'd been through a meat grinder. But she couldn't shake off the persistent thought, and image, of the victim, sitting in the station, waiting for her. That woman wasn't just the victim anymore. She had been here and wanted to see Arla.

What for?

No one knew. She glanced over at Harry, who was poring over the papers. "I can't believe she came here."

Harry closed the file and turned towards her. His eyes were probing. "You sure you didn't know her?"

Arla shook her head, pursing her lips. "Believe me, I've been wracking my brains. She was old, and I don't know many women that age. I've thought of asking my Dad, but I hardly ever see him, and I seriously doubt he'll know anything."

"No family members you can think of?"

Arla shook her head. "But I do know one thing, Harry."

"What's that?"

"She had a reason to come. She wanted help." Arla bit her lower lip. After she had punched the paedophile, and the news hit the papers, she had developed a small fan base. Letters had arrived at the station, congratulating her for the "direct action" she took against the scumbag. Slighlty embarrassing, Arla thought at the time, but it made her smile as well. Now, she wondered if the woman was a mother, or knew a child who was in danger of being abused. But why would she be killed for it?

Arla sighed. Now, she would never know. Which made finding her killer even more urgent. Arla gripped her forehead, massaging her temples. This long day was getting loger. She needed to get some sleep.

"See you tomorrow," she said. He looked up at her, and their eyes met. He stretched out his long legs, bending his ankles.

"Doing anything tonight?" he asked casually. She hadn't seen him for two weeks, and odd as it sounded, had missed having him around.

"Yeah, wild party. Fancy dress. You know."

"I'd love to see you in a skintight PVC Britney Spears dress." His eyes travelled slowly up and down her. "Bright pink. Would suit you."

Arla grimaced. "Grow up, Harry." He stood up, towering over her. Turned his machine off and reached into his coat. She turned and left, and he followed.

"Uniforms did good today," he said as they walked down the corridor, their voices echoing off the walls.

"Definitely."

At the main desk there was a babble of voices. Arla saw the tall crest of a mound of dreadlocked hair before she saw the rest of him. An average-height Rastafarian man, wearing a bulky, tattered Army coat and a collection of heavy red, gold and green beaded chains on his neck. He was pointing his finger at the duty sergeant and saying something with conviction. The sergeant looked bored. He turned away, and the man slapped his hand down on the desk. It made a loud sound.

The sergeant turned back quickly and gave him a warning. A door opened, and another uniform officer came out. Arla stopped as the Rastafarian man was blocking her way. Harry was behind her.

"Excuse me," she said.

The matted tower of dreadlocked hair bobbed in her direction. She recognised the face, a long-time visitor from one of the many estates close to the station. She didn't know the name, but guessed the uniforms would. Not her problem anyway. She wanted to get home. A headache was gnawing at the back of her skull.

The Rastafarian man stretched his hands out, expunging a smell of old sweat and cannabis. "Help me, please."

Arla pointed to the sergeant. "Talk to him."

"Him no listen, mon. Me tell you, there's voices in dat house."

The duty desk sergeant was a thin, sallow-faced guy called Peter. Arla glanced at him, and he raised his eyebrows then shrugged. Arla turned her attention back to the Rasta.

"Like I said, he will help you. Ask him."

Rasta's brows creased, and he raised his voice. "No one listen to me, mon."

Harry spoke from behind Arla. "Move to one side, please." From the corner of her eye, Arla saw Peter and another uniform lift the counter lid and come out. Irritation surged inside her. A situation like this was just what she didn't need.

The uniforms grabbed the man's elbows. He tried to jerk free, but they held fast.

"Dean," Sergeant Peter said, "that's enough. You can't keep breaking into that house. Leave it alone."

There was a brief scuffle, and Harry moved in front of Arla to help the uniforms. They struggled to make Dean sit down on one of the green plastic benches.

"Wait," Arla said, stepping past them and facing Dean. He was breathing heavily, and the stench of cannabis was even stronger. "What house do you mean, Dean?"

Dean was angry, and he bellowed at the top of his voice. "Across the Common, mon. Me always sleep there when council don't pay rent on me flat."

"Shut up or lower your voice!" Peter shouted back. Dean scowled at him and tried to stand up, but two men pushed him back.

Arla put her hands out. "Leave him," she said. The uniforms hesitated. She had the highest rank, but they had a job to do.

"It's OK, lads," Harry said softly. He stood close to her, ready to intervene.

Arla said, "Dean, can you tell us where this house is?"

"Opposite the church. No lights in there, mon. But last night me hear voices."

Peter said, "I really wouldn't pay any attention. He hears voices in his head all the time. He breaks into any derelict house he finds and squats in there. Got a history of mental illness as well."

Dean glared at him. "Me not mad."

Arla was thinking fast. The church wasn't far from the bandstand. She couldn't remember a derelict house in any of the expensive rows of mansions opposite the Holy Communion Church. Then again, she hadn't really looked, and she might well have walked past it several times in all probability.

She asked the uniforms. Peter said, "There's one or two around, we know that. But I don't know which one he's talking about."

If it was in the place Arla was thinking of, then it would be a vantage point to watch the church and bandstand. A good place for a murderer to hide? She could think of worse. She turned to Harry.

He caught the look on her face, and his shoulders slumped. "Come on."

"Fine, then. See you tomorrow."

Arla said, "Thank you, Dean." She walked off, leaving the men standing at the counter.

She was going down the steps into the freezing chill when she heard Harry behind her.

"Do we have to?" he complained. "Talk about shot in the dark."

She sauntered along. "Like I said, you don't have to come."

He muttered something under his breath, then touched her arm. "What?" she asked.

"Better to drive up there. It's a long walk, and it's freezing." She conceded. He had a point.

They walked into the parking lot, and he flicked the remote of his blue BMW. The lights beeped, and headlights gleamed to life. Harry drove out of the station and into Patmore Estate. A Legoland of housing complexes, lights glowing in endless rows of windows and balconies. Like a cruise ship docked at port. Only this ship had nowhere to go. Forever mired in the staid poverty and despondence of inner-city London.

Arla turned to look at Harry as he went around the bend of Union Road into the traffic lights of Clapham Park Road. "You know where to go?"

"Taking the back route. You want to come out opposite the church, right?"

"Uh-hmm."

As they came out into the main road, traffic increased. A fine rain had started, and Harry flicked on his wipers. Yellow lights blurred and sharpened. Arla kept a look to her left as the row of buildings began opposite the Common. To her right, in the front, she could see the lights of the church. A car behind them flashed its headlights, and Harry turned on his blue beepers.

"Pull over," Arla said. Harry kept his flashing lights on and came to a stop. Arla got out on the rain-slicked pavement. She put her hoodie up, but the slanting drops found a way to sting her eyes. Bright lights lit up a wide, red-brick and white-corniced house opposite her, tall and handsome, the best of Victorian architecture. Two doors down, a smaller structure hunkered between two similar terraced mansions. Smaller in height, but just as wide. Unlike the others, it was sunk in darkness. They strolled over. Harry took out a torch and trained it on the building.

It had seen better days. Paint was flaking off the walls, colour indistinguishable from the rancid yellow of bare plaster. Weed plants sprouted from the cornices and eaves. The silver beam of the flashlight danced around, lighting up the windows that stood like hollowed eye sockets. A fence separated the property from the pavement, with a gate in the middle. It had fallen off its hinges, and dangled on its side, useless. Harry trained the beam on the main door. It was thick, brown and stout with a large brass ring in the middle. The front garden was unkempt with wild brush.

Arla moved past the gate. She stopped near the door, Harry behind her. She looked up at the black expanse of the building looming above her and shivered. A sense of foreboding, and a peculiar claustrophobia, despite being out in the open, jarred her senses. Wind creaked one of the window joints. Whispering rain fell like secret sighs against the desolate bricks.

Arla shook, a weight suddenly heavy in her throat. She felt a compulsion to move back into the road, to get away.

"Weird place," Harry said.

She brushed past him and out into the road. She faced the wet cars spraying rain under their wheels, and the night shroud of the Common.

"What's the matter?" Harry asked.

She pointed in the direction of the tube stop. "Nothing. I'm off home. Catch you tomorrow."

Arla watched Harry get into his car and drive off. She turned and faced the house again. Then she looked up and down Clapham Common Road. A long stretch, and these large mansion houses on it faced the Common. An important road for Arla. She had walked up and down this road, so many times in her life. Looking at every house, poring over their histories. She had knocked on doors and asked the people who lived in them. She had followed them in the hope she might uncover a clue. She had waited in her car, keeping watch. Hoping to see a woman who reminded her of Nicole. Arla had searched every nook and cranny of the Common, day and night.

But she still hadn't found who she was looking for. And she would never stop.

Memories opened up like rain falling from clouds.

CHAPTER 13

It was the May half term, and the sun was shining. Arla woke up and lay in bed for a while. She could hear her dad snoring in the bedroom next to hers. Her room was the smallest, barely enough space for a single bed, but a desk and chair had somehow managed to fit in. Nicole's room was almost as big as their dad's. Arla got up and changed, hoping her dad didn't wake up anytime soon. He was always in a foul mood in the morning till he had his drink.

She went downstairs and found Nicole dressed already.

"Good morning," Arla mumbled and opened the fridge. It was usually empty and today was no different. The bottle of milk was fermenting, cloudy. She didn't even smell it. She dropped it in the bin and turned to the loaf of bread, but there wasn't any butter.

Nicole was watching her as she munched on a piece of toast. "Wanna head to the shops?" she spoke between mouthfuls.

"I'm hungry" Arla said.

"Come on."

"You got money?" Arla looked at her askance.

"Yes."

They went out and walked across the road to the parade of shops on the main street. They headed to the corner shop, bypassing the supermarket.

"Arent we going to Asda?" Arla asked.

"No. Mr Roy's wife's got cancer, and she needs a treatment that the NHS won't fund."

"You mean the hospital won't pay for it."

"Yes."

"So what can we do?"

"We can give him some business, can't we? We should do all our shopping at his place from now on."

The door chimed as they walked inside the corner shop. It was stacked full of food and groceries. Nicole picked a basket and gave Arla one as well. They went around putting food inside.

Arla pulled on Nicole's arm. Her voice was stressed. "How we gonna pay for this? Must be thirty pounds worth of food in here?"

"I got money," Nicole said calmly.

Arla frowned at her. "Liar."

Nicole shook her head and showed Arla the wad of notes in her pocket. Arla's eyes widened. "No way. Where did you get that money from?"

Nicole hardened her features. "Keep it quiet. Just get the food and let's go."

They paid, and Arla eyed her sister as she peeled off the notes and gave it to Mr Roy, the shop owner.

"How's Anna?" Nicole asked the white-haired man.

Sadness lined his face. "Still the same. I might have to fly her to Germany for this treatment. Let's see what happens."

Nicole smiled at him. "Let us know if we can help in any way."

Mr Roy nodded. "Thank you, my child. Look after yourself." He stretched his hand out with the change.

Nicole shook her head. "No, you keep it."

Mr Roy stared at them for a while, and Arla could see his eyes glisten. Then he looked down and swallowed. "Thank you."

"No problem," Nicole beamed at him.

"Bye," the girls chorused as they left the shop.

Back home, they stuffed the fridge with milk, bread, ham, cheese and ready meals. More food than Arla had seen in a long time. Her main meals were at school and a box of chips with gravy that she picked up on her way back.

They ate a sandwich each then went out again.

"Where we going?" Arla asked as she kept up with her sister.

"You'll see."

They walked to the bus station and got a ride down to the town centre. The shopping mall was busy, and they hung out, eating an ice cream, and window shopping. Nicole stopped outside Goldsmith's jewellery shop. Arla followed her gaze, Nicole was looking at some earrings.

"Come with me," Nicole said. Arla watched as her sister went up to a sales

assistant and asked to see some earrings. She was proud of Nicole. She seemed so grown up, taking charge of things. Although she was only three years older than her, Nicole just had this way about her, and she could make people feel she was older.

"Do you like them?"

Arla looked down at the blue box that was open. Inside the felt-lined interior, lay two tear drop purple amethyst earrings, with gold circles surrounding the amethyst stones. Purple was Arla's favourite colour. She opened her mouth wide.

"Wow, they're lovely!"

Nicole picked up one and held it against Arla's left ear. She tilted her head. "Yeah, suits you. Have a look in the mirror"

Arla looked, and all of a sudden she could just see herself sitting in a nice posh room with wallapaper, doing her make up at a white dressing table, putting the earrings on. The vision passed as quickly as it came. Well, she could dream, couldn't she?

Speaking of dreams. She turned to Nicole. "What are you doing?"

Nicole shrugged. "What?"

"We can't afford this stuff."

"Do you like them?"

"Yes, I love them but…"

"I didn't get you anything for your last birthday, so this is your present." Nicole smiled.

Arla's mouth fell open. "Nicole, don't be silly. We don't have money to buy each other gifts." She shook her head. "Have you got a job? Where's the money coming from?"

Nicole looked away. "Yes I have job. Just quit asking me, will you?" She composed herself. "Look, I have enough money to buy you a gift, OK?"

Arla snatched up the box and turned it over. Her eyes popped out. "Fifty quid! Flippin' fifty quid, are you nuts, Nicole?"

"Nope."

Arla put the earring back. "No. Don't waste your money on these. Save it for food. All the food we have now will be gone by the end of the week."

"Don't worry," Nicole said. She looked at Arla, and Arla suddenly understood

that Nicole was serious. Something had changed in her sister. Nicole was more self assured and…a bit weird, Arla had to admit. Almost like a grown up, but no way was Nicole, like, all the way grown up. Yes, she had kissed boys and done things Arla hadn't as yet. Well, Arla hadn't even kissed a boy, and the thought made her cringe with embarrassment. There was Charlie who sat three seats behind her and always smiled at her. He was kind of cute, but Arla didn't know how to even begin kissing him. Just thinking about it made her cheeks flush.

"Stop dreaming, silly," Nicole snapped at her. "Do you want these or not?" Her face softened. "It's for your birthday, and you're my little sis."

Arla's eyes shone, and she suppressed the smile that began in her heart and almost made its way to her lips. She pretended to think. "Well," she said slowly, "I'll only get a pair if you get one too."

Nicole opened her mouth and shut it. Then she grinned. "OK, deal. Can I get the same ones?"

"Yes." Arla clapped with joy. "Then we can have a matching pair!"

CHAPTER 14

Arla walked off, feeling Harry's eyes on her back. He was watching her to make sure she was headed in the right direction. *Well, let him.* She did walk towards Clapham Common tube station but then turned left at a brightly lit junction.

The glistening pavement echoed her footsteps. The street became quiet as Arla walked down the road. She passed a busy pub at the junction, punters milling outside with pints and smoking. Another two streets down she saw the sign. Cedarbrook Care Home. The "E" of Care had fallen off, spelling Cedarbrook Car Home. She thought how apt that was – a home for used cars. Teenagers who needed a garage to mend themselves.

Loretta, the tall, black lady with her hair matted up in bob, smiled as the doorbell chimed when Arla came in.

"Working late again, Inspector?"

"First day back, always the worst. Where are they?"

Loretta pressed a buzzer, and Arla pulled on a door that led inside. After a hallway, and a set of stairs, she was in a big, open-plan living room. Three sofas were arranged in a triangle in front of the TV, and a table and chair with bookshelves at the opposite end. Four teenagers lay slumped on the sofas, watching a talk show. None of them looked up until Arla came and stood next to them. One of them blew a bubble gum balloon until it burst. Arla sat down.

Three girls and a boy. The girls were aged between thirteen and sixteen, and the boy was sixteen. All four were between foster parents and had no fixed abode. Their parents were lost beings, sold to drugs and alcohol, or mental illness. A life in social and foster care was a life of rejection, and they had come to accept that. That acceptance came with a price, and it was normally anger, insecurity and poor self-esteem. Arla knew that particular triad of feelings very well.

"Hey," she said to all four of them. One of the girls, the sixteen-year-old called Tara, glanced at her then looked away. Mortaza, the boy, shifted and raised his head.

"Hello," he said. Mort, as he was known, was half-Tunisian, half-white British. He had curly, light brown hair, lovely hazel eyes, and a sharp jawline that made Arla think of a model. His appearance was the only thing going for him. His father had been a drug dealer, and his Tunisian mother the father's biggest client. Both his parents were arrested after his newborn sister died of a brain haemorrhage from shaken baby syndrome.

Arla liked Mort. He was mild-mannered, easy-going. He didn't get angry or raise his voice. In some ways, that worried her more. He buried it inside. She shuddered to think what trees would grow from the horrors planted in his soul.

"How you doing, Mort?" she asked, putting her handbag down from her shoulder.

He did a teenager shrug, his whole body moving.

"Been to school today?"

"Yeah."

Arla engaged him, and they talked about school for a while. She glanced at the girls. Tara was stealing looks at her, and they weren't charitable. Arla responded finally.

"What's the matter, Tara?"

She had auburn hair, combed straight back. She wore a purple T-shirt, tight black jeans, black and white pumps. A striking-looking girl, and all the more reason to be worried about her. She blew out her cheeks and made a clucking sound.

"Nothin'."

"We talked about that, didn't we? It's good to talk." Arla stopped by three times a week, more often if she could. It was called voluntary community support, and once she had the background checks done, she settled into the role with ease. This would've been her career, if not for policing.

Tara shot her a glance, her grey eyes sharp. "You're a copper, right?"

"You know that."

"I also know coppers like to dig for dirt. You come here looking for shoplifters, don't you?"

Arla kept herself calm. "No. I don't deal with shoplifters. I am a Detective Chief Inspector in the Serious Crime Squad."

"Miss too important for her own shoes," Tara spat out. "You think we don't know why you come here? Well, you ain't getting nothin' from us."

Arla nodded then looked down. It had been like this for the last two weeks. Tara was the natural leader of the ten teenage girls who lived here. Sexually abused from a young age, she now mixed with the wrong crowd, dropping out of school frequently. Arla suspected she was a member of a gang, which would explain the tattoo on her left wrist. Someone had paid for her to get that done.

"Do you know what I did today?" Arla asked the other three. They shook their heads. Arla focused on them and told them about her day. Tara feigned disinterest, but she didn't get up and leave. The back door to the large room opened, and two more teenage girls came down. Arla nodded to them in greeting. They weren't interested. They sat down at the table and spoke in whispers.

Arla continued to chat to them, until she noticed Tara leave by the back door. Arla gave her a minute then followed. She heard a door slam upstairs and went up the staircase swiftly. A row of rooms stood to either side of the first-floor hallway. The noise had come from the rear. Arla knew which one Tara's room was. She knocked on it.

"What?" Tara shouted.

Arla knocked again without speaking. Tara opened the door, and her eyes widened. She went to slam it, but Arla already had her foot in. She put her right elbow on the door.

Tara's face was red. "What the hell is your problem?" she shouted.

"Which gang have you joined? The Battersea Boys?"

She sneered at Arla. "You'll never know, you posh bitch."

"No. But I can have you followed, and arrest gang members if they're doing something illegal."

Tara blanched visibly. "What?"

50

Arla wasn't too worried about Tara. Unlike the boy, Mort, she expressed her anger. She was also smart and got what she wanted. With the right opportunities, and some guidance, she could have a normal life, one day. But she had her claws out for anyone who came close. Not surprising, seeing that her own mother made money by selling her as a child prostitute from the age of nine.

Arla kept her eyes fixed on the girl's. "Ever spent time in jail, Tara?"

She tried to be defiant. Lifted her chin. "Maybe."

Arla smiled. "I checked your record. You got cautioned for Drunk and Disorderly twice. Nothing else."

Arla knew it was a slippery slope. Tara had now joined the people who would take her further down. There was no coming up that drain pipe, Arla knew that.

"What do you care?" Tara asked.

"Just saying. Be careful what you wish for. It might come true. You wanna know what happens to girls like you in juvenile prison?"

Tara's eyes were guarded. "What?"

"Let me in, and I'll tell you."

She examined Arla's face for a while through slitted eyes, then stood to one side. The room had two beds, and there was another girl lying on one of them. She moved the glossy magazine she had her nose in and stared at Arla with interest. There were posters of boys on the walls. A desk stood between the two beds, shared by both girls. One large dresser was also being shared. Outside the windows, lights shone in the building opposite.

The carpet was a thin film of cloth beneath which she could feel the floorboards. It was almost as cold in the room as it was outside.

"Hi," Arla said to the girl on the bed. The nose went back inside the magazine without a response.

Tara folded her arms, crossed her legs and leaned against the wall. She had flair, style, a certain presence.

"Talk," she said.

Arla said, "New meat. That's what you're gonna be. If you don't know what that means, believe me, you don't want to find out either. Then you have daily beatings, washing clothes, cleaning toilets."

"Not if I get to leave. Can't be locked up in Juve all my life."

"Most girls in prison leave, only to come back. They have nothing to do outside, so they commit a crime, and bang, back in prison. You want your life to be like that?"

Something beeped inside the desk. Tara was over to it in two strides. She opened a drawer and took out a mobile phone.

"That your phone?" Arla asked with a growing sense of unease. These girls got a weekly allowance, but that wouldn't stretch to a pay-as-you-go phone.

Tara didn't reply. She put the phone in her pocket and sprinted out of the room.

"Tara!" Arla went after her. The girl was quick. She was down the stairs and out of the front door as Arla followed, breathless. Loretta looked up as first Tara, then Arla, streaked past the reception. The girls knew they couldn't be stopped. They could report the carers to social services, which meant reports and assessments, and endless grief. The girls were experts in playing the system.

Arla sprinted down the stairs of the building, and the diesel fume-laden, mineral cold air hit her face like a slap. She could see Tara running down the pavement. Arla ran, and a black Mercedes saloon whizzed past her. Light glowed red as the car braked and stopped next to Tara.

Fear bulged inside Arla. She screamed, "Tara! No!"

The passenger door opened, and Tara climbed inside the car. Arla was running full tilt at the car, trying to fiddle her phone open at the same time. The door slammed, and the tyres screeched on asphalt. With a blast of exhaust, the powerful car took off down the street, engine roaring.

Arla didn't get the registration. She kicked the pavement in frustration.

CHAPTER 15

1999

"What are you doing?" Wendy asked in a thick, drowsy voice. He smiled to himself. He set the camera on the tripod and connected it to the video recorder. The anticipation was growing inside him like a volcano. He had waited all week for this.

"Nothing," he said. "Have you finished your drink?" He knew full well that she was drunk enough already. Actually, he needed to watch that. He didn't want her comatose. She needed to function, needed to participate. He liked that. She was thirteen, and old enough to know how to behave. When they took part, and allowed him to control them, that was when his spirit soared. He was invincible, omnipotent. Sounded childish, but it was true. Women became jaded, lost their innocence as they got older. That wide-eyed innocence when he took control of them the first time, there was no magic like that.

That control. That total submission. When he watched the videos later on, he often forgot to masturbate. The beauty of it made him cry. Sure, it hurt them, but they got used to it.

He licked his lips and looked at her. She was sprawled out on the sofa, her bare legs up on the side. She wore shorts and a T-shirt, with the small bulge of her breasts visible. He quivered with the excitement of touching them. She turned drunken eyes towards him. He found her on the camera lens and focused it on the bed.

He knelt by her side and ran his hand through her hair. Wendy was the same as all the girls who came here. Her care home was up the road, and no one bothered to notice if she was in or out.

He crouched in front of her, and she stirred. He forced himself on her, and Wendy gasped, struggling to free herself.

"Only making it worse," he grunted, as he ripped her T-shirt, then tore her shorts off, holding her down. His eager hands closed around her nipples. They

didn't become erect, and that disappointed him. He liked routine, and the last girl he did this to was much more in sync with his needs. He raised his hand and slapped her hard. She cried out, and he lifted her and dropped her on the bed.

Then he was on top, and looked to the side to make sure the red light of the recorder was on. He moved inside her and closed his hands around her throat. She struggled again, putting her hands on his meaty palms. How small they looked. How insignificant. He quickened his movements, rage and desire coursing through his veins.

He pressed harder on the neck as he saw the veins pop on her forehead. Just as he came, he heard the plop of the trachea collapsing. He smiled to himself. He had perfected it. Her nostrils didn't flare anymore. Her chest stopped rising. He rolled off her, then leaned on an elbow to look at her. The blue tinge was spreading around her lips.

A wave of regret washed over him, leaving him forlorn. He should have kept her for a few more times. He liked using them four times, before he showed them his ultimate control. But she had struggled, and his rage had made him do it. He got up and cleaned himself. Never mind. There would be more. Plenty more where she came from.

He locked the door and went downstairs. Muffled groans came from behind closed doors. In the lounge, he found the landlady who rented the rooms out. She was watching TV, and knitting. She looked up and their eyes met.

"Hi, Katherine," he said. She stared at him for a while.

"Hi."

He walked past her to the main door, where she couldn't hear him. The man on the other end picked up on the first ring.

"I need a clear out," he said softly.

"I'm on my way."

*****

Katherine heard the two men drag something down. When she went to the staircase, she saw them holding the ends of a rolled up carpet, coming down slowly. They walked past her like she didn't exist.

"What's that?" she asked.

"Garbage," one of the men said. This guy came every now and then and helped out his friend. They went out the front door. Katherine followed. Clapham Park Road only had a few cars on it at this time of the night. A van was waiting, and the rolled up carpet was dumped in the back.

Katherine walked up to the man who rented the room. "You can't move furniture without my permission."

His face was mauve with exertion, sweat beading on his forehead. "I'm doing you a favour, trust me. If I left it there any longer, the smell would drive you crazy."

He laughed, and his friend joined in. They got in the van and drove off.

Katherine frowned and went inside, locking the door. She didn't like her husband's friends coming here. The Social Services hired the premises from her for teenage children in care. The few spare rooms were rented by adults, who seemed to know people in the Council. They were friends of Chris, her husband. Chris was never here, and he didn't see what happened behind closed doors. Neither had Katherine, but more than once, she had seen a crying girl rush out of the house.

She climbed the staircase, heart beating loudly against her ribs. She stood in front of the rented room. The handle turned, and she stepped in. There was a stuffy, humid smell. She wrinkled her nose and opened the windows. Her eyes fell on the old sofa. She picked up the torn pieces of clothes. A ripped bra and fragments of a necklace.

Katherine picked them up in her hands and stared at them.

CHAPTER 16

Arla was at the station by 7am. The other detectives hadn't turned up as yet. She went into the kitchen and made herself a coffee.

She lifted the steaming mug to her lips, inhaling the coffee deeply. Her second of the day, with many more to follow.

She busied herself in the office, only looking up when Harry knocked on her door. He looked excited.

"Uniforms have someone who knew her. Recognised her from the photos we stuck on the trees on the Common. He's in the room now."

Arla smiled. "Good work." She got up, and together they strode out to the interrogation chamber where the uniforms had put the witness.

The man sat with his head bowed, hands folded in his lap. A pair of nervous, flickering eyes lifted up as Arla opened the green steel door and walked in. She looked at him carefully.

He was wearing a brown winter jacket and appeared to be in his early thirties. A few days' stubble covered his cheeks. The expression on his face betrayed anxiety. His cheeks were pinched, but his jawline and cheekbones were strong. A curious mixture of strength and diffidence played on his features. A handsome face, she decided. She could tell he was twisting his hands in his lap. Intelligent, sea-green eyes looked at her, then to Harry, and back to her again, as if he was seeking reassurance.

"My name is Detective Chief Inspector Arla Baker," she said in a gentle voice. At this stage, every witness was a suspect, too, but he needed to be at ease if he was going to be of any use. Harry nodded at him, having met him already.

"Are you alright to give a statement now?"

He nodded without speaking. Harry had filled Arla in as they were walking down. His name was Steven Wade, and he attended the church. He had recognised the victim from the photos around the park.

Arla switched the tape on and said their names, time and date. The DVD recorder started, feeding from the cameras on the wall.

"How did you know the victim?" Arla asked.

"She used to attend Sunday mass at the church. She came for charity events as well and volunteered for fundraising."

"Did you meet her anywhere else?"

"No. We run a soup kitchen for homeless people in the church hall every weekend in the winter. She helped us run it."

"What was her name?"

"Charlene Atkins." Arla wrote the name down on her pad and underlined it.

"Do you work for the church?"

"No, I work in a record shop on Oxford Street. I help out in the church." He broke off eye contact with Arla and looked down at his hands again. His voice was shaky. "I can't believe this happened. How did she die?"

Arla watched him for a few seconds, trying to gauge his sincerity. If he was faking it, he was doing a good job.

"I'll tell you soon," Arla said. "Tell me a bit more about her first."

Steven glanced from her to Harry, his manner unsure.

Harry said, "What you talked about, if she told you where she lived, things like that."

Steven licked his lips slowly. "She was a quiet lady, to be honest. Very calm, you know. She lived up the road, off Acre Lane. I can't remember the name, sorry."

Arla had reached for the pad, and she put down the pen with a soft slap. "So you've never been to her house?"

"Apartment, she told me. No, I haven't."

Harry asked, "Did she speak to anyone else in the church?"

Steven shrugged. "Like I said, she kept to herself mostly."

"She didn't speak to anyone you know?"

"No," Steven said quickly. *Too quickly,* Arla thought.

She pressed. "Who else did she speak to, then?"

Steven looked at her, and she remained relaxed, her face impassive. Giving him time.

"The vicar," he said. "They talked. I never heard of what, but they…"

"They what?"

"They seemed to know each other."

Harry and Arla exchanged a glance.

"Do you know *how* they knew each other?" Arla asked.

Steven shook his head. "I never asked."

Arla changed direction. "Did you see her use a phone? Like a mobile."

Steven frowned. "Not that I can think of. She never asked for my number or anything."

They paused for a while. Arla asked, "Anything else about her you can tell us? Did she seem stressed, troubled?"

Steven thought with pursed lips. Then he shook his head slowly.

"Did she talk about any family? Children or husband."

Steven shook his head firmly. "Never."

Harry said, "What were you doing the night of the 24th of November?"

"Was that the night of the…"

"The murder, yes," Harry finished. He fixed Steven with a pointed stare.

Steven seemed to have settled down. He spoke with a newfound ease. "I was with a friend. We went out for some drinks, then I came back home."

Harry took notes. "Your friend can verify this?"

"Yes."

"Name and phone number?"

"I'm not sure if she would mind…"

"Don't worry," Harry said. "You're not doing anything illegal. We destroy all contact details after we have your alibi."

Steven swallowed. Arla said, "Would you like some water?"

He nodded. Arla went to the water machine in the corner and poured him a plastic cup. He sipped it slowly.

Arla stood at the table, watching Steven. "Do you have any questions?"

"May I ask how she died?"

Arla told him. He blanched white as a sheet, then colour filled his face. He closed his eyes and sighed. "Oh my God."

Arla glanced at Harry, who took the cue and turned the tape off. She put

58

one of her cards on the table and slid it to Steven.

"If you can think of anything, Steven. Anything at all, please contact me."

Steven looked at the card, then at Arla like he was seeing her for the first time.

"Yes, sure." He scraped his chair and stood up. His jacket had a nice cut, and it came down below his waist. Underneath, the collars of a black shirt was visible over a blue V-neck jumper. The shoes were pointy and well-polished.

When the door was shut behind him, Harry waited five seconds, opened the door, looked down the corridor, then shut it.

Arla had planted her butt on the edge of the table. "He's hiding something. I can feel it."

Harry nodded. "Reckon it's an act?"

Arla shook her head. Her pearl stud earrings moved. "No. He's too anxious. He's trying to cover something up, and he's shitting bricks for it."

"We have his address and phone."

"Good. Go through his call list and tap the phone. Got anyone to watch his door?"

Harry snorted. "Pigs might fly. We're lucky we got our jobs."

Arla smirked, but she knew the truth well enough. Budget cuts meant never mind the lack of a pay rise, the lack of police officers on and off the street was putting the public at risk.

She headed for the door. If she wanted something done, she would have to do it herself.

"Where you going?" Harry called out.

"Find out where Charlene Atkins lived."

"You could just ask me," Harry said.

CHAPTER 17

Arla watched as Harry's long fingers played over the keyboard. At the Lambeth Council website, he located the electoral register, and searched Charlene Atkins' name. Banners were displayed on the website about the upcoming by-election.

Have I registered to vote, my arse, Arla thought. Voting for yet another Member of Parliament who promised heaven and delivered sweet Fanny Adams. It didn't matter which side of the political divide they came from. They were all the same.

"Bingo," Harry said. Arla peered closer. Under the name Charlene Atkins there was a box with details. Harry checked the address on Google maps.

"22 Lavenwood Road. Two roads up from Elmhurst Drive, where they had the CCTV cameras."

"Does she own it or rent?"

Harry clicked on the keyboard. "She paid the council tax and looks like she owned it as well."

Arla said, "Door might be locked. We need to open it. Take a uniform with us and the battering ram."

Arla went to her office to get her coat. As she came out, she saw a red-faced detective constable rush in with a uniformed officer. They spoke to Harry quickly, who was joined by Lisa. All four of them turned to look at Arla. Her heart sank. With a deep sense of foreboding, she approached them.

The constable, whose name was Rob Pinckney, spoke first. "Another body, guv. On the Common, between the church and the bandstand. Killed by knife wound to the neck."

Arla felt her blood run cold. Fighting the chill, she said, "Don't tell me. Body cleaned, stripped naked."

"Yes," Rob said.

"Same MO," Arla whispered almost to herself and caught Harry's eyes on her. She straightened.

"Fine. SOCO onsite?"

"Uniforms are securing it. SOC not arrived as yet."

Arla said, "Lisa, head down there. Harry and I are going to the last victim's house. Call me when SOC arrive."

They bustled out of the door. Arla saw a shadow to her left on the corridor. Johnson had a grim expression on his face, hands on his waist. She figured he knew.

*****

Lavenwood Road was a long row of terraces, two-up two-down houses that curled around the bend on either side. They were set back from the main road, and despite the grime from London's pollution, there was an air of distinction to the properties. The white eaves stuck out from red-brick windows, and sandstone was carved beneath the windowsills. This was probably an upper-middle-class area once, before the town planners decided to lay a major road right next to it.

Harry pulled up after the hulk of a rust bucket car that had been left to rot on the road. They climbed out with two burly uniformed officers. They opened the trunk, waiting to see if they needed the battering ram.

Arla could see the number 22 written on the black door that faced them. She looked to either side. All the houses looked lived in, which was good news. More neighbours to question. Harry pressed the buzzer. After the third, long buzz, the door opened slowly by a crack. A wizened old face peered out at them.

"It's the police," Harry said. He showed the elderly woman his badge.

"What do you want?" the old woman said in a whining voice that cracked. Arla pushed Harry to one side, and putting her hands on her knees, leaned towards the old biddy.

"We don't want to disturb you. We just need to look at apartment number 22A."

"That's the one upstairs," the woman said, suspicion rife on her face. "What is this about?"

"If you let me in, I can tell you."

The old woman grumbled incoherently for a while, then opened the door a crack. Arla told the others to stay put and went inside.

Arla waited while the old lady sat herself down on the sofa. Then she sat down herself and brought her face closer to the woman's. From her experience of speaking to elderly individuals, Arla knew they were often hard of hearing, and without functioning hearing aids. She raised her voice.

"Did you know the lady who lived upstairs?"

The elderly lady thought for a while. Then she shook her head. "She kept to herself. Saw her out of the window a couple of times. Going in and out. Not the friendly type, you know."

"Did you ever speak to her?"

The woman shook her head. Arla asked her a few more questions, and the answers were all negative. It seemed as if Charlene Atkins' nearest neighbour barely knew her.

"Did she have visitors?"

"No."

Arla pursed her lips and tried a different approach. The older woman stared back at her, her wrinkled skin hanging in folds from her jaws. She rested her chin on her hands folded on the walking stick.

Arla asked, "Did you ever see anyone around the house? Like they were looking for something?" It was a blind call, a shot in the dark. But surprisingly, it worked.

The woman thought for a while. Arla realised that, despite her age, she had her marbles intact. She raised a bent, stubbly finger that waved in the air.

"Oh, yes."

Arla waited patiently.

"There was this young man. He stood opposite and watched the house."

Arla felt her pulse quicken. She raised her voice again, keeping her mouth close to the woman's ear. "Can you describe him for me?"

"Why oh yes, I think so. Hang on." The woman screwed up her eyes until they became slits. "He had long, dark hair. Dark brown or black, I think."

"Anything else?" Arla prompted, bringing out her phone. She dialled Harry's number. He picked up at the first ring.

"Call the image guys. We need a photofit for a suspect. Tell them to come here, ASAP." She hung up.

The woman was speaking again. "He seemed young. Like you, maybe younger."

"Was he tall or short? What did he wear?"

"Not very tall. Not like your friend outside. Oh no, not like that. No, not like that at all." She fell silent. Arla asked the question again.

"Well, he wasn't short either."

"So, average height," Arla concluded to herself. "What was he wearing?" The woman looked at her blankly. Arla wondered if the lady was getting tired.

She got up, went to the kitchen, and came back with a glass of water. The woman took the glass with cold, feeble hands, and drank it thirstily. Arla took the glass away and the woman appraised Arla again.

"What's your name, dearie?"

Arla told her and then asked hers.

"Margaret."

"OK, Margaret, can you remember what clothes he wore?"

She replied after thinking some more. "Black. Or dark. He had a long, black coat on."

"How many times did you see him?"

"Oh, many times. He used to come and stand there like he had no one to talk to. He stood underneath that lamp-post."

Arla went to the window, and saw a car pulling in with the photofit technical team. She saw the lamp-post opposite the house as well. She went out to open the door. She introduced the man and woman of the photofit team to Margaret, then told Harry what she had said.

Arla pointed to the door at the end of the hallway. "That must be for the upstairs apartment." Harry walked forward and took out a pair of gloves from his pocket. He held the top of the handle and pulled with his thumb and forefinger.

"Locked," he said. One of the uniformed officers came in with a bunch of keys and tried them one by one. After what seemed a long time, there was the welcome sound of a key slipping in, and a bolt sliding across. Arla took out gloves for herself and slipped them on.

"Call the SOCO guys," she told Harry. This was not a crime scene, but it was the home of the victim. Vital clues could be unearthed here, and Arla didn't want the place to be contaminated by a bunch of cops digging around. The uniforms stepped to one side, and so did Harry as he fumbled with his phone. Arla took her jacket off, handing it to one of the uniforms.

She felt a sense of trepidation as she put her foot on the first rung of the staircase. A second body had appeared on the Common. She hoped she wouldn't find a third.

CHAPTER 18

Katherine could hear screaming. She went up the stairs quickly and strode across the landing. She didn't have to listen with her ear to the door, she knew which room it was. The scream came again, a girl's voice. Something was thrown inside, it hit the wall with a smash.

She rapped hard on the door. The sounds suddenly stopped.

"What's going on in there?" Katherine said loudly. It was late at night, but she didn't care if she woke up the other children. Voices came from inside, arguing. Katherine rapped on the door loudly again and the voices stopped. After a while, the door opened a crack.

The same man, his belly bulging out, sweat on his forehead. He had thrown a shirt on, but the buttons were undone. His cheeks were red.

"Can't you see I'm busy?" he asked in a flat voice. Katherine tried to look behind him and could make out a shape on the sofa. The shape moved, and she saw a flash of long brown hair. The fat man moved to block her view.

"What are you doing in there?" Katherine asked.

He smiled like he was doing it for the cameras. Perfect white teeth. "None of your business. I've paid you already."

"Who's in there with you?"

"Like I said, none of your business."

Katherine set her jaw. Enough was enough. "I'm calling the police." The man's face didn't change. She turned on her heels to go. He was out the door in a flash and grabbed her arm. Katherine felt his belly shove up against her, pinning her against the wall. He was big. His lips curled, and he got his face closer to hers. It smelled of alcohol, and she turned away, revolted.

"I wouldn't do that if I were you," he whispered.

"Why not?"

"I'd be very caredful of what you're doing."

Katherine met his gaze this time. "I know who you are." She had looked in the papers. His smiling face, arms outstretched, wooing the public at a conference.

He pushed against her harder, and her back ground against the wall, hurting.
"Do you now?"

"Yes. You come here every week, take the children, give them money and booze,
then hurt them. I can tell the press."

The pressure on her released suddenly as he stepped back. His face was purple,
and he panted. Fury blazed in his eyes, and it didn't die as he smiled.

"What do you want?"

"I want you to go. Get the fuck out, and don't come back, you shithead."

He stared at her for a while, and Katherine met his eyes, unflinching. Fear
stormed inside her. Then he stepped back and went inside the room. He didn't
close the door this time. Katherine followed. Her breath caught when she saw the
girl on the sofa, her blouse ripped, bruise on her cheek. The man got dressed
quickly, and she saw the video camera on the tripod. He collapsed the tripod and
packed the camera away quickly. He stood up and looked at the two of them with
a smirk. Then he left.

Katherine sat down next to the girl. She didn't touch her, and the girl didn't
move.

"What's your name?" Katherine asked. "Your real name."

"Nicole Baker." The girl mumbled after a while. Then she looked at
Katherine. "Thank you."

Kathrine hesitated. "You shouldn't let him…"

"Hurt me? He said if I tell anyone my family will be in trouble. My sister will
die, so will my dad."

Katherine frowned. "He told you that?"

"Yes." Nicole bowed her head. "What can I do?"

"You can stay with me," Katherine said firmly. "Then he'll leave you alone."

Nicole's eyes were wide with fear. "But what about my family?"

"Where is your family?"

"My sister is in a foster home, and my dad still lives in our old house, as far as
I know. I don't stay in touch with him. He drinks." Nicole stared down at her
lap.

Katherine reached out and put her hand over Nicole's. "Give me the addresses.

I'll make sure he doesn't go anywhere near them."

"You can do that?"

Katherine said, "I know who he is. We can use that against him."

CHAPTER 19

The smell wafting down was one of stale air and mildew. Arla climbed, hearing the stairs creak noisily. The carpet was the same as on the ground floor, threadbare, ancient. A window allowed in cold, pale sunlight that fell on the landing. She got there and stood for a while, listening. There was a room to her immediate right, and three more rooms across the landing. The door immediately in front of her was ajar. Inside, she could see the outline of a bed and a dressing table. The door next to her right elbow was closed. She touched the tip of the handle and opened it. A bathroom. She left the door open and moved across to the left. She heard creaking and looked down over the railings to see Harry coming up the stairs.

She nudged open the next door with her foot. It fell open soundlessly. Sofas arranged on either side of the wall, and a TV in the far corner. Her fingers groped the wall for a switch and found one. Yellow light suffused the room from a white lampshade on the ceiling. The heavy curtains were drawn, leaving the room in darkness. The walls were bare of photos. A table stood near the bay windows that looked out at the street, with four chairs around it.

She heard Harry go into the room next to her. He joined her shortly.

"There's a fridge in the kitchen. She did eat, just not very much." Arla went inside. The hob was clean, and so was the oven. There was a microwave on the counter, and she opened it. She saw food stains inside. The kitchen window was a sash UPVC, and the blinds were drawn. They looked out at the street as well.

Harry was looking at the cabinet on which the TV stood. A few DVD and old videotapes stood on the shelves, along with some paperback novels. Arla stepped inside the bedroom. The bed had been slept in, and the wardrobes had clothes in them. Nothing fancy, she noted, not even Marks & Spencer. BHS and Primark, if she had to put her finger on it. She opened the drawers on the dressing table. A make-up kit, lipstick, some loose change. No phones or tablets. She heard Harry behind her.

Arla said, "You know what's odd?"

"What?"

Arla cast her hand around. "No photos. No signs of her having friends, never mind family."

Harry shrugged. "Some people don't like photos."

Some people don't like to be reminded of the past, Arla thought. She stared around the bedroom. Something about the place was bothering her, and she couldn't put a finger on it. It was just such a blank envelope. Someone had lived here, but their life had been a featureless white wall. No patterns to suggest who she was, her fears, thoughts, dreams. The things that made her human.

"Get Lisa and Rob up here," she said. "Let them have a look through, after SOCO have been. Are they coming?"

"Yes."

Arla went down the staircase as slowly as she had come up. Harry followed obediently.

"To the Common?"

She nodded without speaking.

*****

Outside, Arla wrapped her jacket around as a gust of wind brought scattered raindrops. Clouds were squeezing light out of the sky, and a cold greyness was leaching into the air.

"Rain's coming," Harry said.

"Shit," she said. "I hope they got the new body covered up, if it's out on the Common."

"SOCO should be on the case. Where are you going?" Harry called out as she crossed the road between fast cars.

She stood next to the lamp-post and looked at number 22 opposite. Harry was watching her, perplexed. Number 22 was an exact replica of the houses on the street. She started from the top and worked her way down. Chimneys, tiled sloping roof, eaves, bay windows. She looked laterally at other houses and compared. Then she found what she was looking for. Many houses had a window in the sloping roof, where there was a loft space. Number 22 didn't. That meant the loft space was used for storage, or not used at all. She made a mental note to check it out later.

The new crime scene wasn't far from the bandstand. With depressing familiarity, they pulled up at the same parking lot, and got out as the rain hosed down. This time, there was no mistaking the two massive white tents that had been raised in the middle of the Common.

Arla stopped and got her bearings. Directly in front, and a few hundred metres away, the A3 ran its traffic-clogged way to the eastern part of the city.

To her right, across the green, stood the Holy Communion Church, the oldest in this part of town. And to her left, the bandstand. Which meant the killer had chosen a point right in between the church and the bandstand.

They approached the tent and saw white suit-clad figures going in and out. Harry stopped where a uniformed officer stood guard and wrote down their names and ranks on a clipboard. Both of them signed it.

It was bright inside the larger tent. Halogen lights, fed off cables from generators, lit up the space in an incandescent white glow. Arla watched as Jeremy Lyons stood to one side, watching the photographers snapping away. Another smaller white-clad figure with glasses leaned over the body, and it looked like Bandy, the pathologist. She walked over to Lyons.

"Busy day in the office," she said.

"Déjà vu," Lyons said with a shrug. "Found naked, body cleaned with antiseptic again. Cause of death probably blood loss from the neck wound. But he can confirm." Lyons pointed to Bandy.

Arla leaned closer to the body. A Caucasian man in his thirties. His jaw was slack, mouth open. Eyes stared towards the sky. The pallor of death was claiming his skin. A dark bloodied line crossed his lower neck from one side to the other.

Bandy straightened, and his eyes met with Arla's. He looked tired, his eyes sunken and hollow beneath the glasses. He took his gloves off and discarded them. Then he lowered his mask.

Arla asked, "Same MO?"

Bandy nodded. "He was just as careful with this one. More in fact, because he didn't leave any chest wounds. But he did leave the same black triangle."

"Where?"

Bandy lifted up the right arm and pointed near the armpit. Arla leaned over and saw the black triangle, hollow in the middle. Looked like it had been drawn with a felt tip pen.

Arla said, "I need the autopsy results ASAP. Have you finished with the last body?"

"Yes, almost. Why don't you come around tomorrow, and I can finish with this one as well, and we can compare?"

Arla didn't like the morgue, but she was willing to do anything to get clues. Years of visiting post-mortems had thickened her hide. Another two bodies wouldn't change anything.

"Sure, about ten am?"

"Make it 1 pm, gives me some time."

"OK."

Arla came out of the tent and tore off her gloves and the covers on her shoes. She threw them into the black bin and stomped away. She stopped and put her hands on her waist, breathing heavily. Mini-clouds of vapour rose from her mouth as she huffed. She turned around to see Harry coming up behind her.

"Take it easy," he said when he saw the look on her face.

"Easy?" Arla exploded. "Apart from a name and an apartment that might as well be empty we have nothing. Nothing! Don't tell me to take it easy!"

Harry dug his hands in his coat pockets and blew out his cheeks. "We got the statement from Steven Wade as well. Time to call in the witnesses from the church." He pointed to the building. "It's not exactly far from either crime scene."

"Can't you see?" Arla seethed. "He's making fun of us. He knows we have no leads, nothing to go on. And is there any form of ID on this body? Wallet, phone, driving licence, anything?"

"Nope."

She raised her arms and let them flop to her sides. "There you go. Another day or two before we get an ID. Who's to say he's not going to strike again?" Arla clutched her head. "Meanwhile, I have King Kong breathing down my neck."

Harry chuckled. "King Kong? I'm sure he'd like that. You should try it."

"Shut up, Harry." She had to admit, the name King Kong Johnson had a ring to it. She smirked inside.

She pointed a finger at Harry. "Let's head back to the station. Gather the incident room. It's time we pulled out the stops."

*****

The Keeper stood invisible behind the trunk of a stout oak tree. He could see the two tents, and the white suited men around it. They couldn't see him. He watched as the female detective and her partner came out of the tent. The woman speeded off, walking furiously. Then she had a tirade at her partner, her arms waving in the air. He could just about make out her face from where he stood, and he paid close attention to the red hair, the fiery, glinting eyes, the lean frame. Her hands were clenched into fists which she kept hitting at her sides.

He had the camera in his pocket, and he looked around. No prying eyes close to him. He took the camera out and zoomed in as much as he could. He leaned against the tree trunk, hiding his body, only the camera visible. He had her face now in close-up. He pressed the shutter several times, hearing the rapid clicks. He lowered the camera quickly, and turned around, his back to the tree trunk. He breathed heavily, sweat pouring down his face, dampening the collar of his shirt. Then he peeked out again.

The female detective and the man were walking off. He gave them a head start then followed.

CHAPTER 20

Jill Meacher looked at Arla as she walked into the living room. Before Arla could go upstairs, she stopped Arla.

"Where have you been, Arla?"

Arla pointed to the sheaf of A4 sized print outs she had cradled on her arm. "Making copies of these."

Each photo was a polaroid of Nicole, taken one month before she disappeared. Nicole had gotten the polaroid camera for Arla as a gift.

Jill said, "You've put photos on every tree and lamp post in this neighbourhood, Arla. Not to mention all the shops, bus stops, and the hospital. Did you know that Mrs Lombard at number 52 complained that you argued with her when she wouldn't let you put the poster up on her front window?"

Arla frowned. Her foster mother was a nice lady, but she could be difficult sometimes. "Well, the more people know she is missing, the better, right?"

Nicole was two months gone. Her school had no idea. So far, the police had come up with a blank.

Jill sat down and gestured Arla to sit. Jill said, "Look I understand. I might not have children, but I did have a sister and a brother. I know you want to find Nicole."

Arla stood. "Then let me put these posters up."

*****

School was finished, and she had picked up more posters on the way back. She nibbled on a Mars bar as she stuck the laminated posters up with blue tack. She came up to the police station and went inside. There was no one at the counter, and she rang the bell and waited.

The uniformed sergent came over and rolled her eyes. "Not you again." Curly blonde hair stuck out from beneath her cap, and her name badge said Wolverton.

"I want to put some posters up."

Wolverton pointed at the opposite wall. "One there already."

"Only one. You should have one on each wall, on the outside and the back as well. As many as possible. Someone might remember something if they see her photo when they walk past."

Wolverton stared at Arla. Arla shrugged. "You never know, do you?"

"Have you rung the missing persons hotline?"

"I ring it every day. They've put messages on national radio and TV. I want to do a TV appeal myself, but they keep saying I'm too young."

Wolverton's face softened. "What about social services?"

"They don't know."

"Did your sister not have a key worker? Most…most girls in her situation do."

Arla wondered what Wolverton had almost said. "Yes, Nicole did have a key worker. But she only met the worker once, and they didn't find her a placement at a care home. This was four months ago."

Wolverton sighed. "OK. Hand some of them over. I'll see what I can do."

"They have my phone number at the bottom, in red. I always answer, even at night. You know, like a 24-hour helpline."

Arla could feel Wolverton's eyes on her back as she walked out.

Jill and Sean Meacher were waiting for her when she got back home. Arla stopped when she saw their expectant faces.

"What?"

"They found someone matching her description. Same age, height, wearing a dark raincoat. She was sleeping in some deserted warehouse, and the builders found her when they came to clear the place out."

Hope flared inside Arla like the sun bursting through clouds. Her pulse surged. "Where?"

"In Glasgow."

"Glasgow? That's the other end of the country!"

Jill said, "Yes, she could have travelled, Arla. You said she had money from somewhere. Now we just have to wait for the photos."

"Where do we get the photos?"

"At the police station. They'll call us as soon as they arrive."

Arla had bitten off all of her nails by the time the phone rung. She almost clung to Sean as he answered. They got to the police station in another ten minutes.

Sergeant Wolverton opened the door for them. She smiled at Arla, who didn't smile back. They followed her down the corridor into an interview room.

"Wait here," Wolverton instructed. The nail biting resumed.

After a while, two men wearing suits entered. They introduced them as detectives. One of them, a tall, thin, young man called Inspector Dixon, looked at Arla with interest.

"So, you are the girl who's been conducting her own investigation?"

"Yes," Arla said impatiently. "Can we see the photos now?"

Dixon tapped out the photos from a brown envelope and laid them out on the table. Arla leaned over and grabbed each one. Then she slumped back in her chair, drowning in a flood of frustration, anger and regret.

"It's not her. It's not her!" She wasn't aware she was shouting.

On the way back, she sat in the backseat as Sean drove and Jill sat next to him. Subdued, Arla watched the lights of the city flash past. Her fingers went to the purple amethyst earring, and she rubbed the stone, feeling its hardness. She wore the earrings every day now.

CHAPTER 21

Arla didn't walk back to the car park. She went on the tarmac road and followed it to the church. She looked at the front garden of the church and the people walking in and out. It was midday, and the lunch crowd were milling around. She couldn't see any CCTVs. Harry was walking ahead of her, and she joined him on the street, looking around.

He lifted a long arm and pointed at CCTV cameras. "There, there and there."

"I want all the images, night and day, all magnified for any suspects. I don't care how long it takes, or how many officers. Just bloody do it." Arla breathed.

"Then you interview a suspect who gives you hell, you snap and punch him."

Colour rose to her face, and she felt the heat. She turned away. "No, I won't." Damn Harry. She felt like punching *him*, right now. At the same time, she felt her frustration and anger drop away. If anything, she felt a bit light-headed. Surviving on coffee alone was taking its toll.

She could punch Harry, but she could also use his lanky frame to lean against. Or was it his arms she wanted around her? Any warmth would be nice right now.

Harry said, "You go too hard at this. You can't let go. I know we don't have much to go on. But it's going to come. Give it a day or two."

Her shoulders drooped. "I don't have a day or two, Harry. Johnson wants a list of suspects. He wants progress."

"Let him talk. He can come and do the work himself if he's that desperate, right? And as for replacing you, good luck to him. He won't find anyone to jump in on a double homicide at this stage. Not unless…" He gave her a warning look.

Arla waved her hands. "Yeah, yeah, I know. I have to be good." She stared at her feet.

"I think we need a coffee and a burger," Harry said.

"Good point."

When they got back to the incident room, it was buzzing. Everyone had heard about the second murder, and the similarity in MO. No one needed to be told it wasn't officially a serial killer until the third body was found, but everyone knew that was a textbook definition. Real life was different.

"OK, settle down," Arla said as she rested her bottom on the edge of the table. To her right, the white board was now full of images. Close-ups of Charlene Atkins, both dead and alive, from SOC photos and CCTV images. Next to it, a line had been drawn vertically down, and images of the new body had been posted. Only two existed so far, both sent by SOC.

Arla walked over to the white board, and she put a big question mark under the photos of the recent victim.

"Right, let's focus on Charlene Atkins for now. We don't have a phone as yet, but we are looking with all the network providers. Right?" She glanced at Lisa, who nodded. Rob Pinckney was standing next to her. They made a nice couple, she thought.

"How about social media?"

Lisa cleared her throat. "She did have a Facebook account, but it's all related to her church work. She didn't post much personal stuff. She only has a few posts every year, mainly during Easter and Xmas. And before 2012, she has nothing. I called Facebook in London, and they confirmed she didn't have an account before 2012."

"Check all her FaceBook friends and all the tagged people on the images. I want everyone interviewed with a statement. Send detectives to their homes, it doesn't matter where in the country they live. Got it?"

Lisa scribbled furiously in her diary and several heads nodded.

"And I want to go through the FaceBook account myself," Arla said. "How are we doing with the door-to-door?"

Rob Pinckney stepped forward from behind Lisa. "I collected the statements from the uniforms and went through them since this morning."

Arla didn't congratulate him. She needed results more than she needed diligence. "And?"

"The night of the 24th of November several residents commented seeing her head towards the church in the afternoon. She came back as well, according to some residents. But no one saw her leave late at night."

"Understandable, because it was dark," Arla snapped. "Anything else?"

"Yes," Rob said, looking pleased with himself. "One of the residents mentioned seeing a stranger on the street she hadn't seen before. She noticed him because he seemed to follow the victim to the church, and then back as well."

"Description?" Arla asked, a fear suddenly slicing inside her.

"A man with long, dark hair. Average height. Wore black trousers and matching long, black leather coat."

"Shit," Arla exclaimed. "That has to be the same guy Margaret, the old lady downstairs, saw. Any images as yet from the photofit guys?"

Harry shook his head. "Should be ready anytime today, though."

"What about Charlene's relatives? Any children, parents, siblings, anyone? There has to be."

Lisa said, "We've asked the Home Office if she ever applied for a passport. She would have put her parents' details in there."

"Good, let's hope we get somewhere. What about a bank account? How did she pay her council tax? Must be a direct debit like everyone else. And utility bills."

"We found a bank account," Harry said. He consulted a printout from the file on his hand. "HSBC. She had a Premier account."

"Premier, eh?" Arla raised her eyebrows. "That's fancy for a plain Jane with no friends or family, isn't it? Which HSBC branch was it?"

"In Oval."

"So not far. We check out the branch manager tomorrow, Harry." He nodded, putting the piece of paper away.

Arla spoke to the men and women facing her. "This guy thinks he's better than us. He thinks he can leave dead bodies in a park and no one can get him for it. Well, we know different, don't we?"

There was a murmuring of voices. Arla leaned forward, turning her ear to them. "What's that you said?"

"Yes, guv!" several voices shouted at once. Arla smiled. It wasn't her usual style, but sometimes a good old pep talk was just what the team needed. Laughter filled the air.

As the team filed out of the partition doors, she beckoned Harry.

CHAPTER 22

Harry put his papers in the folder and walked over to her. "What?"

"Can you call the vicar and set up an appointment? If he can do one now, we can go."

Harry mumbled something about being run off his feet, but she ignored him. She went inside her office and shut the door. She looked up the Met Occupation Health psychiatrist's number. Dr Seddon answered at the first ring.

"How are you, Arla?"

"I'm fine, thanks. I'm very sorry, but I won't be able to attend our session today."

There was a pause. Then his voice came back, slightly strained. "Why is that, Arla?"

"I am leading a double homicide case currently. To say it's keeping me busy is the understatement of the year."

"OK," Dr Seddon said slowly. "But are you looking after yourself?"

She was going to say yes, when she paused. Was she really? Or was she running into this full tilt, trying to solve the case no matter what?

The past was fixed, immutable. She couldn't change what life had done to her, but she could change how she reacted to it. That was what Dr Seddon had said. And she knew he was right.

His voice came on the phone again, a soft and measured tone. "You can't get it your way all the time, Arla. Sometimes you have to let it go."

She sat down on her chair, and suddenly, for no reason, she felt tears prickle the back of her eyes. She rubbed them angrily, embarrassed.

"Dr Seddon, I'll speak to you later," she said.

"Let's meet next week. Remember I have to do your report."

That report was meant to be her fitness certificate to get back to work. She almost laughed at the irony of it. She said goodbye and hung up.

She went outside her office to find Harry just putting the phone down. Lisa and Rob were sitting next to him. Arla said, "Steven Wade, the man who identified Charlene's body."

Harry turned to look at her. "What about him?"

"Did we verify his alibi?"

Lisa said, "Yes, we did. He checks out. He was with his bartender girlfriend, who works part-time at the record shop where he works as well."

"Hmm." Arla was thoughtful. "He knows something. Can someone keep an eye on the record shop? And let's bring the girlfriend in, see what she has to say about him."

Harry held up his phone. "The vicar is there. We can see him in the next hour, he said."

"Good. Guys, give me a minute. I'll see you outside."

They filed out, and Harry closed the door.

Alone, Arla stared out the window. The rain was turning to sleet, and the driving shards of ice bounced off the black asphalt. It drummed on tin roofs and bounced against the window panes of her office. Absent-mindedly, she went to the Met's missing persons website. She searched for the same person she had been looking for for the last eighteen years. Her photo and name were still up there. So was the clear red label that said "Missing". Above the red label was her name.

Nicole Baker.

Missing. An ugly, obscene word. Missing for almost twenty years now.

A lifetime for Arla.

Arla stared at the photo of the teenage girl for a while, feeling familiar emotions surface inside her.

Then she clicked the computer off, grabbed her scarf and coat, and left the office.

Harry was standing at the gates, pulling on a cigarette. She watched him for a while then decided to ask for one. He refused at first, but she won in the end. She had given up smoking well over a year ago. The first few drags jolted her senses, making her dizzy. She leaned against the wall, feeling the cold seep in through the layers of her clothes.

Harry let out rings of smoke then blew them away. "You know what I'm thinking?"

"You think? Really?"

He ignored her. "Someone who has a Facebook account must have a mobile phone. Bet you she's on WhatsApp. Hell, my mother's on it." He looked at her then averted his eyes quickly, shamefaced. He knew that Arla didn't have a mother and had never known the woman who had given birth to her.

She asked, "What do you propose? We have asked the phone companies, and just have to wait to hear from them."

"If we contact her FaceBook friends, won't someone have her phone number?"

Arla looked at him, fascinated. "You do think, after all."

"Question is, can we do it legally?"

Arla pondered. "If we explain to them what it's for, then I can't see why not."

CHAPTER 23

Arla picked up the ringing phone. She was on her way out to school. Jill was in the kitchen, she could hear her pottering around.

Arla pressed the reciver against her ear. "Hello?"

It was a female voice. "This is the Balham Police Station. Can I speak to the legal guardian of Arla Baker, please?"

Arla's heart beat faster. "This is Arla Baker. Who am I speaking to?"

There was a pause. "Can you hand it to your foster mother please?"

Arla licked her dry lips. She was holding the receiver so hard it was hurting her ear. She relaxed her hands, but nothing stopped the surging pulse rate. "Is it about Nicole?" Five months had passed now.

The voice hesitated again. "I need to speak to your foster mother, Arla, or I have to hang up."

Arla put the receiver down and ran into the kitchen. Jill looked up in alarm as she rose from the dishwasher. "What is it, Arla?"

"It's the police, they have some information on Nicole. But they won't tell me anything."

Jill wiped her hands on a kitchen towel and hurried to the front hallway. Arla stood next to her.

"This is Jill Meacher. Can I help?" Jill listened for a few seconds, then nodded. "But she has school now, so..."

"I can come," Arla said quickly. "First lesson's maths, and I can catch up."

Jill raised an eyebrow and spoke on the phone again. "OK, yes. Thank you."

She turned to look at Arla, who was increasingly frantic. "There's a witness at the station. He says he saw Nicole that night she disappeared."

Arla's mouth opened. "I have to go." She reached for the door, but Jill stopped her.

"Arla..."

"Jill, please don't stop me. Please."

"I won't. In fact, I have to take you there and be present. That's not the point. We did have witnesses in the past, Arla. I don't want you to be disappointed again." She sighed and shook her head. "I think this is taking over your life. I know you want to find her, but have you thought she doesn't want to be found?"

"I don't care," Arla said. "What happens if this witness is the one?"

Jill shook her head again. "It's only a witness, Arla. If this comes to nothing, will be alright?"

Arla calmed down. "I know what you're saying, Jill. But imagine if something did come out of this witness. If I didn't follow it up, how bad would I feel?"

Arla rang up school to explain as Jill drove. At the station, they were shown in to one of the interview rooms. The two Detectives were sat inside with an older man who rose when he saw Arla. Hope ignited his Arla's chest. It was Mr. Roy, the corner shop owner.

"Mr. Roy!"

Arla could see the deep lines on his face, and his skin looked more tanned than usual.

He stepped forward and smiled sadly. "Hello, Arla." Then his smile fell away. "I'm sorry about Nicole. Also about everything that's happened."

Arla nodded, but she was impatient. "Did you see Nicole that night?"

"Was it a Friday night in October? The day is clear as I shut the shop for the next three months. I can tell you the date as well. 10th?"

"Yes," Arla said, getting more excited. Then it struck her. "Why did it take you so long to come forward?"

"Because I've been away. I sold my shop and took my life savings to get Lisa treated in Florida. That's where I've just come back from."

Light dawned in Arla's mind. That's why he had the tan and the…sadness. Arla whispered, "Lisa…"

Mr Roy shook his head. "She passed away." He looked down at the floor. Jill said, "Shall we all sit down."

Arla faced Mr Roy. "Tell me about Nicole."

Mr Roy frowned. "I knew it was her from the raincoat. Not all 16-year-olds wear long black leather coats, do they? Anyway, she was walking very fast, it was raining, and I almost missed her as I walked past."

"What happened?"

"She stopped to say hello and ask about Lisa. I asked her where she was going. She said to Clapham Common. As it was raining, I offered to call her a cab, but she said she had the money. But my friend owns a cab company, and I called him then and there. Your sister was always kind to me, Arla. I could see she was troubled."

Mr Roy paused to take a sip of water. "So we stood under the bus stop shelter till my friend pulled up. His name's Gavin. As far as I know, he took her to Clapham Common."

Arla stared at Mr Roy, her eyes like saucers. For the first time, she felt like a ray of sunlight was poking out from dense clouds.

"Where's your friend, Gavin?"

Detective Dixon cleared his throat. "We have called him in too. He should be here soon." As if on cue, the phone on the desk rang. Dixon spoke for a while, then got up and left the room. He came back with a man the same age as Mr Roy, dressed in an old crumpled linen suit. He looked scared.

"Hey, Gavin," Mr Roy said.

"George, what's going on? The cops are saying it's about the girl I drove to Clapham Common in October. You put her in my cab, remember?"

"Yes, Gavin. Don't worry. No one's blaming you. We just want to know where the girl is. This is her sister, Arla."

"Hello," Arla said. Before any of the adults could speak, Arla stood. "Look, Gavin, I just want to find out where my sister is. Please. Can you tell me where you dropped her off?"

George was given a chair by Dixon, and he sat, facing the group. His brows were furrowed in thought. "It was a rainy night. Bad weather, you know. I did wonder where a young girl like her was going on her own. Especially in that weather."

"Carry on," Dixon said, impatience in his voice.

"I dropped her off on Clapham Common Road, right in the middle. Between Clapham North and Clapham Common tube station, you know."

Arla said, "So, on the road with all the big houses opposite the Common?"

George looked at her then at the others. "Yes. Right there."

"Did you see where she went?"

"No. I saw her cross the road, heading for the houses. That was it."

CHAPTER 24

The old man had known it would end like this one day. The night before, he had stared at the TV in disbelief. Crimestoppers was on, and the photofit image on the screen had jolted old memories. He could guess why she had died, and who had killed her out there on the Common.

She had been the keeper of secrets that were best left buried. Now she was dead, it would be his turn. The apartment was his, and it overlooked the park and the river. It became quiet in the evenings as the traffic died down on Putney Bridge Road, like it had now. He could hear the occasional car swish past, even the creak of a bicycle.

He didn't miss the faint sound of a key turning in the lock. He stiffened. His nervous, panicked eyes looked around. The walls of the room seemed to be closing in on him. The flickering TV watched like a baleful square eye. He had muted the sound. After a few seconds, he heard the lock turn downstairs, and the door swing open. Then the door closed, and slow footsteps rose up, getting louder.

He could feel his heart slamming against his ribs. A bead of sweat worked down his forehead, despite the coolness in the room. There was nowhere to hide. Even if he were younger, and able to physically escape, they would find him eventually. He knew there was no option but to surrender.

The footsteps stopped at the doorway to the lounge. The old man gripped the handles of his armchair, his knuckles bone-white. He only had to move his face to the right to see the figure, but he didn't want to. It wouldn't make a difference.

He heard the figure step inside the room, the sound of his shoes swallowed by the carpet. When he heard the voice, a blue flash of electricity streaked down his spine, and he closed his eyes. He had hoped he would never hear that voice again.

"Did you tell her?"

The old man shook his head. Words failed him.

"Answer me." The voice was calm but persistent.

He cleared his throat. "No."

"Then who did?"

"If I knew, I would tell you." He moved his head slightly and saw the figure standing in the middle of the room. His hands were in his pockets. The glow from the silent TV fell on his face, lighting one side but leaving the other in darkness. He looked disfigured, disembodied. The old man shivered.

"You are lying," the figure said.

"No," a hint of panic entered the old man's voice. "Why would I lie, after all these years? I could have... Why now?"

"I don't know. But someone has to pay." The figure moved. He slid into the shadow beneath the armchair, and the old man couldn't see him anymore.

With a gasp, he felt the cord rope around his neck. It tightened and pulled upwards, almost pulling him out of the chair. The pressure increased, and his eyes bulged. His hands became claws, clutching at the rope. There was a woman on the TV, laughing hysterically. Her face became big, then distorted. The maniacal smile was the last thing the old man remembered as the lights dimmed in his eyes.

CHAPTER 25

Arla's phone beeped, and she answered. Lisa's voice was strained. "Where are you, guv?"

Arla said, "At the back." She didn't want to mention she'd just had a cigarette when everyone knew she'd given up. "What's up?"

"Another body found, guv. An old man in an apartment. Strangled, it seems."

An unfathomable, illogical panic flared up in Arla's chest. "Where?"

"In Putney."

Arla breathed out, closing her eyes. "Who called it in?"

"The postman found the door open. He knocked and called, then the smell hit him."

"Smell?"

"Whoever did this left the heating on, and body's decomposed."

Arla grimaced. It sounded nasty, but she knew from experience decomposing a body would get rid of vital evidence. But they would still have bones and dental records.

She beckoned Harry, and they walked back inside. Lisa was waiting in front of her desk. She gave them the address.

In the parking lot, Harry put the BMW into gear and swung out with the siren on. Traffic was horrendous, and without the flashing lights, they would have been stuck for ages.

It was past mid day by the time they got to Putney East. Putney was a world away from the seediness of Streatham. A bona fide Royal Borough, it was the home of South London's elite. Riverside bars, moored boats, and glitzy, chic boutiques on the High Street accentuated that image.

She drove down Putney Bridge Road, putting the window down. Freezing cold air blew in like shards of ice, stinging her face. Arla put the heating on full blast, and let the radio play a mindless music channel as she drove. When she pulled up at the address that Harry had texted her, the white SOCO van and a squad car were already there.

The building, like so many of London's homes, was in the middle of a long line of narrow terraces. She spotted Harry standing outside, smoking.

The white smoke clung to the air as she approached him. He blew it away.

"Watch it up there," he said with a nod of his head.

"Why?"

"You'll see when you step in."

The smell hit her like a wall as she stepped inside the doorway. She crinkled her nose: it made her gag. The heat was still present, and she knew why Harry had kept the door open. Someone had left the heating on full blast. The body must have decomposed. One of the SOCO guys came down, dressed in his white overalls and face mask. He pulled it down and nodded to Arla.

She didn't know his name. "How's it looking up there?" she asked.

"Not good. Body's decomposed, been dead for 24 hours at least. Not much we can tell due to the advanced stage of decomposition."

"Any point in heading up there?"

He shrugged. "I wouldn't. Nothing identifiable on the body. Face is gone. We've taken prints, DNA swabs, fibre and hair samples, the lot."

"OK. I'll still have a look around." She put on the blue sterile shoe covers and placed her foot on the first step where the mat had been placed. A series of mats went up the stairs, then continued into the room. Arla donned gloves and overalls and put a mask on her face. The apartment was old, but in reasonably good condition.

The walls were whitewashed, bright in the light from inside the lounge to her right. Further down the small hallway there was another room, and she could see the corner of a bed. Another door opened to the bathroom. She stepped inside the lounge. The sash had been opened, thankfully, and there was a draught of air coming in.

The body was breaking down rapidly. Flesh had separated from the facial bones. She looked at his clothes for blood splatter or other marks. Nothing. The walls were similarly bare. A sideboard contained some books and DVDs. The TV was flat-screen, modern.

She checked the door. No signs of struggle on the carpet or breaking and entering. Whoever had come in either was let in or had keys.

In the bathroom cabinet she found two boxes of medication. The name on the box was of a Christopher Crichton. The white label said quetiapine 200mg twice a day on one, and temazepam 20mg once a day, on the other. She knew what temazepam was for. It made you sleep and less nervous. Several druggies they had pulled off the street were on it. The bottles were almost empty. She put each in a separate specimen bag and put them in her pocket.

Outside, she handed them to Harry, who took it without a word. "Any ID?" she asked.

"Some letters to the name of a Chris Crichton. Bills mainly, so unless there were any other residents, that must be the victim."

CHAPTER 26

It was the morning after Crichton's body had been discovered, and the department was busy. Three homicides in the space of one month was big news, and Arla knew very soon a nosy reporter would put two and two together and camp outside the station, looking for answers. Which meant the investigation was more of a priority now than it had ever been.

Rob and Lisa straightened as Arla walked in. Rob held out a piece of paper. Arla took it and read the dental report from the lab. It confirmed the latest victim as Chris Crichton.

"Good work," she said, handing the paper back.

Lisa said, "Background checks on Chris Crichton are done. He was quite rich, in fact. Kind of weird he died as a loner in that crummy apartment. Folder's on your email."

"OK." Arla went to her office and sat down. She had opened up her emails when Harry walked in. He asked, "Have you checked Crichton's report?"

"No, I haven't in detail. I saw that he had some company filings." Arla clicked on it. She read the stuff for a while. Then she frowned. "Company was called St Martin's Estates," she murmured to herself. "So he was a property developer, right?"

"Yes. Scroll down and have a look at the list of properties he owned. Page 24."

St Martin Estate's last filings to Her Majesty's Revenue and Customs were several pages long and dated back to 1998. The photocopied pages were not easily readable. In the Company Assests page Arla found the list Harry mentioned. It was almost a page long, the print small.

"Come on, Harry," she murmured. "What am I looking for?"

He stepped around the table and bent over her, facing the screen. He pointed at a line near the bottom of the page. "There."

Arla squinted. The property address was 243 Clapham Common Road. A memory unfurled in Arla's mind. Eyebrows constricted, she looked up at Harry. She saw understanding in his face.

"It's the derelict house, right? The one that we almost went into."

"Exactly."

Arla tried to concentrate on the screen, but her mind was elsewhere. Her fingertips felt numb, cold. She swallowed and tried to get a grip. "Harry, leave me alone."

She looked up at him to see him gazing at her. Harry knew when something was up, and she could easily lose herself in his eyes.

"Please," she said.

"I'm here if you need me."

"I know," she said. When Harry had left, she locked the door. She reached into the bottom drawer and took out the laptop. She opened up Nicole's investigation folder. Arla had painstakingly listed every single address and their history on Clapham Common Road. The road where Nicole had last been seen. Arla ran her finger down the list of addresses. She came up with a blank between 242 and 244.

She frowned. This list she had was from the local council. History of ownership of every property on Clapham Common Road, and the use of the abode for business or residential purposes was all detailed on her lengthly folder.

Apart from number 243 it seemed.

Arla had seen a few abdondoned houses when she had searched the road as a teenager, and later, as a young detective constable. She had thought all of them had been on her list.

She was wrong.

Arla thought for a while, then did an online search for the address. The property didn't exist on Her Majesty's Land Registry. Arla tapped the desk with her red painted fingernails, thinking. Then she picked up the phone and rang Land Registry. The woman she spoke to was as puzzled as Arla was.

"Is there anywhere else you can look for the address?" Arla asked.

The woman thought for a while, then said, "Yes. There is the Crown database."

"What's that?"

"About 15% of land in the UK is not registed under HM Land Registry. That's because those lands or addresses are owned by the aristocracy, churches or the royal family. They've never been sold, so there's no need for registry."

"So, this property on Clapahm Common Road could be one of them?"

"Hold on, let me search for you."

Arla waited. The woman's voice came down the line after a long wait. "OK. The address you gave me is Bona Vacantia."

"What does that mean?"

"It means empty goods. When the owner dies without any relatives or a will, or if a company is dissolved, then the assets are transferred to the Crown Treasury."

Arla digested this in silence. Chris Crichton had only just died. Had he given this property away to the Crown? It didn't make much sense to Arla. A place like that would be worth a few million at least, in today's market.

"Can you check who the last owner was?"

"Christopher Crichton. He bought it in 1991."

Arla gripped the phone tighter. "And what was it used for?"

"A residential home."

"Nothing else?"

"Like what?"

Arla gulped then steeled herself. "How about a care home for children? From broken homes, or under social services."

The woman's reply was almost instant. "There are no records for anything like that. I have a list of the owners before Mr Crichton, if you wish. There is a fee to have this record, by the way."

Arla paid, got the record sent to her via email and hung up. Then she paced her office.

She lifted up the phone and called Lisa into her office. When the plump blonde woman bustled in, Arla asked, "Did we do a check on all of St Martin's Estates properties?"

"Yes. Most of them were sold, and four are still under the name of Robert Crichton, his brother."

"We need to see him."

Lisa tucked a stray strand of hair behind her ear. "Have tried to call him already. He doesn't answer his phone. Lives in Croydon, in a nice new apartment complex. No other living relatives as far as I can see."

A sliver of anxiety sliced through Arla's guts. "Send some uniforms to check out his apartment. We need him alive. He could have vital information about his brother. Does Robert work?"

Lisa shrugged. "Not that we can see. He owns a property company as well, called Coral Property Management. The four buildings he owns are on it. If I had to guess I'd say he lives off the rent."

"Alright. No police records?" Lisa shook her head.

"OK, good work. Let's keep looking for him."

There was a knock on the door, and Rob poked his head in. "Sorry, guv."

"What is it?" Arla asked, as Lisa moved to one side.

"Just got Robert Crichton's credit card statements. He booked a flight for Alicante, Spain last week. Not sure how long he's gone for, but we got the resort address as well."

"Excellent. Let's get in touch with him."

Lisa and Rob left, closing the door behind them.

Arla made sure she was alone and locked the door again. She opened St Martin's Estates property folder and looked down the list of addresses. None of them were in Clapham, apart from the derelict house. Arla picked up the phone and called the council.

When switchboard answered, Arla asked, "I have an electoral roll inquiry. Could you please check if a Chris Crichton lived in 243 Clapham Common Road, in 1988?" Arla knew records went back 30 years and were digitised.

The man's voice came back soon. "We have no records to suggest that, sorry. It means he never registered to vote. Have you checked HM Land Registry for his address?"

"Yes, I have. Do you know if anyone of that name registered to pay council tax?"

"Hold on." The voice came back in a few seconds. "Nope, sorry. No records of a Chris Crichton."

Arla thanked him, hung up and called back the woman at Land Registry.

"Hello, it's Arla Baker. Is that Janice Longhorn, Registrar?"

"Are you the lady who just called about the Bona Vacantia property?"

"Yes. You mentioned the property was used as a residence in 1998. Is that correct?"

Janice hesitated. Arla prompted her. "Janice?"

There was a longer pause, and Arla could hear clicks on the keyboard. She began to feel uneasy.

Janice said, "I'm not sure what I can tell you."

"What do you mean?"

"The property was used as a private residence before. But from 1998, there is no record of its use."

"No record?"

"The records are closed under Crown Restrictive Covenants. These covenants decree any property belonging to the Crown can be used for undisclosed purposes."

"So, the records aren't public?"

"No."

Arla thought before she asked her next question. "What if there was a law enforcement agency inquiry?"

Janice cleared her throat. "A court hearing is needed to make CRR records public, Miss Baker. May I know what your interest in this property is?"

Arla paused. "It's worth a lot to someone, I guess."

"Right. We do get asked these questions occasionally. Good luck to you."

Arla hung up, sunk in thought. Was it just coincidence that the property's details were conveniently hidden under the Crown Restrictive Covenants?

Or had someone made sure of that?

There was something about that derelict house. She could feel it deep inside her, pulling at her guts.

CHAPTER 27

The hailstones were dying down. The Holy Communion Church took up quarter of an acre on Clapham Common. It was an imposing structure, a large, rectangular building made of red bricks. Three doors led into the front entrance and the nave of the church, but other entrances existed at the sides.

Harry parked in the church parking lot. Arla looked up at the tower rising up from the rear, and the large clock face on it. The time was almost midday, and it was correct.

They had to walk around the front, crunching leaves that blew against their feet in the stiff November breeze. The middle door was open, and they walked into the main area with a low roof, that gave way through a red draped screen into the nave and pulpit. The silence was suddenly absolute, and there was no one to be seen. They stood there, necks craning at the curved porticoes in the ceiling, and the stained-glass windows through which coloured shafts of sunlight slanted in. In the front, to one side, there was a large organ, with stands for the choir. High box seats were visible in the nave, distinct from the rows of plain benches in front of them.

Arla whispered, "What do we do now?"

"Search for divine inspiration," Harry whispered back.

Arla was getting ready for a suitable retort, when she spied a black-cloaked figure emerge out of a side door to the right of the nave. The man walked forward with purpose. He smiled in greeting as he approached them.

"Good morning, or almost afternoon," the man said, white teeth flashing. He was shorter than Harry, but close to six feet. Black hair tumbled with grey and white on a receding hairline at the front and sides. His green eyes were open and friendly, and the smooth cheeks smelled faintly of cologne. Late-forties, Arla reckoned. Her eyes went to the white collar then back up to his face.

"Detective Chief Inspector Arla Baker, Vicar…"

He laughed and waved his hand. "Oh, Sean is fine, Miss Baker. Sean Decker is the full name, but Sean will do." He shook hands with Harry, who introduced himself. He pointed to the seats closer to the nave. Arla and Harry followed him.

"We could go inside," Sean Decker said, "but as there is no congregation today, we can talk here if you wish."

"No problem for us, Sean." They sat down side by side, the vicar turning his body to face them. He arranged his cloak and crossed his legs.

Arla took out her pad and pen. "I take it you heard what happened in the Common over the last two days."

His voice was grave, like his manner. "I have, and how terrible it is. To have such acts committed a stone's throw away from a place of worship is dreadful. Utterly dreadful."

Arla noticed he had green eyes, with black pupils. She said, "One of your congregation, Charlene Atkins, was the first victim. Have you heard about that?"

He nodded, his face twisted in a frown. "A few members mentioned it. Like I said, I cannot believe this could have happened."

"The person who identified the body, Steven Wade, is also a member of the church. Do you know him?"

He creased his brows, and his eyes took a faraway look. "You must forgive me, Inspector. As much as I prize each member of this church, I would be amiss if I said I knew everyone personally."

"Steven mentioned that Charlene spoke to you frequently. Is that true?"

He nodded. "Charlene was one of the leading lights in setting up a winter camp for the homeless. We run a soup kitchen, and we also have three beds here for vulnerable adults, funded by the council. Charlene was instrumental in setting this up."

"How do you mean, instrumental?"

"Well, she donated money and wrote to the council. An application that we supported, of course."

"Do you know who she wrote to at the council?"

The vicar shrugged. "No. But there is a Safeguarding Department in the council, for vulnerable adults and children. I presume it was to them."

Arla scribbled on her notebook. Then she looked up at the pleasant features of the vicar. "Did Charlene donate a lot of money to the church?"

His face changed then became neutral again. "The church subsists on council funding as well as private donations, Inspector. Yes, Charlene did donate money, but I am not at liberty to discuss how much."

"Would you say it was a significant amount, compared to other private donors?" Arla pushed.

He shrugged and pursed his lips. "It was a generous amount. I really cannot tell you anything more than that, simply because I don't remember it."

"Was she a wealthy woman?"

A slightly perturbed look flashed across the vicar's face. This time it remained on his features. *Good*, Arla thought to herself. She needed to get past the polished exterior.

"I am not sure what you mean by that, Inspector. I do not concern myself with the wealth of my congregation. I am a man of God."

"Of course. My question was merely to see if she displayed any signs of wealth." Arla shrugged.

"Not that I could see," replied the vicar stiffly. His eyes moved to Harry then back to Arla.

"What did you talk about the last time you saw her?" she asked.

He appeared lost in thought for a while. She took the time to study his hands. Neatly cut nails, no wedding ring. Smooth skin. Not a workman's hands.

"It was Sunday mass. We had a question-and-answer session on religion, aimed at children. She helped manage one of the stalls. We talked about that, and the weather, I believe. Nothing out of the ordinary."

"What were you doing the night of the 24th of November?"

"I was here. I live onsite, my quarters are behind the west gallery of the church."

"Can anyone alibi?"

His face brightened. "Yes. One of the nuns, Sister Meredith. She has her own quarter, but she prepares dinner for me."

"Did she see you for the whole night?"

The vicar's bland green eyes looked deep into hers like he was probing the innards of her soul. She met his gaze, undaunted.

He spoke very quietly. "After dinner, I read, then I pray. Then I go to bed. All three are solitary activities, as you can imagine. That night did not deviate from the norm."

Arla persisted. "But Sister Meredith didn't see you, after dinner?"

"She was aware of me getting ready for night prayers, as she cleaned up. She would have been aware if I had left the apartment, as we share a common entrance."

"I see." The atmosphere between them had become charged, and static seemed to crackle as they stared at each other. Harry intervened by clearing his throat.

"In the future, Vicar, we would like to see the apartment, if you don't mind."

"No problem."

*****

Vicar Sean Decker bid them goodbye from the front entrance of the church. As soon as the policemen rounded the building, he stepped back inside and literally ran across the nave. He opened the side door and went up a narrow flight of stairs to a landing covered by a stained-glass window. From there, he could see the couple get into a black BMW in the car park and drive away. When the car disappeared around the corner, he went up the stairs again to the second floor. He opened the door to his study and sat down at his desk.

He thought for a while. Then he opened the top desk drawer and took out a key. He went to a framed picture of the Virgin Mary next to his bed. He took the picture off the wall, revealing the door to a safe. He inserted the key and unlocked the safe. Inside there was a three-pack box of pay-as-you-go mobile phones, each with its own SIM card. He had been instructed to use each phone once only then discard it.

He charged up one of the phones then inserted the SIM card. He looked in his diary for a number he had now forgotten. With trembling fingers, he dialled the numbers. He wiped the sweat from his forehead. The line connected. He was silent, listening to the heavy breathing on the other end.

Sean Decker cleared his throat. "It's happening," he said.

"Yes, I know," the voice said. "What did you tell them?"

"Nothing."

There was silence for a while.

Sean Decker said, "I think it's time we had a meeting."

CHAPTER 28

The tyres of the BMW crunched gravel as it left the church car park.

"That was interesting," Harry murmured. "Suspect?"

Arla's mind was busy. The interview had started off friendly, but after she probed Charlene, Sean Decker became defensive. She wondered if that was a natural reaction to her questions, or if the vicar had something to hide.

Aloud she said, "He certainly had the opportunity. Once we have a more precise time from Bandy, we can squeeze the Vicar again."

"No motive, though."

"Unless he could get hold of her money. But I can't see how that could have been, unless he knew Charlene some other way."

"Charlene. It keeps coming back to her." Harry said.

"Yes," Arla whispered. She stared at Harry as he drove then looked away, her mind flying off as the traffic went past them. Who had Charlene Atkins been? A woman with plenty of cash, it seemed. But who lived a prosaic life in an ordinary, two-bedroom apartment.

"Back to the station?" Harry asked, breaking into her thoughts.

Arla squeezed her forehead. "Stop for a coffee, then head to the morgue. Bandy should be ready for us."

The mortuary was located inside St George's Hospital in Tooting Broadway, a place Arla knew well. From the west side window of her apartment, she could see the hospital.

The examination chambers were underground, and as they descended in the lift, Arla had the familiar sense of claustrophobia. The lift doors opened into a wide hallway. The cement floor was occupied only by a few empty gurneys on the side. Dark liquid slicked the black leather surface of one gurney. The ceilings were high, and their footsteps echoed in the cavernous space.

"This place gives me the creeps," Arla muttered. Without noticing, she had shuffled closer to Harry. When Harry pushed the double doors open, the smell of disinfectant, damp and dead bodies hit Arla like a wall. She wrinkled her nostrils and breathed through her mouth. That was somehow distasteful, so she snapped her mouth shut and nose-breathed. She had been here and to other public mortuaries numerous times, but she never got used to it.

They pressed the buzzer, and a Chinese woman with a surgical mask and blue overalls opened the door. Her name was Lorna, and she was Dr Bandy's assistant. She pointed to the operating theatre scrub-wearing Dr Bandy, leaning over a gurney in the middle of the floor. The pathologist looked up, took the mask off his face, and waved at Arla. He shuffled over in his lumbering gait, not taking off his gloves.

"You are just in time. I was going over the first body once again. Quite common, in my line of work." He smiled. He pointed in the direction of the gurney. "Shall we?"

Harry followed as Arla stepped towards the gurney quickly. The sooner they got this over with, the better. Bandy took off his old gloves, folded one over the other, swung them around and threw them into a nearby bin. Lorna put a new pack of sterile gloves on the push trolley next to the gurney.

"Come closer," Bandy said, as he stood over the head of the dead body. Lorna adjusted the light over his head, until it illuminated the head and neck area. Arla looked at the chest and abdomen quickly. A Y-incision had been made and sutured up as well. Which meant Bandy had checked the organs, looked for internal damage, and sent off samples for toxicology.

"Here," Bandy commanded. Arla looked at his pointed finger. He had dissected the neck.

Arla could see the tube-like structure of the trachea inside the V-neck of the cut bellies of muscle. A portion of the trachea had been cut and held to one side by clips, showing two thick, cord-like structures inside a compartment.

"See that?" Bandy asked.

Arla nodded. "What is it?"

"The voice box. Larynx. Those two cords vibrate when air passes in the throat, giving us a voice."

"Mine must be pretty," Harry piped up. "Because I can sing."

Arla elbowed him in the ribs and shot him a look. "Bet you they're ugly. Shall we have a look?"

Bandy raised his eyebrows and went back to his work. "Look around the larynx. The small bands that hold the cords to the flesh. Can you see them?"

Arla looked closer. Several bits of tissue had been ripped and torn around the larynx and inside.

"Yes. They're damaged, aren't they?"

"Yes. Why do you think they are?"

"Someone squeezed her throat?" Harry ventured.

"Not just squeeze. When you squeeze someone's throat, the big muscles bulge up to protect the trachea. It's actually quite hard to kill someone by strangulation, especially if they resist. Only with sustained, heavy pressure on the neck will you snap the trachea, and thereby stop air getting into the lungs."

They stared at the neck in sober silence. Bandy continued. "What gets damaged before the trachea is the laryngeal cartilages. The woman was screaming loudly, and the shearing pressure forces snapped the cartilages. It happens to every strangled victim."

"Hang on," Arla said. "I thought she died from the neck wound."

Bandy smiled underneath his mask. "That's why I am showing you this. She was strangled to death before her neck was sliced." He released the clips and smoothed the skin and facia back over the open dissection. He pointed to black marks on the skin.

"These are the thumbprints when the killer pressed on her neck." He pointed to the smooth, linear cut below the thumbprints, going all the way across the neck. "See how straight this line is. Not jagged, no deviations. It would be impossible to do while the person was alive."

Arla shook her head, unable to speak. She finally found her voice. "So, he strangled her, then cut her throat?"

"Yes. And he cut from right to left, which means he is right-handed."

"One sick bastard," Harry muttered darkly.

Bandy moved down the body, and they followed his hands. He pointed at the brutal, haphazard stab wounds on the chest wall.

"Then he went into a frenzy. I think he lost control. In a blind rage he stabbed the chest again and again."

"Weird," Arla said, shaking her head.

"You could say that again."

"Have you found anything else?"

"No signs of sexual assault. Waiting to hear from toxicology."

"Any DNA on her nails, when she fought the attacker? On her hair?"

Bandy shook his head. "No. This killer is very careful. There are some fabric fragments on her hair, but no DNA. On her fingernails, nothing either. Nails were cut short, which is unfortunate. I can tell from the bruises on her hands she fought this guy. But I did get fingerprints."

Arla stared at him, suddenly hopeful. "Did you run them through IDENT1?"

"Yes, and sorry, but nothing. But both bodies have the same black triangles drawn on them."

"Near the right armpit?"

"Yes. Drawn with a felt tip pen. Apart from the type of ink, we can't get much else out of it."

Arla's shoulders slumped. She blew out her cheeks. "We can keep those prints for later use. I know they could be anyone's but more likely they are the killer's?"

"Almost certainly," Bandy said.

Harry asked, "What about the second body?"

"Do you have an ID?"

"Not as yet."

Bandy shuffled over to the next gurney along. Lorna unzipped the cover and took it away.

CHAPTER 29

"Now, my work on this isn't complete, but I have started." Bandy pointed to the wall behind him. A series of colour photographs of the body from every angle and close-ups had been taken. Arla saw the Y-incision had stopped at the level of the upper abdomen. The head and neck had been dissected, and so had the chest wall. She saw the bone on the limbs also exposed.

Bandy pointed to the neck first. "Death by strangulation as well, but this time he did stab him first. In the neck. He was a more potent adversary, so he disabled him with a neck wound, then moved in to strangle him. And this time, no fingerprints. He wore gloves."

He pointed at the neck. "See how crooked the neck laceration is compared to Charlene Atkins. This was a wound of necessity. But he still had to strangle the poor man. See the gloved thumbprints on the neck?"

Arla and Harry leaned closer then back. Bandy said, "Time of death was sooner than Charlene's. The body was found by a passer-by at 11.00, and I arrived on the scene at 13.00. He had been there for about sixteen hours. Which puts the TOD at around 20.00 the night before."

"The 26th of November," Harry said.

"Yes. But I didn't take a rectal temperature. I stabbed into the abdominal cavity." Arla had seen Bandy do it once before. And she knew why he had done it.

"Signs of sexual activity?"

"Yes. Small lacerations in the anal passage, which denotes forced, non-consensual sex. The anal canal does show signs of previous sexual activity as well."

"So he was gay, but someone raped him that night?" Arla asked with an involuntary shiver. She couldn't imagine a worse thing to happen to someone.

"Yes. I think while he was still alive, as he must have struggled." Bandy looked sad, and his eyelids drooped. "Poor bloke."

"He could have gone to meet someone he knew. But then things went wrong," Harry surmised.

Arla asked, "Anything else?"

Bandy moved up to the right arm. "Come around," he said. Arla and Harry walked around the gurney, keeping their hands firmly inside their pockets.

Bandy pointed to the bone of the upper arm. "This is the midshaft of the humerus. The long bone from the shoulder to the elbow. See this thickening in the middle?"

"Yes."

"It's called a callus. Bone grows around a fracture site, forming new bone to heal. It leaves a bump that remains for life."

"So he fractured his humerus. So what?"

Bandy lifted a finger, his face serious. "The growth of callus shows the healing is many years old, probably decades. And it seems like a spiral fracture to me, caused by a twisting injury."

Arla raised her eyebrows. "English, doc. What are you saying?"

Bandy took his gloves off, and grabbed Arla's upper arm. His grip was surprisingly strong. He shook her arm. He smiled. Arla wouldn't have let any other man but Bandy do that. She could feel Harry tense beside her.

"What are you doing, doc?" Harry asked quietly. She looked up at him and saw frank concern in his eyes. She didn't understand why that pleased her.

Bandy looked at both of them and said, almost in a whisper, "Imagine you are a child. I grab you by the arm and shake you because I'm angry. Now imagine I'm a grown man."

Arla closed her eyes as Bandy let go. Her hand flopped to her side. She said, "The bone snaps."

"Yes", Bandy said. His shoulders were slumped, and he put both hands on the edges of the gurney. He lowered his head. There was deathly silence for a while, broken only by the dripping of a tap in the distance.

Bandy said, "The bone breaks with a twisting injury, leaving a particular type of callus formation. It's called a spiral fracture, and it is well known in cases of Non-Accidental Injury."

Arla knew Non-Accidental Injuries or NAI were the result of suspected physical abuse in children.

He moved up to the chest and pointed at the open ribs. "Multiple broken ribs. Again caused many decades ago. Caused by punching and kicking." He looked up at them, his eyes hollow and sunken. "No child gets multiple rib fractures like this from a natural accident. The ribs show the callus formation in adult life."

Harry said, "So he was definitely abused?"

"Without a doubt."

Arla asked, "No such signs of abuse on Charlene Atkins?"

"None whatsoever. Most adults don't have signs like these. These are typical of NAI. I will go on to do a full forensic skeletal survey and call in a specialist. I'm sure there'll be more signs."

He looked away from them and threw his gloves in the bin. He took off his scrubs as well and did the same.

"Coffee?" he asked.

Arla shook her head. A new sense of purpose was filling her mind with a steely resolve. "No." She glanced at Harry. "We are going back to the Common."

CHAPTER 30

Harry drove while Arla flicked through a folder on her phone. She had a portable file where she had stored all the evidence gathered for Nicole's missing persons investigation. She went throught some of it, but it was already firmly committed to her long-term memory.

Gavin, the cab driver, had spoken the truth. Every inch of his house and car had been searched. On the handles of his cab Nicole's fingerprints were seen. But there was nothing in his house. SOC officers had searched for hair fibres, blood spills, everything.

What hurt Arla was that the same treatment was dished out to Mr Roy. His home was ransacked too. For more than a week the two houses where searched relentlessly.

Arla remembered the broken, sad face of Mr Roy now. He was childless, and Lisa had been his life. His only fault had been to help Arla. She could see why investigating him was necessary. His call data showed he made the call to Gavin at 20.24 on 10th October 1998. He was the only witness who had known Nicole personally. But there was no evidence against him, and Arla knew he wasn't guilty. From his shop floor a fragment of Nicole's hair was found, but so was Arla's and that of other shoppers.

The search around the Common, and on Clapham Common Road had gone on for several months. No one had seen Nicole that dark, rainy night she vanished. Gavin had been the last person. Arla had checked on him extensively. He had no police record and lived with his wife and three kids.

All vehicles registered to the houses had been searched. No witnesses came forward. Arla had always wanted a reward to be announced, but she never had the money, and her foster parents Jill and Sean, as good as they had been to her, turned her down.

The police investigation, and Arla's own enquiries, had drawn a blank. Nicole's disappearance stood like a desert in the middle of Arla's life, sucking her life blood into its dry, shifting sands.

But now, she had a new angle to look into.

"Where we going?" Harry asked.

"243 Clapham Common Road," Arla said.

Harry glanced at her. "Crichton's derelict house? Not much point in heading back there."

"I know that, Harry. I just want to have a look around. You can drop me off."

Harry parked on a side road, and Arla waved at Harry then walked away. She was standing in front of the house when Harry appeared. He shrugged. "No one has to know, right?"

Arla tried to keep the grin off her face. She pushed the rusty gate aside, and it sagged on its hinges. The front lawn was overgrown with weeds, and some of the plants stood up to her shoulder height. The old wooden door, scarred by weather and neglect, was locked as she had expected. She desperately wished this was a crime scene. Even though it wasn't, she had pleaded with Johnson and gotten a warrant. It had to be indemnified by the Crown, and it was hard work, but they had managed.

The front windows were boarded up, so they walked down the right side. The garden was in an even worse state. It was roughly fifty feet long and about the same in width. Harry stood with his fists on his hips, staring at the masses of weeds and shrubs.

"What are we looking for, boss?"

Arla gave him a pair of gloves. "I don't know. Just start looking."

Harry muttered something under his breath, and they waded into the undergrowth. It was hopeless. The brush was thick and came to their waist level. The ground was barely visible.

"OK, stop," Arla panted after a while. She swatted at some flies and walked towards the rear of the house, feeling for the screwdriver in her pocket. She had gotten it from Harry's glovebox.

"You got the warrant?" Harry asked. Arla nodded. He took the screwdriver from her, and they took turns in loosening one of the planks that covered a rear window. When it was down, Arla stared at the black hole inside. The glass was broken, and she could just see a bare wall inside.

A fear rose inside her, shrouding her mind. Was it wise to come here? If she found anything about Nicole, would she be able to deal with it?

Harry pried off the remaining shards of glass and clambered in. He helped her inside. Arla smelt dust, animal waste and air that had been trapped for decades. Both of them turned their Maglites on. The daylight helped, but the gloom inside was still foreboding.

Arla kicked away bits of fallen plaster from the walls. Damp reached up from the skirting boards, marking wet levels. Floorbroards creaked under their weight. They came to a hallway and a large staircase. The rooms on the ground floor were large, and they went through them one by one. Each was the same – devoid of furniture, flaking walls and peeling wallpaper.

"Let's go upstairs," Arla said, her voice echoing. As she put her foot on the first stair, something caught at the back of her throat. A sense of danger, and it made the hair stand up on her neck. She heard it then, a faint creaking. It came from upstairs.

Harry pointed his beam up before she could speak. It was silent now. Arla nodded at Harry and pointed. She held the flashlight in front of her and mounted the stairs.

The wallpaper whispered against her coat as she went up. The landing was broad, with six rooms in total leading off it. Harry pointed to the left, and Arla went right. All the doors were open, and two of the rooms didn't have doors any more. Each was a copy of the rooms downstairs. Empty, and forgotten.

But Arla couldn't forget that sound she had heard. She went from one room to the other, flashing her light inside.

The blank walls seemed to stare back at her. Listening, watching.

CHAPTER 31

Katherine shut the door and listened. She could hear muffled thuds. She put down the packet of groceries from the supermarket. It was afternoon on a Sunday, and the rest of the house was silent. The teenagers were out mostly, in the sunshine of Clapham Park. But she could still hear the sounds from upstairs.

She was still in the hallway when a door banged open upstairs, and running feet came towards her. Katherine flinched, her back against the wall. But she relaxed when she saw who it was. One of the boys, about fifteen or sixteen years old. She had seen him come in a month ago with his social worker, and Katherine had signed the necessary documents to allow him to stay.

Vincent, his name was, and she had forgotten his last name. Sounded foreign, German. The boy appeared on the landing and looked down to see her. Katherine's heart plummeted when she saw his face. His eyes were wild, terror stricken. His mouth was open, panting, and his face was drenched in sweat.

"Vincent!" she called out and went for the stairs. He struggled to come down, and she could see that he was limping.

"Stay there," Katherine called out. She got to the landing and pulled him off the stairs. He was a thin, gaunt looking boy. His long eyelashes fluttered, and his eyes rolled back. He collapsed on her lap, and she cradled him, calling his name.

Vincent's eyes remained shut, and his breaths came in gasps. She looked at his left leg – below the knee it was bent at a strange angle. She knew without examining further it was broken.

The door at the end of the corridor opened and two men stepped out. One of them was the fat man she knew well now. The other was younger, a man she hadn't seen before. Both of them wore suits, like they were going to a business meeting.

Anger flared inside Katherine. "Did you do this to him?" she yelled as they walked past her. The fat man gave her an evil, lopsided grin.

Katherine heard them go out and slam the front door shut. She got up, leaving

Vincent on the floor. The boy's name had come to her now. Vincent Bruhn. She took her phone out and dialled 999.

"I want an ambulance and the police," she said. She couldn't bear it anymore. She hadn't seen the girl called Nicole for days now. Now this.

Fifteen minutes later the ambulance arrived. The paramedics trudged upstairs and put Vincent's leg in a mobile cast. He used scissors to cut his trousers, and grimaced.

"How did this happen?" the paramedic asked.

"He was assaulted," Katherine said. She turned to the policeman. "Men come here to assault these vulnerable children. I know the name of one of them."

The policeman looked at her inquisitively.

"Not here," Katherine said. She glanced at Vincent. "I'll take him to the hospital, then come to the station to give you a full statement."

CHAPTER 32

As Harry drove, Arla wound down the window, letting the icy blast of air blow away the mountain of memories that were threatening to overcome her. She had struggled to keep them at bay since the investigation started, and now they were pushing to the fore of her mind.

"I'm freezing," Harry complained. She wound the window up a little, just to shut him up. Fat chance.

"What's the matter?" he asked. He knew something was wrong, but that didn't mean she had to share with him. Share with anyone, in fact.

Harry parked in the lot overlooking the bandstand. Blue and white tape still covered the area. A few hundred feet to their left they could see the big white tents at the second scene.

Arla got out first and walked off towards the second site. She stepped on the soft grass, mushy, muddy from rain. The SOCOs were still working, hunting around the tents, spreading down. A line of uniforms had joined them. A sergeant, whose name badge said Bradley, was directing the search for evidence. She flashed her badge.

"Anything?"

Bradley said, "Yes. We found some footprints."

"We did?" She felt her excitement rising. "Show me, please."

Sterile hardboard planks had been laid on the wet earth, leading up to the footmarks. Arla bent her knees and crouched lower to the grass. Large feet, definitely a man. The stripes across the front could be the soles of a trainer. But maybe not, she chided herself. No one would wear a trainer to a rainy, wet park. Had to be hiking shoes. She straightened.

"Have we sent the images to the footprint database?"

"Yes," Sergeant Bradley said. "Nothing as yet."

Arla sighed. So much of police work was sitting around waiting for people to get back to her. She followed the footprints until they climbed onto another tarmac road a few yards away. She followed the road around with her eyes. It went past the pond, and the parking lot, towards... *Hang on.*

Her eyes moved sharply back to the pond. It was overgrown with moss, a few straggly weeds poking out of the green top. Doors were opening and closing in her mind, air rushing around. She turned towards Sergeant Bradley.

"Have we looked around the pond?"

"No."

Arla waved at Harry, who waved back. Then he started walking. Arla spoke to the sergeant quickly. "Can you get some men to come with me to the pond?"

He grimaced. "Sorry, guv, but we have orders to finish the search here first."

Arla took a step forward until she was under Sergeant Bradley's nose. "Do you know who the SIO in this case is?"

He faltered. "You... You are, guv."

"Good. Then consider this an order. I want two men to come with me to the pond right now."

She turned and strode off, squelching mud, splattering her trousers. When she got to the pond, she cast her eyes around. The pond was no more than ten feet wide, but twice as long. Its banks were muddy, covered with reeds, wild plants and what looked like a duck's nest. She sensed Harry next to her.

"What?" He was out of breath.

"We didn't find any ID near the body, did we?"

"Nope. Body was naked, cleaned. No clothes found." He twigged. Their eyes met. "You think..."

"This guy is good, but he's also mortal. He's got an armful of clothes, a wallet, maybe a phone, and he needs to get rid of them, right? What better place to chuck a phone than into a pond?"

She pointed to a sign sticking out of the pond that said, "Caution, Deep. No swimming allowed."

Two of the uniforms had arrived. Arla turned to them. "Please do a sweep of the area around the pond. We're looking for victim's clothes, wallet, watch, phone, anything at all."

As they walked off, Harry shook his head. "There's only one way to do this right."

Arla nodded. "Dredge the pond."

"Gotcha. But you need clearance. He's gonna kill you."

Arla grimaced. It was time to face Johnson again. She was looking away from the pond, when she noticed a white van drive up the road and park next to the BMW. It had a satellite dish on top. She saw a woman jump down, followed by two men. The woman was smartly dressed in a skirt suit, and her hair was sprayed and done up. One of the men reached inside and pulled out a shoulder-held camera.

"Oh no," Arla said. "Here comes the cavalry." She wasn't surprised. The media had been around. The white tents had already appeared on the front page of *The Daily Mail* with the lurid headline, "Murder on the Common."

With growing alarm, she saw the woman heading towards her, clutching a microphone in her hand. The man with the camera was right behind. Arla turned to Harry. "You heard anything about this?"

"Nope."

"Shit. Let's get out of here." She cast a venomous look in the direction of the uniforms. All of them had their mobile phones on them, she was sure. The temptation to make a few quid by selling the news to a tabloid had obviously been too much for one of them. She didn't believe it was a coincidence that the TV camera crew had arrived after she had.

Arla rushed off towards the parking lot. The reporter woman saw her coming and moved to cut her off. Harry spread his arms, trying to shield her from the camera's angle.

"DCI Arla Baker, are you in charge of this investigation?"

Damn it, they even know my name. Now she knew for certain this was an internal leak. She gritted her teeth and kept walking, bowing her head. The reporter kept up her questions.

"DCI Baker, is it true that we have a serial killer on our hands?"

Arla remained quiet, and they reached the BMW. She was about to slide into her seat, when the next question hit her like a sledgehammer.

"DCI Baker, you were recently suspended for assaulting a witness. Are you the right person for this job?"

The window was up, thankfully. "Move it!" she screamed at Harry. His face was a mask of composure. He revved the engine and the tyres skidded back, churning up dust from the gravel. The sudden backward thrust of the BMW made the cameraman jump to the side, and the camera almost fell off his shoulders.

Arla covered her face in her hands. Harry reversed the big car all the way up the entrance, and pulled out into the road, turning his siren on. Several cars beeped as they slammed on their brakes. With a lurch, the BMW zoomed down the A3, heading towards Oval.

CHAPTER 33

Wayne Johnson kicked the armchair behind his desk, and it smashed into the wall behind. The leather-bound journals wobbled on their shelves before settling down.

He turned towards her, his jaw working, face a mask of red rage. "Who?"

Arla shrugged. "Don't know, sir. But I bet you it was one of the guys out there."

"I want to know how the press knows about your suspension." He stopped and clutched his head. "Someone's trying to undermine me."

"You?" Arla asked, incredulous. "With all due respect, sir, it's my name they were yelling out."

Johnson brushed past her and sat down on his high-backed chair. "Can't you see, Arla? They know it had to be me who authorised your return. I wonder who it could be." His face became thoughtful.

Anger pulsed through Arla. She was being used like a pawn, to further Johnson's career, while three innocent people had died horrific deaths. She leaned forward and raised her voice.

"Sir! With all due respect, I don't care who said what. And I don't care about your fancy new job either!"

Johnson looked up at her in shock. It was replaced by a dangerous look. His eyes became small and calculating. "Mind what you're saying, DCI Baker."

Arla pointed outside. "I have three victims killed by a psychopath. He knows what he's doing, and I don't think he's going to stop. I don't give a toss about office politics, sir, I just want to do my job!" Arla stood back, her nostrils crimson and quivering.

Johnson stared at her for a while then got up. He put his hands behind his back and paced up and down. He stopped abruptly in front of her.

"You're right. This is why I got you on this case. I knew you would chase

117

it intensely. Let's stop wasting time and crack this." He sat down heavily on his chair again. "Do you have a report for me?"

Arla told him what she had seen in Charlene Atkins' house, her meeting with the vicar, and the findings of Dr Bandy. A shadow crossed Johnson's face as he heard about the second victim's life.

"Do we have an ID?" Johnson asked softly.

"We might do, soon. But first, I need clearance for something."

Johnson's expression was wary. "What?"

"We need to dredge a pond on Clapham Common. The deep one near the church."

"What? Why?"

Arla told him. Johnson shook his head. "Out of the question. See what a media circus this is becoming already. Now you want to get a dredging machine there? Never mind the SOCO tents, the press will start camping there soon!"

She stood her ground. "We need an ID quickly. You know that better than I do. I have a strong feeling about this, sir."

"We follow process, DCI Baker. These *feelings* of yours get you into nothing but trouble."

Arla winced, but she wasn't giving up. "No witnesses have emerged. Fingerprints have shown nothing and neither has DNA. If I'm right, and we find his possessions, then this whole investigation changes. We get a mountain of evidence. If I'm wrong, we just move on."

Wayne Johnson tapped a well-manicured fingernail against his lips. He let out a long sigh. "OK. Do it. The press will be all over this now. We might as well give them a statement." He jabbed a finger in her direction. "They will ask you personal questions. Can you handle it?"

Arla lifted her chin. "I can tell them the truth. I did nothing wrong."

Irritation flashed across Johnson's face. "No, you will *not* tell them that. Let the Press Liaison decide what needs to be said. You keep your mouth shut. Got that?" He glared at Arla.

She glared back. "Got it. Sir." She turned and left the room, leaving the door open.

The Incident Room was slowly filling up. Harry had the projector up and running. He beckoned to her. "What happened?" he whispered. Arla told him.

"It's getting heavy," he said in a low voice. "I want to know the name of the arsehole who leaked your file to the press." He swore between tight lips.

"Thanks for getting me back," she said. Their eyes met briefly, and between the rush and bustle of the room, a moment flickered then faded. Arla was the first to look away. She didn't know what she felt, but now was not the time to analyse it.

Lisa came up to her. "CCTV images have arrived," she announced triumphantly. "Got something interesting to show you."

Rob Pinckney was at the desk, and he brought the time lapse images up. "These are from the cameras facing the entrance that victim number two entered from. There he is." He pointed. Four heads craned to get a better look. The grey images were not ideal, especially as they showed the back of a solitary man.

"Show up the opposite image," Arla snapped.

Rob clicked on the keyboard, bringing up another file. More dark grey and black shapes filled the screen. But this time the man's body was clearer. Rob zoomed in and paused the image on a close-up of the face.

"That's the second victim," Rob said, with a hint of pride.

Lisa said, "But that's not all." There was excitement in her voice. "Go on," she told Rob.

He pulled out folders and laid them out as thumbnails on the screen then clicked on three in series, getting smaller images up on the screen to play simultaneously.

"This is a time series," Rob said. "Victim 2 enters the gates at 19.30 hours. But before that, we see another man approaching and entering the same gate. Time is 19.10 hours." These were dark, quiet parts in the evening, and no other pedestrians were visible on the screen.

Arla leaned forward, something about the new figure familiar. "Who is that?"

Rob zoomed in again, and with a flourish stopped at the close-up of the man's face. Arla's eyes widened and breath caught in her chest.

"Shit. It's the witness, Steven Wade."

"The guy who ID'd Charlene Atkins," Harry said, his eyes locked on the screen.

"What the hell was he doing there, just before victim 2 went in and got murdered?" Lisa asked finally, voicing the question in all their minds.

Harry straightened his long spine. "Let's bring him in."

"No," Arla said. Everyone looked at her. "Did we put a tail on him?"

Harry shook his head mournfully. "No manpower. Unless Lisa or I did it ourselves."

Arla thought for a moment. "OK, bring his girlfriend in. Let's make sure the alibi is watertight." She turned and crossed the glass partition to the incident room. It was full.

Arla stood in front of the whiteboard. It had been divided into two parts now, one for each victim. She circled the name of victim 2.

"Alright, people," Arla spoke as she wrote with the black marker on the white board. "We are getting closer to an ID for victim 2. A witness is now definitely a suspect. We are dredging the pond nearby to see if the killer dumped evidence there. Anyone want to sort that out?"

One hand shot up. A young black man, wearing a sergeant's uniform. His name was Toby. Staying seated, he said, "When I was in the Royal Engineering Corps, we used dredgers in Afghanistan. I can make enquiries."

Arla said, "You need to do more than that, Toby. I want a dredger onsite today, and the pond cleared out by first light tomorrow. If it's gets dark, we use the generators that SOCO have at the site. Clear?"

"Crystal," Toby said. He got up and left the room, giving Arla a thumbs-up. Arla looked at the guy approvingly. She liked someone who took action.

Lisa said, "We have the name of Charlene Atkins' parents. I had to trawl through Home Office records to get it. She has a driving licence and a passport that she's never used."

"Don't care if you had to speak to the Prime Minister." Arla softened her voice with a smile. "We need to check that out ASAP. Well done."

"Steven Wade's girlfriend is coming in at 17.00," Harry said. Arla looked at her watch.

"OK, we should be back by then. I need two volunteers to monitor Mr Wade. Drop what you're doing now. Don't worry, I'll clear it with your unit boss." A few hands went up slowly. Arla chose a woman and a man and gave them instructions.

"That's it for now, people. We meet back here in the evening."

To Harry she said, "We're going back to Charlene Atkins' house. Something there I want to check out."

CHAPTER 34

Harry parked in front of 22 Lavenwood Road, letting the engine idle for a few minutes. Arla didn't mind. Warm air blasted from the heaters, and she held her hands up to them. The throbbing of the engine sat between them, a presence that insulated them from each other. Harry stared straight through the windscreen. She sneaked a glance at him. His black hair was gelled back immaculately, and his coffee-coloured skin was stretched smooth on his cheeks. His large right hand rested on the steering wheel, thumb caressing leather. The prominent cheekbone had a dull glow as the wintry sunlight fell on it. She swallowed, then looked away, trying to quell her heartbeat.

"Let's get going," she said, opening the door. Harry followed after a beat. Arla had keys, and she opened the door, which creaked loudly in protest. *Margaret must be inside,* she mused: lights were on in the hallway. She opened the door that led to the staircase. SOCO had been already and dusted for prints, taken hair and fibre samples. Apart from Charlene's DNA, nothing had been isolated.

She stood on the landing, staring up at the ceiling. Doors to the three rooms were open, but she ignored them. Harry joined her.

"What are you looking for?" he asked.

She took out her flashlight and pointed the beam at the ceiling. It was painted dark burgundy, an unusual colour for a ceiling. She couldn't see much on the first pass, only the light bulb that dazzled her.

"Take out your torch, and switch the light off," she said.

"What's the magic word?"

"God, Harry."

"That's two words, but I'll take it for now." He switched off the light, and it was dark inside, despite the zero-watt, watery sunlight on the street. Two pairs of high-voltage beams played on the ceiling.

Arla stopped when she saw the outline of something different. A different shade of burgundy. She pointed it to Harry.

"It's tape," she said. "Peel it off. I'm not tall enough." Harry reached up, scraped the ends of the tape, and it separated from the ceiling. He pulled it, revealing a faint black line. Arla followed it with her torch as Harry pulled it down and around. It made a square shape on the ceiling. She looked at Harry. "See that?"

His eyes were focused on it. "Yes." He stood next to her, and she moved to make space. He rose on his tiptoes and stretched his long arm to full length. His fingers reached, then his palm. With a grunt of effort, he pushed, and there was a soft click. A smoothly oiled trapdoor descended from the ceiling, with a steel, folded ladder attached to it.

"There's the loft space," Arla said softly. "Gloves on."

Harry turned to her. Arla rolled her eyes. "Please."

"Thank you," Harry said and put his gloves on, then lowered the ladder. The rungs snapped into place.

"She tried to camouflage the trapdoor," Arla thought to herself out loud. She put her foot on the first rung and started to climb.

"After you," Harry muttered. She ignored him. Breath fluttered in her chest, and her heart was thumping fast. Without lifting her head into the darkness illuminated by Harry's torch beam from below, she groped around the opening of the trapdoor at the top. She found the switch and flicked it. A naked yellow bulb in the middle of the room sprang to life. Arla took a deep breath and raised her head.

Wooden rafters criss-crossed the ceiling space, wreathed in cobwebs. Blankets covered objects on the floor. She climbed up and stood inside. Plumes of dust rose as she walked around, flashing her light. Old suitcases stood in one corner. Harry came up behind her. Arla sniffed the air. It smelled dank, musty. Nothing to indicate rotting flesh. No chemicals.

With a gloved hand, Harry squatted down and gingerly lifted one corner of a blanket. He looked under, shining his light. Arla watched.

"Rolled carpets," Harry said. "Look expensive. Maybe Persian rugs."

"Take it off," Arla said. He did so, standing up. Together, they rolled the rug out. The pile was deep and luxurious, with elaborate patterns. But there was nothing else. Arla felt around the edges of the carpet. Nothing. They took the covers off another two rugs and repeated the process. Nothing again. They opened the suitcases next, flinching as they did so. Apart from layers of dust, they found nothing.

Arla stood up, consternation etched on her face. The rafters made ghoulish shadows on the wooden floor. Next to them, the brick wall of the next house. Arla ran her torch on the bricks. She walked to the other end of the loft, checking the corners. She went up and down methodically, examining each brick.

She almost missed it. Her beam went past it then jerked back.

A brick with a crack down the middle. No other brick she had seen so far had it. It was at her head height, and she reached it easily. One half of the brick came off in her hand. She pulled it out, put it down, and pulled the other brick out. The brick below came loose as well, and soon she had exposed a one-square-foot boxed area. There was a compartment inside. A bundle lay there, covered in a red rag. She reached for it. It was heavy, but it came into her hand easily. Harry took it from her. He took a specimen bag out and inserted the rag bundle into it.

"Bingo," he said. Arla looked at him and raised her eyebrows. Then she looked at the ground. Something had fallen down from the bundle by Harry's feet. She cursed and bent down.

It was a business card. It was new, and the name "Richard Bromsgrove, Councillor and MP, Battersea" was written clearly on it.

The smiling face of a fifty-something male was circled to one side of the card. Arla turned the card over. A logo of UK Parliament was embossed in the middle, with the title – Under Secretary for the Minister of Work and Pensions.

Arla glanced at Harry, and their eyes met. Both stood up at the same time, and they went down the ladder.

The heating was on full blast in the car. Arla put the specimen bag inside the dash and shut the door. Harry was searching for Richard Bromsgrove on his phone.

"Here he is," he said. "His homepage is on the Conservative Party website, and he has his House of Commons site as well."

"MPs do surgeries, don't they? Where they sit and listen to their voters' problems?"

"They do, and his is listed here. He has a phone number as well. Hang on." Harry rang the number, and Arla turned the heaters down. Harry spoke quickly, without giving his name and title. He hung up.

"It's on Battersea Park Road. He's there now, doing a surgery. First come, first served."

"Let's go, Harry. Let's see what he can serve for us."

Harry indicated to pull out and Arla said, "Turn the siren on. We need to get to him before he gets out of there."

CHAPTER 35

Battersea Park Road was long and bendy, with the large expanse of the park on the bank of the Thames. Adjacent to the park, the residential dwellings were old and immaculately maintained. Most of them were Edwardian apartment complexes, grand, old mansions divided into apartments, built before the turn of the century.

Harry pulled into the former school that was opposite Battersea Library. The red-brick building was now used as council offices. They were shown into a large reception area that had "Richard Bromsgrove" written in large blue letters on the wall.

"Working for you, all the way", the slogan read below his name. Flyers were strewn on the seats and the counters, exhorting people to vote for in the upcoming by-election. It was a chance for the candidates to test their constituency support before the general election in two years' time. Arla knew it was an important event in any politician's calendar.

She went up to the reception desk and flashed her badge. Harry did the same.

"DCI Baker, London Met," she said, fixing the woman with a stare. "We have something important to discuss with Mr Bromsgrove."

The woman looked flustered. "Does he know you're coming?"

"No, and it couldn't be helped. Like I said, it's urgent."

"Take a seat, please," the woman said, pushing the glasses up her nose. "I shall speak to him."

After ten minutes, during which time Arla looked up Mr Bromsgrove's website on her phone, they were shown into his office.

Richard Bromsgrove was a chubby, heavy-jowled man in his mid-fifties. His full head of hair had turned white, and a pair of intelligent blue eyes shone brightly in a swarthy, ruddy face. He wore a blue suit, jacket unbuttoned, and white shirt that strained at his belly. The blue tie had a perfect Windsor knot at the neck and pushed up the fat fold above.

They introduced each other and shook hands. The door shut behind them.

The MP spread his hands. "How can I help you, officers?" His expression was blank, and carefully controlled, Arla noticed.

She got straight to the point. "Do you know a woman by the name of Charlene Atkins?"

The MP frowned, then looked confused. "I am not sure that I do."

He paused, Arla thought to herself.

"So you are certain that you have never met this woman?" Arla pulled out one of the photofit pictures, as showing images of the deceased was not allowed. The MP looked at it carefully, then returned it to Arla. His expression had gone back to being blank.

He shook his head. "No, I have not, Miss…"

"Baker. DCI Baker."

"OK, Miss Baker, can I ask you what this has to do with me?"

"Your card was found in the possession of this woman."

"My card is in the possession of many people, Miss Baker. It's part of my job to make myself available to everyone in my constituency."

"Only this person is dead."

He raised his eyebrows. "Dead?"

"Yes. She was murdered, and her body was left in the bandstand of Clapham Common."

His expression was shocked. He looked from Arla to Harry, then back to Arla again. He shook his head. "I don't know what to say."

Arla waited a spell, during which she kept her eyes fixed on his vivid blue eyes.

"So this woman is a total stranger to you?"

"Yes, I'm afraid so."

Harry asked, "Can you think of a reason why she would have your card?" He looked at Arla, and she nodded very slightly, a movement that would be missed by most casual observers.

"No. As I said, many people have my card," the MP said.

Harry leaned closer. "She hid this card in a special place. She didn't want anyone to find it. Do you know why that might be?"

A frown creased Richard Bromsgrove's face. "I really don't understand this. What does any of this have to do with me?"

Arla changed direction and asked, "Do you attend church, Mr Bromsgrove?"

He nodded, still looking perturbed. "I do, yes. My parish is at Claygate in Surrey. That's where I live."

"Do you know of the Holy Communion Church on Clapham Common?"

"I have heard of it, yes."

"Have you ever been there?"

"No, I have not." He shrugged his shoulders, and his eyebrows knit together. "Look, Miss Baker, I am sure you are busy and so am I. I would love to help you, but I cannot see this line of questioning going anywhere."

"That church got funding from the council to provide respite care for vulnerable adults. Do you know anything about that?"

"No. If this is a council matter, I would advise you to ask them directly."

He stood up, scraping his chair back. "I thank you for coming, and if there is anything I can help you with, please don't hesitate to call." He smiled and stuck his hand out. Arla shook, feeling his heavy grip.

As they walked to the car, Harry said, "Did you see his face when he saw the photo?"

Arla nodded. "He did well, but he was acting. Well practised. But we don't have enough to bring him in for questioning."

"Where to now?"

"How far do Charlene's parents live?"

"Only her mother's alive. Not far, in Streatham."

Arla fleetingly thought of her own father, alone in his apartment, shut out from the world. She doubted she would even know if he died. She banished the morbid thought from her head.

"Time to check it out."

"You head back to the station," she said, "I'll check out Charlene's mother."

"OK," Harry said, handing her the keys. "I'll take the tube back. Sure you'll be OK?"

"I can take care of myself, Harry!"

He walked off, but spoke over his shoulder. "That's not what I was talking about."

*****

The Keeper pressed himself against the wall of the corner building and watched as Arla Baker got into the car on her own. The tall man stood there, watching her get in. His excitement mounted. She was going to be alone. He ran back to his car, gunned the engine, and drove up to the Give Way sign. He indicated right and took off, having already spotted the BMW further up the road.

CHAPTER 36

Arla had gone past Streatham High Road, with its row of cheap shops, pubs and the cinema. The ice rink followed, its blue and red neon lights lit up garishly. Youths loitered on street corners.

Arla parked the car, got out, and looked up at the grimy apartment block rising above. The colour of its walls was indistinguishable from the pavement. A drunk lurched out of the entrance, almost bumping into her. He burped into her face, and she dodged him with a frown, smelling his whiskey breath.

The narrow hallway inside had stained walls, and it stank of piss. A dim, naked bulb glowed feebly. Charlene might have been wealthy, but Arla wouldn't have known that if she had come to see her mother first. Arla stepped inside the narrow, humid elevator, and pressed for the fourth floor. The rheumatic drone of the machine was annoying as it climbed slowly. She was glad to step off it.

She came onto a narrow balcony that stretched around the floor, all of the doors opening out to the balcony. A cement railing came up to her waist level.

She walked to number 42 and knocked. The light was on inside. She knocked three times before she got an answer.

An old woman's shaky voice. "Who is it?"

"The police. Here to ask about your daughter."

"Who?"

"If you open the door, I can tell you."

"Show me some ID first." Arla pushed her badge through the letter box. The door opened after a while. She found herself looking at a very old woman, skin wrinkled and sagging from her face. She was balanced on a Zimmer frame. The woman turned and slowly shuffled her way back inside the apartment. Arla stepped in and shut the door behind her.

She followed the woman into the small living room. It was stuffed full of junk – old sofa, newspapers, gramophone, and radio. A TV was on in the corner. There was a coffee table with a remote on top. The woman sat down on the armchair and picked up the remote. She pointed it at the TV and turned it off.

Arla bent one knee and got closer to the woman. "Miss Atkins?"

She turned her head slowly towards Arla. "Yes?"

"I am a police officer."

"Yes, you said."

Arla hesitated. She gathered her thoughts. "I need some information about your daughter."

The woman's face creased into a frown, and her lips turned down. "What?"

"Your daughter. Charlene Atkins."

The woman appeared confused. She shook her head, getting agitated. She squinted at Arla again. "What are you talking about?"

Arla raised her voice and got closer, wondering if the woman could hear her. She noticed the hearing aid attached to the right ear. "Your daughter, Charlene."

"You don't have to shout, I can hear, you know."

"Sorry."

The woman was staring at Arla with an expression that bordered between curiosity and hostility. "I don't understand. Why do you want to know about Charlene?"

Arla pursed her lips. "We just need to find out more about her. Did she have any belongings that she might have left with you?"

The old woman lifted both her hands, then put them down. Her head sank down on her chest. "Oh, Lord. Oh, good Lord."

Arla waited. When the woman didn't respond, Arla asked again. The woman lifted her head slowly and stared at Arla for a few seconds. Then she shook her head.

She said, "You don't know, do you?"

Arla felt a sudden uneasiness. Light was fading outside, and the apartment was dark. She turned from her sitting position and looked around the small room, and the dark hallway outside. Empty, but eerie. She had shut the door, and she couldn't hear anything. She looked back at the woman, whose eyes were fixed on her.

"Don't know what, Miss Atkins?"

She cleared her throat, and her next words punched Arla deep in the gut. "Charlene is dead."

Arla struggled to regain composure. "Who... Who informed you?"

The old woman smiled, showing the black gaps where teeth should have been. It was a mirthless, bitter smile. A hollow dread was spreading across Arla's chest, squeezing her lungs. The musty, closed air made it hard for her to breathe. She took a breath, feeling small fingers crawl up her windpipe.

"Miss Atkins, did you hear what I said?"

In response, the woman pointed to the wall. Arla couldn't see well in the gathering gloom, but she saw a row of photos. She got up and switched the light on. Yellow light flooded the room. She stepped closer to the photos.

They were of a little girl, in various poses, and in the hands of a younger man and woman. When Arla got to the fourth photo in the row, she had the sudden sensation that she was falling, the floor having slipped from underneath her feet. Her hands were flaying for support, and she was screaming, but no sound came from her throat.

The black and white image was of a gravestone. On it was clearly written: *Our beloved Charlene. Taken from us after three years. Rest in Peace, Forever Love Darling. 1970-1973.*

A sickness was spreading inside Arla, poisoning her insides. She turned to the old woman, unable to speak. The old woman wasn't smiling anymore. An infinite sorrow was marked in every crease line of her face, a map of grief that all her years on earth had deepened, stamped, made permanent.

Miss Atkins lowered her face, and a teardrop coursed down her cheek. She rubbed it with a sniff.

"My Charlene died of fever all those years ago. I wonder why God left me. I want to join her, you know."

Arla knelt by her chair and touched her arm. "I am so sorry, Miss Atkins." She struggled with her words. What could she ask?

Are you sure your daughter died in 1973?

Arla said, "Miss Atkins, I will go soon, but before I do, I need to ask you something."

The woman nodded, sniffling.

"Did you ever have a burglary in your apartment? Did any of Charlene's papers get lost? Like her birth certificate?"

Miss Atkins raised wondrous eyes to Arla's face. "How did you know about that?"

"When was it?"

"About fifteen years ago."

Arla's head dropped on her chest. She gripped her forehead, fighting the spinning sensation that threatened to overcome her. She swallowed, fighting the nausea.

"Because without the birth certificate, she couldn't have applied for a new passport," Arla whispered, almost to herself.

She said goodbye to Miss Atkins, then stood up. She opened the door and stood there for a while staring at the buldings opposite. Rust was layering over the diesel exhaust fume-ridden, broken dream skyline of London. Punctuated by pinpoints of light that lit miserable lives, like glistening teardrops. She thought of what she herself had lost, perhaps forever. She thought of her father, dying slowly in his grief, wrapping it around him like an iron cloak.

Just like Miss Atkins.

She went back and sat down by the old woman's feet. She smelled of old age, dry skin, soap, old, yellow papers that held memories of a life together. Arla closed her eyes and rested her forehead against the old woman's wrinkled, inelastic skin.

"I'm so sorry," Arla whispered.

"It was a long time ago," Miss Atkins said. "But it never leaves you."

Arla felt a sob catch in her throat, and she swallowed the tears away like she always did. Like she had done for the last fifteen years.

"I know," she said. "I know."

CHAPTER 37

The Keeper was sitting down on a chair at the streetside café, drinking his coffee.

Scarcely three doors away, he spotted Arla Baker step out into the street. Adrenaline surged through him. He stood up. The street was busy with people, and that made the ultimate task difficult. But as with all his preys, he liked to get close before he got them for good. To smell them and even make them aware of his presence. They needed to know who he was.

Arrogance came naturally to him. What no one understood was his desire to establish order. His own sense of justice in the world, where no flaws would be tolerated. He was the Keeper of that perfect world, and when the ordinary men and women saw that, they would convert to him. He smiled. Yes, of course. He could be a messiah, a prophet who let loose the rivers of blood to cleanse the souls of the few survivors. This horrible, dirty world would then be free, empty of faults.

He put the hood of the jumper on his head and shuffled closer to Arla. She was about to cross the road, standing at the edge of the pavement. He could almost smell her. He stood behind her and got closer. His heart was hammering, mouth dry. He looked at the lines on her long, black jacket, the small white mark on the side. He could almost reach out and touch her.

Smell her. He inhaled deeply.

The lights changed, and the cars stopped. She stepped out on the road. The Keeper followed, walking fast to match her steps. She was tall, almost his height. The thought of fighting her made his pulse pound. How much fun would that be?

He picked up his pace and ran past her to the other side. Grinning inside, he turned around on the pavement and faced her full on. She barely glanced at him. Her face had a sad expression, and he wondered why. He wanted to reach out and brush her cheeks, soothe her worries. He didn't understand sadness very well. It was a strange feeling, like watching his mother die slowly. He remembered the hospital, the nurses and doctors. All asking if he was OK, and him shrugging. Death just happened, right? What was the big deal?

He moved towards her. She looked at him finally. He lowered his head at the last minute and brushed past her shoulder.

The contact was like a burn on his skin, making him alive. His mouth opened, hot air dancing out of his lungs. Did she see him? He glanced back, and she was getting in the car. Eyes wide with excitement, he breathed out. She was wearing a perfume, light and summery. He inhaled it deeply again. It flowed in his veins like an intoxication.

I'm getting closer, he thought, as he watched her inside the car, only a few feet away. She was obsessed with something and ignored him completely. He smiled. He was going to change that.

*****

The green iridium arms in Arla's watch said 17.00 as she left the apartment. Thoughts were twisted in her head like a spaghetti junction. Nothing made sense anymore. Charlene Atkins wasn't who she was. She had applied for a passport on a stolen birth certificate. Her Majesty's Passport Office looked at birth and address details, and two witnesses. She must have faked them or gotten someone to act as her witness.

Arla got inside her car, and leaned back on the seat, leaving the keys dangling in the ignition. Traffic moved slowly past her window, lights flashing momentarily on the rear-view, like sudden ideas that came and left her consciousness.

She rang Harry. "Are you OK?" He kept his voice calm, but she heard the concern behind it. It made her smile. She told him about Charlene.

"Fuck," Harry said.

"My sentiments precisely. Did you look inside the specimen bag we got from her loft?"

"No, I left it with SOCO and came down to Putney."

"Then there are the witnesses in the passport application. We can ring the Home Office and get a copy of the original application."

"Good thinking." After a pause he said, "You need to get down to Putney." He gave her the address.

She asked, "How about the dredger?"

"I heard from Lisa. She's onsite. Apparently, Clapham Common is lit up like a fairground right now. Bags of fun, especially for headline-hungry punters."

Arla's voice was tight. "Keep the media out of Putney. Tell as few uniforms as you can. We can't let this leak as well."

"Keep the media out? That's like saying keep flies out of a road kill in Clapham High Road."

"Do your best. I'm heading down to the Common."

CHAPTER 38

Harry hadn't been exaggerating: the area around the pond did look like a fairground. Two light sources were shining on the long arm of the dredging machine, which looked like a forklift truck, with a long jib arm attached to it. The arm extended several metres, and a large claw at the end scooped up silt from the pond, lifted, then dumped it on the bank. Two men with rakes were going through the silt to see if there was anything of value.

Arla spotted Lisa and Rob in high-visibility jackets. Both wore yellow hard hats as well. Lisa spun around when she tapped her on the shoulder. The noise was too loud for conversation. They walked away to the car park. Lisa removed her hat and blew her loose hair strands away. A sheen of sweat plastered her forehead.

"Right," Arla said, looking around them. "Is this our new incident room?"

"If you say so," Lisa said. "Though I'd take the office any day."

Arla felt a twinge of guilt. It was almost 8pm, and she had left the team out here working. She hadn't been back to the incident room to see if others were still at work.

"How has it been?" she asked Lisa.

She shook her head. "Nothing as yet. They're scooping up mud from the pond, but no sign of any evidence."

Arla nodded. "Why don't you two now take the night off? It's been a long day."

Rob still had the hat on his head, and he looked comical in his new outfit. "No, boss, it's fine. We need to secure the place anyway before we go."

Arla shook her head. "No. I can call some uniforms on night shift to do that. We can set up a perimeter. Go home now, because I need you fresh for tomorrow." When Lisa and Rob went off, Harry and she walked towards the group of men who were doing the dredging.

The machine shut down with a shudder as Arla approached. She showed her badge to the men standing near the cabin of the forklift machine, and the two guys raking the silt.

Their leader came forward. Dressed in hi-vis jacket and hat, he was a tall, wide-shouldered man with a beer belly, matching Harry for height.

"My name's Adrian," he said, opting not to shake hands with mud-caked gloves on.

"How long till you finish?" Arla asked.

"Another three to four hours," he said. His face turned uneasy. "Your officers wouldn't tell me. But we're not looking for a dead body or anything, are we?"

"There were no bodyparts missing from the victim, so it's not likely," Arla said in what she hoped was a reassuring voice. "We're more interested in clothing, mobile phones, any personal belongings."

The machine started up again, and Adrian waved at the driver to shut it down.

"Anything else?" he asked.

"Yes. No talking to anyone about this, please."

Adrian nodded, but Arla knew there was nothing she could do to keep them quiet. She looked at the small hill of silt that had already been scooped up and felt a sense of futility run through her. If this was all in vain, Johnson would have her guts for garters. But she wanted to carry on. In the mid-distance, she could see the lights of the church shining brightly, reflecting a white glow on the leaves of the trees that came close to the watchtower. Her instinct told her she would find something in this pond.

Adrian said, "You're lucky it's winter. Newts and frogs hibernate till Feb, so we can dredge ponds now, but not in summer."

"I'm not looking for frogs," Arla said sharply. She indicated the driver. "Let's get cracking." She turned to leave, brushing against Harry. He had his phone to his ear. He caught her questioning look.

"Calling the uniform sergeant on for nights."

"Good." She waited until Harry finished his call. She looked at her phone again. Johnson hadn't called, but she would be facing him tomorrow, and he would want answers. Answers she didn't have at the moment.

Three bodies. No leads.

Worse, in her own mind, it was opening up old wounds. Sores she covered up under sealed bandages. She had a headache and knew sleep would come only after a few glasses of wine. A solitary night was not something she was looking forward to, but she had no choice. Her eyes fluttered over to Harry, his broad back to her, phone to his ear. Then they fluttered to the ground.

She didn't need a man. Oh, she did need a man. Not a man like Harry, anyway. She'd probably run him over with his precious BMW one day.

She was no stranger to men, but the overarching theme in all of them had been self-indulgence and egos. Maybe she did need that wine bottle after all. Safer to cling to that tonight than a man.

Her thoughts turned to her father, and she felt another stab of anger mixed with regret. Frustration followed. She shoved it back in the dungeon, choosing not to think about it.

Harry's shadow moved ahead of her, and he trudged back. The dredging machine had started up again, and the ground was shaking.

Harry said, "Uniforms are on their way. You go home. I'll stick around till they turn up."

Arla shrugged. She feigned nonchalance, but she was the SIO here. Harry couldn't, and shouldn't, tell her what to do. Her jaws clenched.

"No, you go home. I'm fine to stay."

He crossed his arms and looked at her before looking away. He knew. "I wasn't… I mean I didn't…"

She felt bad. Both of them had had a long day. Harry knew something was bugging her, and it was bigger than the case. He was being nice, and she was being a bitch.

"When are the uniforms turning up?" she asked after a pause.

"21.30."

"OK." She nodded. "In that case we can both go home, as it's almost time for the uniforms to show up."

"Sure," he said, glancing down at his shoes, then kicking a pebble away. It was his turn to feign nonchalance.

They drove off, and Arla took one last look at the red eye dredging machine. She hoped it would have some answers for her tomorrow. Otherwise, *she* would be covered in silt.

When they arrived at the station, Harry kept the engine running, and she was aware he was staring at her.

"Goodnight, Harry."

"Yeah, Goodnight," he said in a light voice. "Sure you don't want me to swing by after I've dealt with the uniforms?"

She slammed the door shut. "No. Go home and get some sleep. That's an order."

He grinned and gave her a salute. "Aye aye, cap'n."

Arla looked at her watch. It was almost 21.15. She thought for a while then rang the Cedarbrook Care Home. Loretta was at reception. Arla hung up and went down the stairs of the tube station.

It was raining when she arrived at Clapham Common and walked down to the care home. A few of the teenagers were sitting around, playing darts, pool and watching TV. It was bedtime for most of them, but in most Secure Children's Homes (SCH), the older children were given some laxity.

She spotted Tara playing pool with one of the girls. She felt guilty for not having seen her for the last two days. Although every child here had a personal officer, and Arla saw them on a voluntary basis, she felt responsible. Tara straightened after taking a shot and looked at Arla. Arla waited as the girls played around the table. She tapped on a ball close to the green.

"Take this shot, it's an easy one," she told Tara. "Hit it on the angle and it rebounds off the edge, then goes in." Tara thought about it, then took the shot. It went in. She gave Arla a look and the corners of her lips twitched.

When the game finished Arla edged closer. "Who was driving that Merc you got into the other night?"

Tara grimaced. "A friend. Why?"

"I want to know the name. He has to be older than you."

"How do you know it's a he?"

Arla didn't say anything. Tara said, "Have you guys put all those posters up of that woman?"

Arla stared at the teenage girl. Something constricted at the back of her mind. "What woman?"

"You know, the one who got killed or something. And now you guys are dredging the pond as well. Man, that's crazy." Tara smirked.

"Tara, listen to me. Did you know that woman?"

"Who, Charlene? Yeah, man. She used to come here, gave us food and stuff."

Arla felt her limbs become cold. She focused on Tara with an effort. "Can we sit down and talk about this?"

Tara looked at her suspiciously. "I'm not gonna get done for this, am I?"

"No, don't worry. I give you my word, OK?" They sat down at the table, away from the TV.

"You know, she asked about you," Tara said. "Charlene."

"Asked what?"

"About who you were. When she found out you were a copper, I reckon she wanted to talk to you."

"I want you to think about this carefully, Tara. Did she say anything else to you?"

"Nope."

"When was the last time you saw her?"

Tara screwed up her face, thinking. "Almost a week ago, I reckon. She came with a basket of food and gave it to us. She came in the mornings mostly but sometimes late afternoons. I reckon that's when she saw you one day."

After a pause Tara said, "She wrote down your name on a piece of paper and looked at you from the window. For a long time."

Arla leaned back on the chair, thinking. Charlene Atkins, or whoever she was, had known who Arla was. She had come down to the station. Why did she want to contact the police? Was she scared for her life? But she took down Arla's name, and…what did Charlene want from her?

CHAPTER 39

Arla came up to ground level on the elevator, then out through the gates to the familiar squalor of Tooting Broadway. A drizzle had started, the cold, miserable type that slanted into the face, directed by a malicious wind. She bent her head and hurried along with the other pedestrians.

The light was on in the porch, which meant one of her neighbours had arrived recently. She bumped into the woman as she opened the door and stepped inside quickly. She trod on a bunch of magazines on the floor, and almost slipped. The older woman looked up, unsmiling.

"Mind yer step," she barked in a heavy Irish accent. Her back was stooped, and her washed, loose grey and white hair hung in clumps around her face and shoulders. She never wore make-up, and tonight was no exception. Arla put her age in the late-60s, and she was a cantankerous old grouch.

"Hello, Miss Raymond," she said.

"Hello yourself, Miss… Uh." She turned away and stumbled on the stairs then corrected herself.

"Do you need a hand?" Arla asked.

"We have to make do with what God gave us, like," she rasped, without turning to face Arla. Slowly she climbed up the stairs. Arla watched her, wondering how Miss Raymond had ended up here. Maybe that was what someone thought of her dad, she reflected. Old and bitter, waiting to die a solitary death. She suppressed the thought and the conflicting emotions it raised. Her phone beeped. She saw Dr Seddon's number, and her heart beat faster. Did they have a meeting scheduled?

She answered and asked the question. His resigned sigh was an adequate reply. "We were due to meet at my office at 21.00."

Arla mentally smacked her forehead. "I'm so sorry. You did send me a text."

"I can't send the progress report if you don't see me, Arla." He was stating a fact, but the tone of his voice suggested something else. Did he want to see her? She swallowed. She knew that *she* wanted to see him.

"I am still at the office. My office, that is." His voice was deep, warm, like molten chocolate. She realised with a jolt how much she liked listening to it. He said, *his* office.

"Where is your office?"

"At London Bridge." He gave her the address. Arla glanced at her watch. It was 21.30, and she could take the Northern line tube up there in twenty minutes. "I can be there by 22.00," she said. She needed to make sure Johnson got her report. Keep the boxes ticked. That was what this was about.

"Good. I'll be waiting."

Arla hung up and headed out again. She sat back in the train and leaned against the glass wall at the corner. Her eyes were closing with the rhythmic jolts, much-needed sleep teasing her mind. But she couldn't sleep. Charlene Atkins' dead face kept appearing in front of her.

By the time she got to the address, half-walking, half-running to avoid the rain, it was past 22.00. It was inside an office block on the main street, five minutes' walk from the busy station. She could see the tall spire of the London Shard gleaming up into the velvet night sky like a bejewelled finger.

The reception of the office block was dark, and Dr Seddon came down himself after speaking to her on the buzzer. He slid bolts and opened a side door. She stepped inside. Street light cast a limited glow, and the giant space was sunk in darkness. She could make out the counter tables at the end and found the absence of security guards strange.

Dr Seddon's face was barely visible. "This way," he said, walking towards some lights in the distance.

"Where's security in this place?" Arla asked as she walked. He turned to her, and she could see his teeth flash.

"Spoken like a true cop. The night shift doesn't start till 23.00, and I guess the day shift went home a bit early."

"They shouldn't."

"Are you worried about my safety?" They had reached the elevators, and the sudden bright light as the door parted was blinding. They got inside and stood apart. Arla rubbed her hand, feeling awkward.

"I hope you didn't mind coming to my chambers," he said.

"Not at all. I know I have to do the reports."

"Good. We missed a session already, so this one was important."

"Sure."

The elevator pinged, and they came out into a dark corridor where light sprang into life as they walked. Dr Seddon opened a mahogany door that bore his name and title and walked inside. He flicked lights on. Arla saw a wide desk in the middle, with a white laptop, and no papers. The walls had two certificates, and two modern, framed canvases. Half of the glass wall at the rear had drawn curtains. The other half showed The Shard opposite, and London Bridge below, sparkling like fireworks. The office gave her a feeling of calm, like the man standing opposite her. It was almost relaxing after her hectic day so far.

"Have a seat on the sofa," Dr Seddon said, walking to a cabinet behind the desk. He poured himself a drink then lifted a glass. "Coke or orange juice?"

She wanted a glass of wine but suppressed her reply. "OJ is fine."

Arla reclined on the warm, brown leather sofa. She wondered how many clients he saw at his office. He came forward and gave her the drink. Her coat was folded next to her, and he put it up on the coat hook on the door.

"How are you?" he asked, sitting down.

"Busy with the case."

He inclined his head, observing her closely. He smiled, and it made her less self-conscious. He looked handsome as ever, a white shirt clinging to a muscled, trim body. The tie was loosened at the collar.

"Not getting too busy, I hope."

"What do you mean?"

He swirled the dark liquid in his glass and she heard the ice chink. It was very quiet. "You get obsessed with your job, don't you?"

She bristled at his judgement, but knew it was true. "Doesn't everyone, to some degree?"

He laughed, a rich, warm sound. "I can't deny you that." His face grew serious. "But there are dangers with getting too caught up. Right?"

"Yes."

"Any problems with work?"

Arla shook her head. "Apart from the usual."

"You can talk to me, you know. That is the whole point, after all. Everything you tell me is strictly confidential. Several senior detectives have received therapy from me. So don't worry."

Hesitantly, Arla opened up about the case. He listened calmly, his eyes not leaving her face.

"Are you getting frustrated when dealing with an authority figure like the MP, Richard Bromsgrove?" he asked.

She shrugged. "I guess so."

"Frustration is a warning sign for you. Do you agree?"

Arla frowned. "What do you want me to do?"

He shook his head vigorously. "It's a natural emotion when dealing with something tough. But you have to watch it doesn't lead to anger and then impulsive behaviour."

She rubbed her forehead. "It's hard."

"I know, Arla. Look at me." His eyes penetrated hers. She felt her heartbeat skip, and her mouth go dry.

"We talked about control last time. When faced with an angry situation, turn off. Move away."

"Do you turn off?" she found herself saying, for no apparent reason. She couldn't stop looking at him. His grey eyes were cloudy, but they held her in a rigid grip.

"Not always," he said in a husky voice. "But I try not to lose control." He blinked then and moved back in his chair. Arla swallowed. Something had passed between them, solid and tangible. She could feel it, crackling in the air. The lights were dim, casting shadows around them.

"Do you think this could be a serial killer?" he asked.

"I don't know. But I can see a pattern forming. We have to wait and see."

"Serial killers are interesting."

"How do you mean?"

"Everyone thinks they are psychopaths. But not all psychopaths are serial killers. If you are driven to succeed, have loose morals, and can't form close emotional connections, chances are you are a psychopath. Many important people in society are like that. CEOs, lawyers, doctors – take your pick. But it doesn't make them serial killers."

"Then what does?"

He shrugged. "They just don't feel emotion at all. Most psychopaths have some feelings, but serial killers are"—he smiled—"what we call cold-blooded. They don't make friends."

Arla shivered despite herself. "But many serial killers come from good families and have children who grow up loving them."

"Absolutely." He was silent for a while, observing her. "Enough talk about them. Let's talk about you. What are you suppressing today?"

Arla said, "Nothing."

"We need to talk about that, right? In order to make progress, you have to bring it back."

The wall returned, staring at her. She could feel its oppressive weight. No, she couldn't go there.

"I can't." Her voice broke, and she took a hasty swallow of her orange juice.

The intense look was back on his face. "It's going to be painful, Arla, and emotional. But I am here. You are not alone. I understand."

She looked at him, the table lamp illuminating half of his face. His hair was slightly dishevelled from running his hand through it. The top button of his shirt was undone, and she caught a glimpse of his chest hair. A heat fanned her face, and she looked down, avoiding his gaze.

His voice was gentle. "It won't go away at the same time, Arla. Slowly, piece by piece. Start at the beginning, it will be easier. There's no rush."

"I wish I could," Arla whispered.

"You do. I know you want to." Their eyes met again and locked. Arla saw warmth in his eyes, and frankness. "Don't be afraid," he whispered.

She reached for the glass of juice and found her hands shaking. She forced herself to drink, closing her eyes. "I'm tired. I should go." Her voice was thick, and like the drink, the words felt insincere. Her head felt light, her heart flirting with a flurry of rapid beats. A deep breath did nothing to dispel the feeling.

She watched as he leaned back in his armchair. "OK. As you wish. Remember what we talked about. Dealing with the frustration."

"Yes."

"I will send the report to your superior." His eyes gave nothing away. She felt he had retracted into his professional shell.

"Thank you," she said, standing up.

CHAPTER 40

Tara James looked at her pay-as-you-go phone in the street light. The corner she was standing on had a tree leaning over a fence, and she could merge in the shadows, hidden from passing cars. She wore make-up and had washed and dried her hair. She felt the dampness, then looked at the bright red of her fingernails. She checked her phone again. 8.30pm. He was late. She thought of calling him, but then decided against it. Fewer calls, the better, he always said. In fact, he kept his phone turned off and the battery separate, most times. Every month, he bought Tara a new phone, like the one she had now.

She heard the screech of brakes and looked up expectantly. Her heart fluttered wildly. The black BMW was waiting, engine running. Deep bass music sounded from inside. She could see his silhouette, and he was looking at the rear-view mirror. Tara looked around her, then opened the passenger side door quickly. The familiar smell of leather and a masculine cologne enveloped her. She strapped herself in. Without a word, he pulled out into traffic.

He spoke after a while. "Anyone seen you?"

Tara shook her head. "No."

"That woman who ran after you two nights ago. Did you find out who she was?"

"No," Tara lied. She couldn't tell him the truth. He would go apeshit. He was scary when angry, and the total opposite when in a good mood. Jekyll and Hyde. She had read that book in the library.

"You need to find out, OK?" His voice took a hard edge.

Tara nodded. "I will. She comes to talk to us now and then, check on our studies. Like some people do, you know."

She looked at his face, lit up by the lights from the dashboard, and the occasional headlight of a passing car. He remained impassive. He was so handsome. She looked away, her heart racing. He drove until they came to a block of council estates. He drove inside and followed the narrow paths until he came to a clearing, surrounded by tall council apartment buildings. Lights blazed in the open-air balconies. He stopped the car. He reached inside his pocket and took out a plastic packet. Inside it, several small paper wrappings were present. He took out four and gave them to her. She took them, feeling her heart thump against her ribs.

"Hey," he said. She looked at him. His normally bright eyes were hidden in the dim light. She could make out his strong jaw, the slight stubble on his cheeks. He smelled nice, like he always did.

"Sure you can do this?"

She held his eyes. "Yes, I can."

He breathed out. "Always ask to see the money first. Real customers have the cash in hand, ready. Time-wasters and junkies make excuses. Got it?"

"Yeah."

His voice dipped and became steely again. "I'm trusting you on this, big time. Come back down straight away. If this goes as planned, then we can party." He stared at her, then the corners of his lips twitched. Tara smiled back. She loved it when he was nice to her. She thought of what lay ahead, and excitement mounted inside her.

She opened the door and stepped out into the cold night air. The buildings stood like sentinels guarding the area. Vapour rose from her mouth, and the tip of her nose went numb in the cold. Her fist closed around the four small paper packets, and she thrust her hand deep inside her pocket.

She crossed the courtyard quickly and got into the building. The hallway was coloured the usual bland yellow and white of a council complex, tainted by graffiti on the wall and spray paint. She looked around and, seeing no one, thrust her hand inside her knickers and put the packet inside. Tara got into the lift and pressed for the fifth floor. She walked out along the open balcony, the freezing cold stinging her nose and cheeks as she hurried down the garishly lit passage.

She knew why he had sent her. This was her second job, the first had been a drop of only one packet, a test drop. She had succeeded. No one would suspect a well-dressed teenage girl to do what she was doing. A man, on the other hand, could be stopped and searched.

She reached the door. Bright green, like every other regularly spaced door along the balcony. She knocked twice. There was a sound of voices inside, then someone shouted. She heard footsteps, then the door opened. She had already taken the stuff out. The man who came out was naked from the waist up despite the weather, and the cloud of cannabis smoke hit her nostrils hard. He looked down at her, and his lips split into a slow smile. She saw the gold tooth and shivered as his eyes ran up and down her body.

"So, you T's new bitch, huh?"

She swallowed and held her ground. "Where's the money?"

"Where's the gear?"

"I need to see the money first."

"Fuck you, bitch."

"Fine, see ya." She walked off with purpose. She heard the man swear.

"Whoa, whoa. Hold up."

Tara turned. The man had stepped outside the door, notes in his hand. She glanced at them. Four fifties, the correct amount. She took the money and handed over the goods.

"You're lucky you got T's protection, bitch," the man called out as she walked off. Inside the lift, she sank against stainless steel wall and let out a long breath. This scared her. But she could do it. She had been nine years old when her mother's friend tried it on with her, while her mother jacked up in the next room. She had bled, hurt, scarred and bruised, and her whole life had been on the run.

Yes, she could do this.

She hurried across the courtyard. The black Merc's lights came on. She slipped inside the passenger seat, and the car took off without a sound. They drove out of the estate then parked inside a dark alley. She showed him the money. He counted it and put it into his pocket.

Tara asked, "Where's my cut?"

He turned his head to her. She could smell the heady scent of his cologne. His hand reached out and pressed on her breast. She wanted to stop him but knew it was futile. He leaned over, and his lips sank on hers.

"You're gonna get your cut, don't worry," he grunted, as he ripped her bra down, and thrust himself on top of her.

CHAPTER 41

Arla jumped the last few steps of the stairs leading up to the double doors of Clapham London Met station. John Sandford, the desk sergeant, caught her eye as she came in.

"Boss wants to see you," he said darkly. "Told me to let you know as soon as you arrived."

"Yes, I know," Arla sighed. "Is he in his office?"

"Yes."

Arla walked down the corridor and took the lift to the first floor. She knocked on Wayne Johnson's door. She heard his voice and entered.

She was surprised to see Harry in there. He was dressed immaculately in a navy-blue suit, only the scuffed shoes from the mud giving away where he had been last night. Johnson was wearing his uniform again. *Probably another press release,* she thought. Harry turned to look at her, and she saw anxiety on his face. *Great start to the morning.*

"Good of you to join us, DCI Baker," Johnson said. Arla didn't miss the sarcastic note.

"Well, you did ask to see me, sir," she said pointedly.

"I called you several times, as well, in the last day and a half. Yet you choose to ignore my calls."

"You called me once, sir, last night. Before that you told me to report to you."

Johnson raised his hands. "Enough. Save your breath, 'cos you're gonna need it."

Harry shot her a look and gave a little shake of the head. It didn't escape Johnson, and she realised Harry hadn't intended it to, either. Johnson's expression darkened.

"What the hell are you two up to?" he asked.

Arla asked, "What do you mean, sir?"

"Yesterday, you went to see Richard Bromsgrove, the Battersea MP."

"Yes." She glanced at Harry. He was looking forward, his lips pressed tightly together.

"Yes? I have been asking DI Mehta what it was about. Perhaps you can enlighten me now that you have arrived."

"The first victim had his card in her possession. She had hidden it, like she didn't want it to be found."

"Why the hell would she do that?"

Arla shrugged. "She didn't want the outside world to know about her relationship with him? I don't know. But you can't deny it's not worth following up."

"No, I can't. But you can see it doesn't mean anything, can't you? There could be a number of reasons for it. Maybe she just wanted to have a chat with her MP about the pollution in Battersea."

"Then why would she hide it?"

"How do you know it was hidden? Maybe it was coincidence."

"Sir, I…"

Johnson spoke over her, his voice rising to an authoritative pitch. "DCI Baker, do you know who Mr Bromsgrove is?"

"An MP, sir."

"Not any MP. He is the leader of the Commons Select Committee on Policing and Criminal Justice. Did you know that?"

Harry and Arla exchanged another glance. This was news to both of them. Arla said, "No, I didn't know that."

"He is also widely tipped to become the next Policing and Fire Minister." Johnson put his knuckles on the desk and leaned forward. "In fact, I have it on good authority that letterheads in the House of Commons are being prepared right now for a change of Minister position. With his name up there."

Arla struggled to contain her anger. She was aware of the warmth on her face. "Sir, are you suggesting I stay away from a potential suspect in a murder case because of their political position?"

Johnson glared at her. "Harassing important public servants is not the way

152

this department works, DCI Baker."

"Harassing?" Arla laughed. "All we did was ask some questions. I can't believe he lifted the phone and cried to you. Ridiculous!"

Johnson squared his jaws and his nostrils flared. "I'm warning you, I don't want to hear from him again. Leave him alone. There are multiple directions in which this case is moving, and I understand you have a new homicide to deal with as well."

Arla should have bit her tongue, but she couldn't help it. "What is this really about, sir? About you getting the top job?"

Johnson's face blanched white then flushed a deep crimson. He bared his teeth. "How dare you?! I put you in charge of this case, and now you dare accuse me of...of..."

"I'm sorry, sir," Arla said quickly. She had overstepped the mark. But she knew she was right. She looked at Johnson plainly, and she knew that he knew it, too. He pushed his shoulders back, clasped his hands behind his back, and walked around behind them. Then he walked back to his desk and faced them.

"Leave, DI Mehta," he said to Harry. Harry looked at her, and she nodded. He mumbled a goodbye to Johnson and left. Johnson waited until the door had shut.

"Be careful of where you point your finger, DCI Baker," he said in a quiet voice, eventually. "You know the Independent Police Complaints Commission have looked into your case. You need to be very careful of where you tread, and on whose toes."

Arla didn't say anything until she saw the hostile look in his eyes. "Yes, sir," she murmured.

"Have you seen the psychiatrist?"

"Yes, last night."

"Good. From now on, before you go to see the MP, you have to clear with me first."

Arla frowned. She wasn't a trainee detective constable who had to ask permission at every turn. "But, sir," she protested.

"Remember the media have your file." He lifted up his hands. "I am as annoyed as you are. The truth is, I don't know where it came from." He sighed heavily. "It just means you and the SCS are now under renewed pressure to sort this mess out." He sat down on his armchair and waved at Arla to sit down.

"Tell me where we are," Johnson said.

After ten minutes of debriefing the boss, Arla came downstairs. She went straight into the incident room, as she knew it would be packed. She was right. Men and women stood along the walls, nursing cups of coffee in their hands.

Harry had the white boards ready, with the victims' names on it. Charlene Atkins, Victim 2, and on the next white board, he had written down Chris Crichton.

"What did we find in that red bag in Charlene Atkins' house?" she asked Harry.

"An old VHS videotape recorder with a tape inside it. Tape is blank. Two sets of fingerprints on it, one of them is hers. The other – nothing as yet on IDENT1."

"DNA?"

"Again, some skin cells from her and someone else. Nothing on the DNA Database."

Arla thought for a while. "OK. The tape recorder must have a serial number. What company, is it?"

"Panasonic," Harry said.

"Call up Panasonic UK, give them the serial number, and they can work out which year that model was made. Get a list of authorised Panasonic retailers in London, active that year. Many would have shut down by now. Panasonic should have a record of which items were sent to which retailer. Then we narrow the field and visit the shop if it's still open. Got that?"

"Yup."

"Are we looking into Bromsgrove?" She noticed a few uneasy looks pass between Rob, Lisa and the rest of the team.

Harry said, "Squeaky clean. All the way from college in Oxford to his current post in the government."

"Basically, untouchable," Arla said, rolling her eyes. "Is his blood blue?"

There was a smattering of laughter. Lisa was sitting at her table, and she spoke with her eyes on the screen. "Actually, he does have an interesting business profile."

Arla sauntered over to Lisa. "Like what?"

Lisa pointed at the screen. "This is the list of his companies. He owns two hotels, a spa, and several properties across the South East and North West."

Something tingled Arla's spine. Chris Crichton had also owned a property company.

"Are these companies live?"

"Yes. We are downloading documents as we speak, and I'm going to go through the filings once we have them."

"Good," Lisa said. She straightened and faced the rest of the team. "Any news of the dredger?"

Toby, the black sergeant who had taken the lead role in organising the machine, spoke up. "I was there after the detectives left," he said, nodding to Harry. "They went through all the mud: nothing was found."

"Nothing at all?" Arla felt her heart sinking. "Is all the dredging done?"

Toby said, "The pond is almost done, guv. There's a smaller marsh area next to it, they're looking at that now. But so far, nothing."

Just great.

Arla said, "Did we get hold of Charlene's FaceBook contacts? Any sign of a phone?"

She looked at a row of blank faces then at Harry. He shook his head. "We asked the majority. They all said she didn't have a phone."

Why would someone not have a cell phone? Arla pressed her temples. None of this was going to plan. But she needed to maintain her sanity.

"As you know," she said, "Charlene Atkins was a fake identity. That woman"—Arla pointed to Charlene's photo on the whiteboard—"got hold of my number, and then came to see me as well."

"She didn't leave any other name in the care home. Her bank account, National Insurance number, passport, everything is in Charlene Atkins' name. But that's not who she is."

Arla stood up from where she had perched herself on the table. "This woman had a life before she became Charlene Atkins. A life she wanted to leave behind and forget. If we find out about that life, I reckon we crack this case."

She turned to Harry. "Did we pull in Steven Wade?"

"He's coming later today."

"And the girlfriend?"

"In the next hour."

"Good. I will do the interviews. Lisa, Rob, call Panasonic and dig around. Anything from Bandy after the autopsies? Any dental records?"

Lisa and Rob shook their heads slowly. Arla tried in vain to hide her disappointment. Something had to give, and soon. "OK, team, let's get to it."

She left and walked back to her office.

CHAPTER 42

Arla folded her hands and stared at the confident young woman staring back at her. She was tall and sat straight-backed in the chair. Her dyed blonde hair was long at the back, and she was dressed in a dark green, furry jacket with a black turtleneck top underneath. A gold chain gleamed on her neck. Arla peered at the paper in her hand. Harry was sitting next to her. He made sure the tape was on, and the DVD player on the wall was recording. Arla introduced herself on the system, then glanced at the woman.

"Monica Pawlowski."

"Yes, that is me," Monica said in a Polish accent.

"You work in Starbucks as a manager, and you are the girlfriend of Steven Wade's."

"Yes."

"Was he with you on the night of the 24th of November?"

"Yes, he was."

"And on the 26th?"

Monica's eyes crinkled slightly. "26th?"

"Yes, the 26th of November, two days later. Was he with you that night as well?"

Monica frowned. "Why are you asking me about that night?"

"Can you please answer the question?"

She shrugged. "Not sure. I need to think."

"OK." Arla nodded. "This is important, and we need you to get it right."

Monica's confident frontage developed a crack. She blinked twice and cleared her throat.

"What is this about?"

"Nothing, we just want to know about Steven's and your whereabouts that night."

Monica stared at Arla for a few seconds. "That was not an answer to the question."

Arla normally had a laid-back approach to interrogation. She got more clues from observing behaviour than being forceful. But for Monica she decided to do an exception. Time was short, and her boyfriend would be arriving soon.

"I would like to remind you that you are in a police station, and you are giving a legal statement that can be produced in court, and you can be called to testify. Do you understand, Miss Pawlowski?"

Monica blinked again. "In that case I need a lawyer. Yes?"

Arla sighed wearily. Harry was sitting motionless to her right. He asked, "Is Steven Wade your boyfriend?"

"You asked me that already. Yes." She shrugged in irritation.

"And you can't remember if you saw him three nights ago?"

Monica shrugged, and Arla could see the studious effort on her face. Her senses began to twitch. Something was wrong here. Monica was trying too hard. She was too careful. Maybe a blind alley, but it wouldn't hurt to tread softly.

After a pause, Arla said gently, "You can have a lawyer if you want to, no problem. Shall we take a break?" She rose from the chair and gave Monica a glass of water from the drinks machine. She spoke for the recorder and turned the machine off.

Monica said, "Can I leave now and come back later?"

Arla and Harry looked at each other. Then Arla shrugged. "You are not under arrest, Miss Pawlowski. But we do need you to answer our questions."

"So I can go?"

Arla sighed, trying not to let her irritation show. "I thought we were going to take a break, and resume."

"No, no. I go now, and back later. OK?" Monica stood up, and her height matched Arla's. The two women locked eyes, and Monica was the first one to look away.

Harry watched her go, heels clicking on the laminate floor. "If that was a dress rehearsal, I would love to see the real show."

"Call Steven Wade. Bring his appointment sooner if you can," Arla said, leaving the room.

CHAPTER 43

Steven Wade looked better than last time, Arla thought. He was more poised and calm. Harry moved a screen closer to them on the table but didn't switch it on. Arla started the questions after a brief introduction.

"Where were you on the night of the 26th of November?"

A look of surprise appeared on Steven's face. His clean-shaven jaws clamped shut before opening again. His aftershave was faint, and his blue suit pressed neatly. The black shoes had polished tips, an achievement in this weather. Harry had a competitor.

"The 26th of November? Why do you want to know?"

"Please answer the question, Steven." Arla watched him closely. He seemed flustered all of a sudden. He passed a hand over his moist forehead, rubbing it.

"I went for a walk, I think. Down to the Common." They had already established that Steven lived in Nine Elms, an area near Battersea Power Station.

"You came for a walk on Clapham Common, and not Battersea Park?" Arla asked. She thought she saw a hint of colour appear in Steven's cheeks before it died.

"I...I go for a run, you see, and as I always run in Battersea Park, opted for a change."

Arla nodded, giving him some time. He had chosen for the truth, she thought, and that was the right option. But again, he had a simmering undercurrent of anxiety that was now rippling up to the surface. He was trying his best to hide it, and that was making it worse.

"So you ran from Nine Elms, down to Clapham Common, and you used the entrance for the Holy Communion Church?"

The mention of the location had been intentional. She saw a splurge of red on Steven's face, like he had been slapped. His spine rocked back, and his face came up to level with Arla's.

"How did you know that?" he asked, eyes narrowed. "What's going on here?"

Harry reached out and pressed on the monitor screen. Then he picked up a remote control and activated the CCTV spool in the DVD recorder. All eyes were now fixed on the screen, showing a black and white image of Steven walking towards the gate.

Arla said, "That is you, Mr Wade, right?"

Steven was hunched close, eyebrows joined at the middle. He looked up at them, his face pale and drawn. "Yes," he said. "Why do you have this?"

Arla said, "Because an hour after you went in those gates, a man was killed, in exactly the same manner as Charlene Atkins was."

Steven sat back in his chair, his face white, body very still. "And you think the same man killed…"

Arla shook her head. "No one is saying that, Mr Wade. We are making enquiries. Soon we will have the victim's identity. But we have to ask you if you know him."

"Know who?"

Harry reached inside a brown paper envelope and shook out the photos of Victim 2. Arla watched as Steven's eyes widened in shock. He pushed the photos away and averted his face to the side. He looked as if he was going to vomit.

"Are you OK?" Arla asked with genuine concern. He looked back at her, eyes still wide. He licked his lips.

"This is horrible. Horrible," he repeated.

"Have you ever seen this man?" Harry asked, leaning in. Steven stared at him blankly for a while.

"No."

"Are you sure?"

"Yes. Yes, I'm sure."

Harry tapped the photo. "What you say now can be given as evidence in court. You know that, don't you?"

Steven closed his eyes before replying. "Yes, I do."

"When did you get back home that night?" Arla asked.

"Not late. My runs are normally an hour to an hour and a half. Can't remember the exact time."

"Is Monica Pawlowski really your girlfriend?"

Steven seemed perturbed by the question. He bit his lower lip. "You have seen her already today, haven't you?"

"Yes."

"Then you must know the answer. Yes, she is my partner."

"She didn't seem to remember if she had seen you the night of the 26th, but it was only three nights ago. Maybe your partner has short-term memory loss."

Steven stared at Arla then smiled weakly. "Maybe. I don't know. Look, am I free to go?"

"Sure. We will call you if anything else comes up."

When Harry shut the door, he folded his arms and leaned against it. "He was wearing jogging clothes. Likes his Lycra, doesn't he?"

Arla shrugged, deep in thought. Harry said, "Steven goes in before the victim, but there's no images of Steven coming out. And yet, he says he got back home after one and a half hours?"

Arla said, "Have we checked all the cameras?" Clapham Common was 220 acres of triangular parkland, and almost a square kilometre.

"Most of them," Harry said.

"Even if we don't see him running back it doesn't mean anything. He could have used a different route."

"You don't think he did it, do you?"

Arla lifted her eyes to his. "No. I reckon he's thrown up at the sight of a victim. He's too nervous."

Harry nodded. "I agree. But then why don't I trust him?"

Arla pursed her lips and frowned. "I was thinking the same thing."

CHAPTER 44

The sun was slanting its last rays over the golden spires of Westminster Palace. Victoria Tower, the largest of the towers built in the New Palace, stood watch over the Old Palace Yard, where concrete fences restricted access to the public.

The portly figure of Richard Bromsgrove hurried out of the gate into Old Palace Yard, and crossed across the barriers into the street. He walked over to the white, Gothic magnificence of Westminster Abbey Church. Dodging tourists, he continued with the Abbey on his left, walking straight down Victoria Street. Traffic buzzed around the gyratory of Parliament Square Garden.

Bromsgrove walked as fast as his corpulent figure allowed and turned left into Great Smith Street. He followed a series of left and right turns until he came to the street he sought. Rows of golden brick buildings lined the street, stunningly built terraces with long windows and elaborately carved eaves. He took out the keys from his pocket and watched up and down the deserted street. There were no CCTVs here.

He opened the door and slipped inside. A dark hallway greeted him. Despite the appearance outside, the building inside was empty, and had been derelict for many years. He reflected on how most of Westminster lived up to that truth. All bluster and not much substance. The electrics didn't work, so he switched on the torchlight he had brought. A massive, sweeping dusty staircase went upstairs, but he ignored it and headed towards the door at the end of the hallway. It was unlocked. He shone his torch inside and found a landing, with steps at the far end leading down to the basement. The smell of animal excrement hit his nostrils, and he curled his lips. This place gave him the creeps.

He could hear voices as he went down the stairs. At the bottom, a yellow bulb illuminated a stark scene, moulding concrete walls, and an old, bricked floor. Three other figures stood in the centre, casting long shadows on the floor. Bromsgrove walked up to them.

Sean Decker, dressed in jeans and jacket, turned to face him. Bromsgrove knew the other two as well. James Percival worked for the Home Office; the other was a retired politician called Alistair Brown. The four of them stood in the halo of light.

Alistair Brown, once a senior Cabinet member in a 1980s government, spoke first. "How did it start?" he asked calmly.

James Percival, who was in his sixties, replied. "With Charlene. We don't know how she knew, but she did."

"Someone told her," Brown said. "We have a leak."

Decker shook his head. "It doesn't matter anymore. Fact is, this has the potential to become big. Very big. And it's not just the four of us. There are others."

Neither of them looked at each other. They silently weighed up the ramifications, none liking what they saw.

Brown said, "We need this to go away. Who can make that happen?" He looked from one face to the other.

Bromsgrove said, "The cops came to my office." His audience stirred. "They asked me questions about Charlene. I denied ever knowing her, of course. They found my card on her. Nothing else."

Decker said to Brown, "Charlene was going to come to you next."

Brown said, "It doesn't matter. She's been dealt with. It's about the police investigation now. We cannot afford for it to go through." After a pause he said, "This woman, DCI Baker – she's quite tenacious, isn't she?"

Bromsgrove nodded. "She's the one who came to my office. With a male detective."

The vicar said, "We can't just get rid of them. It makes the current problem a hundred times worse."

The man from the Home Office was silent. Presently he said, "We can't get rid of them, but we must do something. If they have got to you"—he indicated Bromsgrove—"then they can get to us as well."

"The by-election is a problem now," Bromsgrove said with a curse.

"No, it's not," said Brown forcefully. "We have to nip the investigation in the bud and get rid of any remaining evidence. Then we carry on as usual. Remember what the fallout will be if we don't."

Decker looked at them steadily. "That means getting rid of that pesky Detective Arla Baker."

All four voiced agreement.

CHAPTER 45

Harry knocked on Arla's door. It was unnecessary: the door was ajar. He pushed it open after a brief pause. Arla shut down the screen she had been browsing. The usual cold cases, and the same missing person. The file still had Nicole's photo in black and white, staring out with an arrogant, confident stare. Most days, Arla had trouble looking at the photo, as it seemed to be staring at her directly. Today was no different.

She drained her coffee, her fourth of the day. "Please tell me you got an ID on the second victim."

Harry shook his head. Arla slumped. "But I got something on Chris Crichton," Harry said.

"Go on," Arla was mildly interested.

"That apartment was his, and he used to work in the Home Office."

"Which branch?"

"Communications Unit at 2 Marsham Street. That's their HQ. He worked there most of his life, and was a senior strategist, helping the way the HO handled media enquiries. He was a civil servant and had close contacts with Ministers."

"And MPs." Arla sat up straighter.

"Yes." She saw the corner of Harry's eyes crinkle, and she knew he had something.

Harry said, "So I looked up all the policy documents Crichton had published for the HO over the years. Stuff about how to deflect questions from the media, aimed at ministers. Guess who was his co-writer in several of the documents from the late-80s and 90s?"

"Tell me."

"Richard Bromsgrove, MP."

"Good work." Arla clutched her hands together under the table, excited.

"Bromsgrove wasn't an MP then. He worked for the Conservative Party

Office as a media analyst and had contact with the Home Office's civil servants. Maybe that's how he met Chris."

Arla was lost in thought. "And maintained a professional relationship over more than a decade, publishing papers together. Maybe friends as well, we don't know."

"And now Crichton is murdered."

Arla looked at Harry, her eyes shining. "Good work, Harry. It's all coincidence right now, but we need to push this, see where it gets us." The phone rang on her desk. It was the call she had been waiting for. "Stay," she told Harry and answered the phone.

Bandy's measured voice came over the line. "If it isn't my favourite DCI."

Arla smiled despite herself. "Flattery will get you everything, doc."

"Except the gift of your company, evidently."

"You have it now, you old charmer. What have you got for me?"

Bandy's voice changed and became brisk. "Not much left to see on the surface or the insides of Chris Crichton. The heat has played havoc with my time of death calculation. The charts are all off the scale."

Arla knew pathologists used multi-axis charts with many variables to get a final time of death. It was tough, and an imprecise science at the best of times. Temperature, moisture, environment chemicals – all played a part.

Bandy continued. "Given the advanced state of decomp, I would say the body's been there for two days." Arla scribbled on a piece of paper. Harry walked behind her and watched her write. That time meant the date probably was the 27th, one day after the death of victim 2.

"MO?"

"Again, hard to tell, but found some interesting clues. Petechial haemorrhages in the eyes, and similar on the tongue. Both identified by jagged black marks. Rupture of laryngeal cartilages, along with tracheal cartilages. All caused by…"

Arla cut him off. "Increased pressure from strangulation."

"Yes. No flesh in the neck remains, apart from heavily decomposed tissue. Unfortunately, fingerprints and fibres have all degenerated in the heat as a result. That was the killer's intention, I believe."

She said, "So, the same basic MO as the other two. But we don't know if he cut their throats as well, as we don't have the tissue."

"Exactly."

"Thank you, doc."

"Keep me posted, and let's hope the bodies stop here. I have other work as well, you know."

Arla grinned and hung up. She turned to Harry who was waiting expectantly, and explained what Bandy said.

"Shit," he said. "This is now stacking up. Has to be the same killer."

Arla had her thinking hat on. "We know Crichton and Bromsgrove started to collaborate in the late-80s, right?"

"Yes."

"What if they started earlier? I mean, if they knew each other personally, or as colleagues before?"

Harry was silent. Arla said, "Find out their college degrees, and where they went to university. They both must have CVs online, right?"

Harry dashed out of the room. Arla's fingers danced on the keyboard, searching for Chris Crichton. She found nothing. The Home Office website was just as bland. Harry dashed back in, his face animated.

"We know where RB went. Oxford, I did the check myself. All we have to find is if Chris went to the same college in the same year. I've told Lisa already, she's calling the university up."

Arla said, "How did you find out about Chris's publications?"

"It's not on the HO website," he said with a satisfied smile. "I had to ring up and speak to Human Resources about Chris. The publications were tagged to his file."

There was a knock on the door, and Lisa poked her head in. "That was quick," Arla said.

Lisa was beaming. "The University Registrar was super helpful." She fluttered a piece of paper. "I've written it down and am waiting for the fax to come through. Chris Crichton and Richard Bromsgrove went to St John's College in Oxford. Attended from 1980 to 1983, and both studied PPP. Physics, Politics and Philosophy."

Arla leaned back in her chair. After days of deadlock and frustration, things were suddenly on the move.

CHAPTER 46

"Well done, Lisa!" Arla called out as a flushed, excited Lisa left the room. Arla stood up and grabbed her badge and coat. She stuffed the badge on her belt line.

Harry said, "Let me guess. A visit to the MP?"

"Yes, but before that, have we checked all the CCTV cameras on Chris Crichton's street for the last three days?"

"Nope, and it's gonna take time."

"Get it done, Harry."

"Team's on it, boss." He looked at her with a level-eyed stare.

"What?" Arla asked, knowing what he was going to say.

"Are you sure this is a wise move?"

"Two of the three victims know the same person, and all three died in similar fashion? Yes, I'd say this is a wise move. He knows more than he's letting on, and if I had my way, I'd arrest the fat fucker and bring him to the station."

"Whoa."

"You're just scared he's a potential Minister."

Harry followed as she stalked down the corridor. "Am I heck! Since when has being nice to a Minister helped?"

They parked the car outside the large complex of the Battersea Leisure Centre where Bromsgrove was conducting a meeting with some of the local business leaders. The media had arrived as well, and TV crew were getting cameras ready, anchors powdering their faces on make-up mirrors, smoothing down skirts and suits.

The general crowd around the mouth of the car park stopped their car. Harry beeped once, but no one took notice. Arla flicked the siren on the dashboard before Harry could stop her. The siren wailed suddenly, drowning out the hubbub. The blast of sound got everyone's attention. The crowd parted, and Harry turned the car inside the car park. As Arla came out, she noticed some of the reporters leave their ranks and run up towards her. Cameras flashed as Harry stepped in front of Arla, and together they ran towards the doors.

Security stopped them, and Arla showed them her badge. They were shown inside a large space that housed tennis and badminton courts. The area was full of people, with desks and stalls arranged around the sides. Supermarkets and local businesses had booths advertising their wares, and above their heads, a big banner in blue and white proclaimed "Making Britain Better". The crowd was denser at the middle, and a group stood around a person who was talking. A recording camera was pointed in his direction, and several people were doing videos on their iPhones.

Harry pulled on Arla's sleeve. "We should be discreet. Wait till he finishes."

Against her better judgement, she agreed. Surprising Bromsgrove was what she had in mind, to see how he reacted. Being caught in the middle of a public event would make him think twice of their encounter, she hoped. She waited impatiently while he finished speaking for the camera and turned to the assembled public to take questions. Arla pushed forward. His eyes fell on her, and he frowned.

"Mr Bromsgrove," Arla called out. Her voice was low in the general commotion. She raised her voice. He ignored her and turned away, showing her his wide back. Arla surged forward, pushing people away. She grabbed his shoulder and pulled him back.

"Mr Bromsgrove!" she shouted at his astounded, red face as he turned around. She held up her badge. "DCI Baker, we need to have another chat."

There was a sudden quiet in the middle of the room. The bubbling voices around them died down. Arla ignored it. She focused on the perspiring Bromsgrove. The flesh on his neck spilled out over the edge of his white shirt collar. His cheeks were heavy, sagging. Wet beads glistened on his forehead. He glared at her with undisguised hostility.

"I told you last time, Inspector, I have nothing to say."

"Detective Chief Inspector, actually, Mr Bromsgrove," Arla said calmly, noting his infuriated expression. "We need to question you regarding another murder in the area."

There was an audible murmur from the group around her. Bromsgrove's face turned a deep shade of mauve. With an effort, he checked his anger.

"I have nothing to add, Miss Baker, as I informed you last time."

Arla noticed that he knew her name. It made her uneasy. "This is for a new line of enquiry, regarding a new victim."

He was seething. "Please see my secretary and make an appointment to come to the office."

"I'm afraid it cannot wait, Mr Bromsgrove. Do you know someone called Chris Crichton?"

Bromsgrove paled visibly. He swallowed and, despite the battery of eyes now focused on him, raised his voice at Arla. "I cannot comment on these matters at the moment, Miss Baker. Like I said, please make an.."

"Are you denying that you knew Mr Crichton?" Arla persisted. She could feel the bodies pressed together tightly around her, eagerly listening to the exchange.

Bromsgrove softened his stance. "Miss Baker, I can answer your questions later. As you can see, I am not at liberty to do so now." He made to move away, but Arla called out to him.

"You went to the same college and published papers together, didn't you?"

The murmur of voices around them grew stronger. Men and women looked at them and spoke in hushed tones. Bromsgrove's mask slipped, and he lost his cool. He stepped up to Arla, his face working.

"Harassing an MP isn't the correct way to conduct an investigation, Miss Baker. I suggest you remove yourself from the premises, before I call security." He stormed off, elbowing his way past the crowd. This time, Arla didn't chase him.

Like a punctured balloon, the bubbly atmosphere in the auditorium had deflated. Instead of the chorus of voices, whispers made the rounds. Bromsgrove strode to a stall at the far end and shook hands with a group of men in suits. Harry leaned close to Arla.

"Reckon it's time to go, boss. You got what you came here for."

Arla nodded. She had indeed. Bromsgrove was hiding behind a mountain of denials and smoke, and he couldn't hide for long. He must be doing it for a reason, and Arla couldn't think of anything but buying himself time. Well, she wouldn't be giving it to him.

Eyes and whispers followed them as she followed Harry's lanky frame out of the room.

CHAPTER 47

Light faded fast from the ochre and gold sky over the dense clump of green trees on Clapham Common. It was barely 4pm, and the fuzzy orange glow from street lights already cast conical shapes mid-air. The tangled knot of traffic seemed to grow as darkness claimed London's streets, headlights glowing like an army of feral creatures on the prowl.

Arla held her coat tight around herself, face numb from the biting wind. She had decided to walk from the station today, partly because she needed space to think and partly because she wanted the exercise. She was beginning to regret the decision now. The invariable whispering drizzle had started, light enough to be thwarted by her hooded jacket, but a nefarious partner to the biting cold. Thoughts came and went from her mind like the passing traffic.

Who had Charlene Atkins been?

How was she connected to the other two victims?

Arla crossed the junction of Clapham North and walked down the bar and restaurant-filled High Street. Music pulsed from one of the double-storeyed nightclubs as she walked past. She dodged the crowds but kept her eyes open as she walked. She was going past the Sainsbury's when she noticed a dark-haired man leaning against the entrance, staring at her. They both looked away at the same time, but she couldn't shake off the feeling she had seen him somewhere before. As she went past him, he slipped off the entrance and followed her.

Arla's sixth sense started ringing. She could feel his presence behind him. A disturbing thought tingled the back of her mind. A dark-haired man had also been spotted outside Charlene Atkins' house. Her pulse quickened. Inside the coat pockets her fingers squeezed into fists. Suddenly, she dived into a newspaper kiosk and snatched up a newspaper. She looked over the edge of the paper and caught the dark-haired man just in time as he lowered his head and snuck behind a family of four. He wasn't tall, about her height of 5' 9". He wore a dark overcoat that came down to his knees.

Arla clenched her teeth and waited. There was a bus stop between them, and a red double-decker screeched to a stop. A cloud of passengers descended, and she couldn't see the man anymore. She cursed and moved forward, smacking the unfolded paper back on top of its pile. People moved to board the bus, and she caught sight of the man, darting on-board from the back gate.

Arla shoved people aside and charged through the crowd. Angry shouts followed her. The back doors closed before she could get to them. She grabbed the rubber gaskets and tried to pry open the door. She saw a man's feet running up the stairs, vanishing from view. The front doors shuddered close and the bus began to move.

"Stop, police!" Arla shouted, but the bus had left the kerb already. She ran to the front and waved at the driver, but he was busy navigating traffic. With a curse, she noted down the registration number. She phoned the station and gave them the bus number and reg then stood staring at the red behemoth as it drove away, belching out exhaust fumes.

Arla shook her head then resumed walking. The neon craze faded, and the light grew dimmer. The looming mansions of Clapham Park Road began, old buildings built for wealthy Victorian merchants. All were preserved in a pristine state. All but one.

The squat, ugly structure stood between two well-restored, tall, terraced buildings. Arla came to a stop outside it. She was drawn to it for some reason, but she couldn't fathom why. The boarded windows had weeds growing out of them. Suspended in time, it was also sunk in the darkness between the orange penumbra of two street lamps. The crumbling red-brick façade stared out at the expanse of the Common. The wide, once stout wooden front door was covered in mould and scars. The tall triangle of the roof was still intact, with holes at frequent intervals. That told her the building wasn't set on fire. The roof would have collapsed, and the black smudges outside the windows were also missing.

No, someone had locked up the secrets in this place and thrown away the key. She wondered why the building hadn't changed hands. Surely a new owner would be keen to exploit the über-high land prices in this part of London? Arla wasn't into property: she never had the money to buy herself an apartment within a short commuting distance. But she knew this place, if renovated, would cost several million pounds.

A cold gust of wind blew a smattering of rain on her face. Like a skull with hollow eyes, the derelict building gazed back at her. She shivered and moved on. After a brisk, ten-minute walk, she turned left and crossed into the road for Cedarbrook Care Home. As she walked she reminded herself to talk to the old Rastafarian who used to sleep in that building. There must be a side entrance that she couldn't see.

As she approached the care home, her breath quickened when she saw a squad car outside. The engine was off, and she couldn't see anyone inside. She walked fast and ran up the stairs. Loretta looked up as she walked in. She said two uniformed officers had arrived and wanted to speak to Tara. An ominous feeling surged inside Arla.

She went through the locked door and entered the common room. It was empty, save the two uniformed officers at the far end. They were sitting at the table, with a frightened Tara opposite them. Arla approached them quickly. One of the uniforms turned and saw Arla. She nudged the man who was with her.

"What's going on here?" Arla asked, slightly out of breath. Both the uniforms stood up. One was a sergeant, the other a constable. Arla had seen them both at the station, but she didn't know them. They introduced themselves as PC Stinson and Sergeant Broad.

In an apologetic tone, Sergeant Broad said, "We had information, guv, that one of the victims in your case used to attend this care home as a voluntary helper."

Arla looked at them, stunned. She hadn't done her report yet, and these guys were not present in the incident room, or part of her team. How did they know?

In a dangerously low voice, she said, "I am the SIO in that case. Who gave you authority to come here?"

The uniforms looked at each other. Sergeant Broad said, "DCS Johnson, guv. Said we didn't have to clear it with you. I did ask."

Arla clenched her jaws then relaxed them. What the hell was Johnson playing at? She glanced at Tara, who looked pale and drawn. It wouldn't be her, she knew that. As for the uniforms, they were just following orders, taking a statement.

She let out a frustrated sigh. "OK. Why are you questioning the girl?"

"We were told she spoke to the victim."

"Who told you that?"

Broad shrugged and said, "The lady at the front." *Loretta.*

Arla thought quickly. She said, "I'll take over the statement. Please go back to the station. I'll see you there."

The two uniforms looked at each other. Arla didn't like the look on their faces. They looked apologetic, but there was something else, too.

Broad cleared his throat and in a nervous voice said, "I'm sorry, guv, but we were told to-

"Leave the statement to me." Arla's voice was like a whiplash. "That's an order, Sergeant Broad."

The beefy man swallowed and stepped back. "But guv, the DCS said…"

Arla's eyes bore into his. "Don't worry about the DCS. I will take it up with him. Nothing will happen to you. Don't worry."

They looked at each other again. Arla softened her voice. "Like I said, I'll see you back at the station. Tonight."

They murmured goodbyes and shuffled away. Arla looked at Tara. The girl was standing, and despite her height, she looked small and vulnerable. Arla felt an urge to give her a hug. She moved forward and took her hand. It was cold and trembling. Tara snatched it away. She lifted her chin.

"I'm fine," she said.

"Tell me what happened."

"Nothing. They just wanted to talk."

"Shall we sit down?"

Colour had returned to her cheeks, and she was angry now. "This is all your fault."

Arla held up her hands. "Now hold on, Tara."

"Don't Tara me!" the girl shouted. "You act like you wanna be my bestie and hold my hand, then you go and dob me to the coppers. Because you are one! I know your type." She turned to move away.

Arla grabbed her arm. "Tara, please."

She shook her arm free. "Let go or I'll complain about you." She had a crafty glint in her eyes.

Arla stepped back, a despair suffocating her inside. This was going wrong. All wrong. Tara ran to the door, stepped out and vanished into the street.

CHAPTER 48

Arla fought the urge to run after Tara. It wouldn't do any good. She could catch up, but the teenager wouldn't talk to her. Tara's attitude was troubling Arla deeply. Anger was a constant among these forsaken souls. They used it as a shield against the cruelty life had inflicted upon them. And often that anger was subverted into something more dangerous. A desire to seek vengeance. That led them down a deep, dark vortex of crime and drugs. Arla had seen it with her own eyes. She didn't want Tara to disappear down that slippery slope.

Arla rubbed her eyes and walked down the steps of the care home. Loretta had gone home, and she would have to question her later. A yawn escaped her lips and an aching exhaustion was resounding in her bones. She desperately needed her bed, but she had other things to do first.

She hailed down a cab and went back to the station. She wanted to type up the flimsy statement before the uniforms had a chance. The offices were dark now, but a light gleamed over a table across the glass partition of the incident room. It was Harry. He leaned his head back and stretched his long arms upward, yawning. She smiled. Nice to see she wasn't the only one who was shattered.

She walked across the dark expanse of the room and through the partition. She leaned against the table, crossing her arms. Harry had a day's stubble on his cheek, and his coffee skin was stretched tight over his cheekbones. He considered her with interest.

Arla said, "Working overtime, Detective Inspector?"

"I could ask you the same thing," Harry said. "Thought you went home."

"I was going to." Hesitantly, she told Harry what had happened. His face creased into a frown. Arla said quickly, "Keep this to yourself."

"I will. What worries me is the intel they had. Only a handful of us in the incident room knew about this."

"It would've been in my report, if I had the chance to write it," Arla said in a resigned voice. She flopped on a chair and massaged her temples. Alcohol. That was what she needed. A bottle of wine. Alone.

"I've been thinking about Chris Crichton and Bromsgrove," Harry said.

"And?"

"When we accosted Bromsgrove, he clearly knew something. It makes sense to speak to former colleagues during their college years, or admin staff."

Arla nodded. It was nice to hear her own suspicions spelt out. "Admin staff from 1981 might well have retired by now. Maybe even the professors."

A thought struck her. "Most universities have a newspaper, right? Maybe we can check copies of that between 1981 and 1984 to see if something happened at St John's during that time. Or in Oxford in general."

Harry's eyes gleamed. "Good idea. But a lot of work."

"We have three bodies, no motive, and hardly any suspects. I reckon we need to work harder." Arla looked around. "What time did the team clock off?"

Harry's voice was gentle but firm. "Give them a break. They were here till well after 6."

Arla stood up. "I hear you. But we need to speed things up. I suggest we look at the yearbook of Crichton and Bromsgrove's grad year and call the men on it one by one."

Harry said, "And Lisa can go through the newspapers."

Arla nodded. "Any news from the pond dredge?"

He pursed his lips. "Nothing as yet. Toby said they had finished everything tonight. I'll get his full report tomorrow."

"What about Crichton's brother? Is he back from Spain?"

"Tomorrow, I believe," Harry said. "He knows that we're coming to see him."

Harry snapped his fingers. "Whoa. Thanks for the reminder." He pulled out a notepad. "We also have the number of his boss."

"Great. Tell his boss we are coming in tomorrow morning, and let's see the brother in the evening."

"Yes, boss." Harry's eyes glinted. Arla looked at him and rolled her eyes.

She walked towards her office to type up the statement and submit it on the online London Met platform. When she came out, Harry was stretched out between a chair and a table, legs crossed on the table top. He grinned at her. She frowned at him.

"What the hell are you still doing here?"

"Stalking you."

She suddenly remembered the dark-haired man at Clapham High Street and her face clouded over. She walked past Harry briskly. "Go home."

"Need a lift to the station?"

She was at the door and called back to him. "No thanks."

The desk sergeant, Andy, waved at her, and she waved back. The cold air turned her breath into fumes, and she considered the dark, serpentine, inner-city streets in front of her. A shiver passed through her. She turned and went back inside, just as Harry was coming out.

"I need a lift," she said.

CHAPTER 49

Arla's face was bathed in a green and red glow from the dashboard as Harry drove. They went past the Common, the dredging machine now silent. She could still make out its black hulk not far away from the church. She leaned back against the seat, weary. It would be nice to let Harry drive her all the way back. She knew he wouldn't mind. Her mind latched onto something she had forgotten.

"Did Lisa find out about the VHS recorder?"

Harry whistled. "Yes, she did. She was going to tell you at the meeting tomorrow morning, but I might as well say it now. She has a list of shops that sold that model number. She rang all of them. About twenty in the South-East. All of them closed bar one, in Soho. It's been there for donkey's years, tucked in some small alley near Chinatown. And most of that model sold in London. It was only around for a few months before they pulled production, as smaller recorders flooded the market."

"Are any of the other dealers in London?"

"Two more, but they've both shut."

"Good. Let's hope this is the place that sold it. We can ask the owner for records. When was that model active, again?"

"1986. For six months, I can't remember the exact period off the top of my head. Computerised records had started, it's just whether the shop was using them."

"If they were an authorised dealer of Panasonic, chances are they were. We take the model with us, and not leave the shop till we have the buyer's details."

The station was approaching. Harry started to slow down and glanced at her. "Sure you don't want me to nip down to Tooting for you?"

What the heck, Arla thought. "OK."

They carried on driving in silence. Harry pulled up outside her apartment. She lingered before opening the door, aware that he was staring at her. "Goodnight, Harry."

"Goodnight. See you bright and early."

She made a lousy attempt at a smile and failed. She got out and shut the door. Harry drove away softly, tyres spinning up water from the rain-slicked road. Arla turned her face upward, the cold and light drizzle suddenly refreshing on her eyes and lips.

There was no one in the doorway. She climbed the staircase up to her apartment, the stairs creaking. She got changed and fixed herself a drink, then sprawled on the sofa. She shook out the papers on Bromsgrove and the file on Crichton. For the latter, they now had printouts of his recent emails, FB account, and his phone log. She looked through the phone numbers. One had been underlined several times, and she squinted closely at it. Question marks had been placed by one of the team next to the number. Which meant they were still chasing it up. She hoped the number was a live one, and they could trace the owner. She stood up, cradling the glass of wine in her hand. She was going to stop at one, and the bottle was near-empty anyway. The tiredness was rearing up inside her again.

She went to the bedroom and her eyes fell on the photo. She picked it up, looking affectionately at the teenager with an arm wrapped around her shoulders. Swallowing the weight in her throat, Arla opened the drawer on her desk. She picked up the purple amethyst earring, with small golden ringlets arranged in a circle around the central stone. Arla shut the drawer gently, watching the light wink off the stone briefly. She wished closing the drawer erased her memories. But they spilled out from the sides like smoke from a fire.

She drained the glass of wine and looked at the myriad of lights from windows that contained lives similar to hers. The continuous strata of small squares and rectangles of yellow and orange, the patterns of death, birth, secrets and sorrow that people lived with and could never talk about.

She thought of Tara, running around on the desolate, twisted streets below her. The girl she wanted to help.

She thought of old Miss Atkins, with her dreams of a dead daughter.

The lights gleamed before her eyes like a signal, a Morse code of a distress call she couldn't read. London, and her life, was a lonely crock of shit.

*****

Arla was at the small canteen inside the station at 7am. No one had arrived. She sat down with a steaming mug of coffee and two hot cross buns, munching and sipping. She went through Chris Crichton's Facebook pages. There wasn't a great deal. He liked fishing, that solitary pastime of men she could never understand. There was hardly anything from his brother.

Chris posted only a few times a year, it seemed, mostly about the fish he caught. A few other anglers liked and responded to his posts. Arla went back to the call list. She needed to listen to the calls as well, or get transcripts from the phone company. She tapped her nail on the number that had been called several times – two to three times every day. The calls were brief, less than a minute. Which probably meant they weren't answered. She looked back over a week before his death on the 30th of November. The pattern repeated itself. Whoever this person was, Crichton was almost desperate in his attempts to get hold of him.

A thought struck her, and she fished out Bromsgrove's card. The number was not the same. She checked the other numbers, but they seemed random, and not very frequent. She flicked the pages back almost a month before she found a call from Bromsgrove's number. The call had lasted for 2.37 minutes. She took out a yellow marker pen and highlighted that line. Lisa would have to get the call data soon.

Arla focused on the emails next. They were a mixture of work and personal emails – Crichton had two addresses. His government email had been decrypted, and most were about standard office work – memos, meetings, deadlines. She found a few from his boss, a Mr Tim Percival. They were short and cryptic – one-liners about meetings. She noted the meetings only referred to Crichton and his boss, with no mention of any other employees. She circled them with the highlighter. She didn't find any emails from his brother.

She was finishing the last of her coffee when people started streaming in. It was 7.45 on the wall clock. She nodded at Rob as he came forward to speak to her.

"Incident room in fifteen minutes," Arla said to Rob and Toby as they stood at the coffee machine.

"DCI Baker!" The voice came from the doorway. Several heads turned. Arla knew who it was.

CHAPTER 50

Johnson made eye contact and gestured towards his office. Arla walked towards him, preparing herself mentally. Johnson walked in ahead of her and held the door to his office open. Arla walked in and tried not to show her surprise when she noted the figure sitting at her boss's desk.

The uniformed, thin, wiry man with large eyes that dominated his face looked up as Arla entered. He wore glasses that hung from the bridge of his nose, giving him the appearance of a college professor. Deputy Assistant Commissioner Nick Deakins had a reputation of being a softly spoken, intense man. One who, as his rank suggested, didn't tolerate fools. Arla had only met him once at a press conference. He had a warm handshake then, and some words of encouragement for the successful prosecution of a recent case. His demeanour was different now, and she couldn't help wondering about the contents of the file he was reading. Johnson shut the door behind him.

"Sit," he said, taking a seat to her right. Deakins remained seated opposite, his attention having wandered back to the papers on the desk. Both men remained quiet for a while.

Deakins looked up after a while and removed the glasses from his face. "DCI Baker." His face was impassive, eyes cold and emotionless.

"Yes, sir." Arla fought to keep her composure.

"Do you know what I am reading?" He held up the papers and stacked them so Arla could see the front page of the sheaf. Her heart sank as she recognised the blue and white logo of the IPCC. Independent Police Complaints Commission. Words died in her mouth before she realised that the men were waiting for a response.

She cleared her throat and told them what it was.

"And I think you can guess it concerns you. Correct?" Deakins looked at her closely.

"If you say so, sir."

He lowered the papers without a sound. "This complaint is from the MP Richard Bromsgrove. A potential Minister of Justice, and a key member of the Law and Justice Select Committee. In other words, a future senior colleague of ours."

"Your colleague, sir, not mine." The words had escaped her lips before she had thought about them. She bit her lip. Deakins remained impassive, but his voice was a shard of ice.

"He might not be your colleague, DCI Baker, but he certainly will be your superior. Have you got that?"

"He's a civilian, sir, not a member of the forces-

"Enough," Johnson interjected loudly from her right. "From now on, just listen to what the DAC has to say."

Arla looked at Johnson, who glared back at her. Arla swivelled her eyes away eventually.

Deakins said, "These complaints are now stacking up in remarkable fashion, DCI Baker. A few months ago, you assaulted a suspect. Someone whom we couldn't successfully prosecute. So you ended up taking the law in your own hands."

He was a child abuser, she thought silently. How much evidence did the court need? She flexed her jaws and looked to the ground.

"DCS Johnson reinstated you and was generous in making you the SIO in a high-profile case."

Arla felt nauseated at the top brass cosying up to each other. *I didn't ask to be SIO,* she wanted to say.

Deakins continued. "Do you know what this does to the reputation of our force?"

"If I may say, sir, Richard Bromsgrove is now a suspect in a homicide. Are you saying he is to be granted immunity from the law of the land because he is a senior lawmaker himself?"

Deakins put his elbows on the table and leaned forward. "No, I am not. What I am saying is there is a due process. You do not barge into his public engagements and make a spectacle of yourself. You inform DCS Johnson when you want to see Mr Bromsgrove, and if he deems it suitable, then see him."

"I did ask him." Arla looked at Johnson, who seemed uncomfortable. "He did give me permission."

"I told you to tread carefully," Johnson said. "Not tread on toes."

"As a result of your actions," Deakins said, "you have now landed yourself in the middle of another disciplinary procedure. You know how much manpower these things take up. And it is your second in six months."

Arla said, "Bromsgrove is hiding something, sir. I know that much."

"Really? And do you have any proof of that?"

Arla assumed that Deakins had read her reports already. "He knew our latest victim, Chris Crichton, very well. They collaborated on papers."

"Politicians and civil servants working together is common. Surely you know that?"

"Yes, but..." Arla shook her head in frustration.

"But what?"

"The first victim had his card hidden away with her personal possessions. She would have done that for a reason. Maybe she didn't want her association with Bromsgrove to become public or knew something about him."

Deakins waved a hand. "Conjecture. Do you have any evidence of this?"

Arla fell back on an old line. It was a cliché, but she felt it was apt in the circumstances. "An absence of evidence is not an evidence of absence. Sir."

"I know that," Deakins snapped. "In this case, you don't even know the real identity of the victim. She could be anyone. The fact that she happens to have Bromsgrove's card is totally random and hardly points the guilty finger at him."

Arla stared back at him, feeling an odd sense of dread at the back of her spine. She was up against a wall of denial. A wall constructed at the highest levels of the London Met, and probably higher up in Westminster.

Deakins pressed on. "We are all busy, DCI Baker, and your actions are now deflecting us from the real job of catching the killer. I came here personally to tell you that from now on you are forbidden from approaching MP Bromsgrove without the explicit authority of DCS Johnson."

Arla stared back at him disbelievingly. "Are you saying, sir, that I cannot take a statement from a potential witness in a homicide case?"

"No!" Deakins said forcefully, raising his voice for the first time. "I am saying you have to follow the system. Senior politicians are to be interrogated by the *most* senior police officers, and you are not that person. Do I make myself clear?"

Arla clenched her teeth, holding her response back. She nodded.

"And, if there is another complaint about you, DCI Baker, you will be suspended until further notice. I am not going to rule out recommending a tribunal in your case. If found guilty in that tribunal, it will be the end of your police career. Got it?"

Guilty of what? Arla thought to herself scornfully. *Stopping you and your politician buddies from exposing the truth?*

Aloud she said, "Of course, sir." Her voice was gentle, almost mocking. She saw Deakins' eyes narrow and his lip curl upwards. He picked up his uniform hat and pressed it on his head. He stood up, indicating that the others should rise, too, which they did. He nodded at Johnson and left the room.

There was silence for a few minutes. Johnson went to his desk and shook his chair for no reason. Without looking at Arla, he asked, "Any progress so far?"

"Following up leads from Crichton and the first victim." Arla told him what she was chasing.

"Anything from the pond dredge?"

Arla rolled her eyes as she replied, "Not yet. But still hoping."

Johnson gripped the chair and pushed it towards his desk. "Arla, I can't keep covering for you anymore. Deakins wanted to suspend you right now. I had to talk him out of it."

"Thank you, sir."

"Don't thank me! Stop creating a mess for yourself and others." He raised a meaty finger in her direction. "Leave Bromsgrove alone. Clear?"

"Crystal, sir."

"I want a report on progress by this evening as usual. And find out who the hell this first victim was."

"We are trying our best."

Johnson lowered his tall, wide frame into the chair ponderously. "Improve on your best, DCI. We need a result."

CHAPTER 51

Harry cupped his palm over his lips and dragged deeply on his cigarette. He put the lighter in his pocket and blew out smoke. Arla looked at him with mild envy, wishing she could have one.

"Want one?" Harry read her thoughts. She shook her head and walked away from him.

The Home Office headquarters on Marsham Street was a modern glass and steel structure. Rows of artificial blinds crossed the office windows, but the main entrance block was of transparent fibreglass. A rainbow pattern of coloured glass stuck out from the roof of the building. Harry finished smoking quickly and followed after her.

Arla showed her badge at the main entrance and was shown into the reception. Chris Crichton's boss was a man called Timothy Percival. After a hushed conversation with him, the receptionist turned to Arla.

"Have a seat please. He will come down soon."

The canvas red sofas were comfortable, and they sat down to wait.

"Makes a change from our green plastic seats, eh, guv?" Harry smirked.

"Don't get used to them, Harry. Your soft bum might not be able to take it back at the station."

Harry opened his mouth for a retort, but the door opened, and a suited man poked his head into the reception. He was older than Arla had imagined. Definitely late-sixties. His bald scalp was covered in moles, and the deep brown linen suit was crumpled. He was short and stocky, but the flesh on his face was losing to gravity. He gazed at Arla with curiosity when she stood up, then walked over to her. He held out a gnarly hand. Arla shook it, feeling the old, cold, wrinkled skin. His eyes had droopy bags under them, and his hazel eyes had glazed with age.

"DCI Baker, is that right?"

"Correct." They exchanged greetings, then Arla introduced Harry.

Percival led them to the elevators, and they climbed up to the seventh and top floor. His office was medium-sized, with a desk to one side, and printer and fax machine to the other. A row of filing cabinets flanked the rear and side walls. From the windows at the back Arla could see a garden courtyard, enclosed by the rest of the building.

"You should have seen the last place we had," Percival remarked as he sat down. Arla looked at the framed degree certificate on the wall which bore his name. She turned her eyes back to him.

"Sit please," he said. "Terrible business, this thing about Chris. How can I help you?"

"How long had you known him?"

He thought for a while. "On and off for the last twenty years. He wasn't always in the Media office. He worked in other departments when our paths crossed briefly."

"Did he have any problems at work, any grievances with other employees?"

Percival pursed his lips then shrugged. "Not that I can think of, no."

Harry asked, "Any drink or other substance-related matters as far as you know?"

"No."

"Did he ever mention his family?"

"I think he has a brother, but I've never seen him."

Arla said, "From our records of his life, there is no marriage certificate in his name. Do you know if he had a girlfriend?"

Again, Percival appeared lost in thought for a while, his eyes staring into the distance. Arla snuck a glance at Harry, who shrugged.

"Come to think of it, he might have mentioned having a partner once. But this was a long time ago."

"How long ago?" Arla asked.

"Well, I can't remember when exactly. He didn't mention anything recently, if that's what you're after."

Arla said, "Do you know of any reason someone would want him dead?"

The old man shook his head, looking sad. "I'm afraid I have no idea. He

188

was a good worker, always punctual. He will be missed."

Arla changed direction. "How long have you worked in the Home Office?"

His lips twitched. "I am a career bureaucrat, Miss Baker. For more than forty years at the last count."

"But not in the same department?"

His voice became guarded for some reason. "No," he said shortly.

Arla picked up on it. "Which other departments have you worked in?"

He shrugged. "All civil servants rotate around in their jobs." A non-committal answer if there ever was one. There was something here, a persistent gnawing at the back of her mind. She pressed on.

"Your department works closely with Westminster, doesn't it?"

"Yes." The guarded voice was joined by a similar look in his eyes.

Arla went for the jugular. "Have you had any contact with an MP called Richard Bromsgrove?"

He paused, pursed his lips and shook his head. Yet, Arla thought, he was slow to respond. Slower than she liked.

"No."

"Have you been in contact with other politicians in the past, Mr Percival?"

He coughed into his hands and apologised. "Where are you going with this line of questioning, Miss Baker?"

"Just something we are looking into." *Non-committal works both ways, Mr Percival.*

"I see. Well, the answer to your question is yes. Most of us civil servants deal with politicians on a regular basis. Surely you know that already."

Arla didn't like the hint of condescension in his voice. "Yes, I do." Her voice hardened. "But I wanted to know which politicians you specifically have been in contact with."

"It's a bit like asking how many police chief's you have met, Miss Baker."

Common as thieves, then, Arla thought in silence. Her sensors were picking something up, but she wasn't sure what it was. His reaction to Bromsgrove was a well-honed one. He was cagey about his politician friends as well. *Almost like he had been expecting her.*

She asked, "In some emails, you asked to see Chris Crichton in one-on-one meetings. Why is that?"

"To discuss confidential matters. He was a senior civil servant, and to discuss other employees' disciplinary issues I had to do it in their absence." He smiled. Arla ignored the barb.

"I get the feeling, Mr Percival, that you knew him quite well."

He spread his hands from the chair handles. "I worked with him for five years. Yes, you could say I did."

"And in those five years, you never discussed his personal life?"

"I've given my answer to that question already, I believe."

They stared at each other in silence. Then Arla rose.

"Thank you, Mr Percival." She handed over her card, and Harry did the same. "Please call us if you can think of anything else."

"I certainly will, Miss Baker. Good day to you."

They took the elevator down to the reception and out into the main atrium. Sunlight flooded in through the glass frontage. Arla's phone beeped as they came out of the sliding doors, and she answered. It was from the station.

"Guv, this is Toby," a breathless voice answered. She picked up on the urgency of his voice and stopped walking.

"What is it, Toby?"

"We found a mobile phone from the dredging. It wasn't in the pond, but good job we drained the marshy bit further back."

Arla felt her pulse surge. *This could be the turning point.* "Fantastic! Is it on its way to the lab?"

"Yes."

CHAPTER 52

The Keeper watched Arla and her tall sidekick get into the black BMW. She had answered her phone and then had an excited conversation with her assistant. They literally ran to the car and drove off. The Keeper was disappointed. He was hoping she would ditch the tall idiot and go off on her own, like when she had gone to look for the old lady. He had almost touched her then, and he shivered at the thought. His skin tingled with anticipation. He would feel her naked skin with his hands soon. That much he knew for sure. It would be a challenge, but she would also become his most prized possession. From then on, his name would be famous.

*****

The Keeper drove quickly and got to the street corner in Clapham where he had told the girl to wait. He liked using her. He had started by buying her gifts then giving her money. He knew these girls were bought easily. His master had instructed him, and he had been right. He had finally had sex with her last week, although she hadn't wanted to. That made it all the more enjoyable. He controlled her now, and she knew it.

He had seen her with the policewoman and knew he could get closer to her real target by using the girl. When he had attained his goal, he would discard the girl as well. Permanently. He saw her standing under the tree and pulled over.

Tara got in the car, her face sullen. He drove off, not paying her any attention.

"I didn't like what you did last time," Tara said.

He drove calmly. "Then why did you come back?"

Tara said nothing, looking down at her lap. He said, "You like the money you are earning, don't you?"

In a small voice she said, "Yes, I do."

191

"Then do as I say," he said in a voice like steel. "You have to deliver eight packages today, to three of my peeps. On your own. Can you handle that?"

Without speaking, Tara nodded.

CHAPTER 53

Toby was hovering near her office when Arla and Harry got back. His face lit up when he saw her. Lisa stood next to him.

"Anything from the lab?" Arla asked. The third party, private provider digital forensic lab the Met used, had the phone in their possession already. She wasn't expecting them to provide the call data so quickly, but the phone owner's name would be a big help.

"Yes," Toby said. "They have the number and provided it. We called up the provider, and we have a name!"

Arla smiled at his enthusiasm, but her own heart fluttered in hope, too. It had been a long, miserable few days without an ID.

Lisa ducked her head into her notes. "His name was Vincent Bruhn. Caucasian, 32 years of age. Lived and worked in Nottingham, at the University Hospital, the city's largest hospital. He was an IT analyst. Lived alone, in a two-bedroom apartment three miles from the city centre. Paid rent."

"Previous history?" Arla asked.

"Going through that. This is what we have right now. Speaking to the Nottingham Special Branch for access to his home."

"Partner or relatives?"

Lisa shook her head. "None that have turned up, but early days yet."

Arla knew how hard Toby and Lisa had worked to get this done. She felt like hugging them, but it would be inappropriate. She smiled instead. "This calls for a celebration." It was 13.00, lunchtime. "Who wants pizza for lunch?"

"I prefer KFC," Harry said breezily.

"I didn't ask you!"

"Actually, guv," Toby said, "I prefer KFC as well."

"Lisa, please ask the rest of the team what they want."

Lisa came back soon. KFC was the winner, and Lisa and Rob went out to collect it with cash Arla gave them. Harry gathered the team in the incident room when the pair returned with boxes of fried chicken. Arla nibbled at a small piece, avoiding the chips and carbonated drinks – the prime source of calories in fast food.

"So." She raised her voice, and the whispers in the room died. "We have an ID for the second and third victims. We don't know if they are related, but the MO is the same in all three cases, it would seem."

A thought struck her. The team had gone through the Crichton house and brought evidence back with them. "Did we find anything else in the last victim's house?"

Rob put his hand up. "Newspapers and books, mainly. A filing cabinet of invoices and tax bills, and an old photo album."

"Anything worth looking into?"

"Not really. The invoices are from repair works done on his apartment, and it seems he owned a couple of properties, as the invoices are numbered for Flat 1, Flat 2, and so on."

Arla frowned. "Was he the owner? Have we checked?"

"Well, there's no address on the apartments. And if he did own them, there are no documents to say that he did."

Arla thought for a few seconds. Without knowing the property address their hands were tied. "Did you search for his name on the property owners database?"

Rob nodded. "Yes. But the only ownership in his name was where he died."

"What about the photo album?"

"Some old photos, nothing else."

"Bring me the album please, I need to see the photos."

Arla said, "Now, Rob." He hesitated, then hurried off when he caught the look of intent on Arla's face.

"Right." Arla went to the white board, wrote down Vincent's name with a black pen and circled it. She jotted down a number of points. Then she turned to the team. "We know from Bandy that this man had a number of fractures on his bones that were old and caused by non-accidental injuries. Which means he was physically abused at some point in his life. That might not have been the only form of abuse he suffered. I want a search of his name on all the children's care homes in the UK." Arla paused, swallowing the heavy, black sensation at the back of her throat. She had always dreaded this investigation would hit close to home, and finally it was.

Rob returned with the old photo album in a plastic evidence bag and handed it to Arla. She updated him quickly.

"Any news from the Panasonic shop in Soho?"

"Yes," Lisa said. She took a sip from her Pepsi Max before continuing. "The transaction for the serial number on that VHS recorder took place on the 10th of January 1991. It was paid for by credit card, and the name on the card is Alistair Brown. I have called the card company, and now waiting for them to get back to me."

"Good. We need an address and DOB, then we can track him down." Arla dismissed the team, all of whom murmured their thanks for the food. There were a few jokes about making a habit of this and getting some exercise instead.

Arla walked back to her room, and flinging her coat on the back of her chair, she clicked on her keyboard. She answered the emails and then checked for Nicole on the missing persons database. It was a reflex habit that was now ingrained in her. She expected to see nothing but the same "Missing" logo in red letters, and this time was no different.

She closed the screen and concentrated on Chris Crichton's photo album. It had a leathery brown cover, inlaid with foam. She opened it and got a whiff of old, moth-eaten pages. The photos were turning yellow at the edges. Several were of groups of children in a school, with their teachers, which Arla assumed were of Crichton's old school. The same woman appeared in several photos, with two teenage boys. She recognised Crichton from his passport photo. She assumed the other teenager in the photos was his brother, and the woman their mother. After that page, the rest of the pages were blank.

It was as if his life had taken a break, or the photographer had forgotten to record the images. Arla was about to close the book, when she caught sight of a photo tucked in the last page. It was unusual because it was torn. The jagged edge showed a smiling Crichton, standing in front of a building. He had his arm around someone, but that person had been ripped off the photo. Arla took the photo out and examined it closely. It was a colour photo, and with age it had turned dull. She put the photo, and one with his brother and mother on the desk, then closed the album. She called Harry.

"Any news of the brother?" she asked when he appeared.

"You said to fix an appointment with his boss, then his brother. That's what I did." He consulted his watch with a flourish. "In one hour, at 15.00. He lives in Croydon."

"Let's get a move on," Arla said. "It'll take us almost an hour to get there."

"Not if I'm driving," Harry said, raising his eyebrows.

Arla grimaced. "I'm worried about getting out alive if you're driving." She stalked out of the room, ignoring his response.

CHAPTER 54

It started to snow as Harry drove out. Arla watched the flakes descend like swirls of white cotton, nodding as they fell slowly. It was the first snow this winter, and for a while, Arla was caught up in the novelty of watching the pendulous drops, a break from the straight falling rain. Questions came and went from her mind.

"Why did Charlene have the video recorder of this man?" Arla asked.

"That is the question."

"There'll be hordes of Alistair Browns in London. After we get the right age group, I mean."

"Needle in a haystack."

A strand of logic penetrated the veil of snow and reached out to her. She fished out her phone and called Lisa. "When you do find the relevant Alistair Browns," Arla said, "drill down to the ones who were in politics, or a civil servant, or policeman, anything. If there are any, call them first."

"Yes, guv."

Lisa had some findings of her own. "I looked into more of the call data from Crichton's phone. The ones you had circled."

"Anything?"

"Those frequent calls were to a pay-as-you-go phone. I traced it; it was bought from a shop in London Bridge."

"We need to check the shop's CCTV."

"I'm on it. But there's something else. I got the call data for the message that Crichton sent to Bromsgrove, a week before his death. He rang, but Bromsgrove didn't pick up. Shall I send you the file?"

"Yes, please do," Arla said eagerly. She hung up and a minute later her phone beeped. The message was disappointingly short and to the point. There was a buzz of static, then a pause and Bromsgrove's voice came on, asking to leave a message. After another pause, Crichton spoke.

197

"We need to speak about the matter discussed. I suggest we meet at the usual place."

There was a prolonged pause after that, during which no one said anything. It seemed Crichton was holding on for Bromsgrove to answer, and he simply didn't. Arla shut the file down, then opened her phone again. She fast-forwarded to the end, and this time listened with the loudspeaker on. She heard it this time. The sound of breathing. Both men were holding onto the line, neither saying anything after Crichton had left the message.

Arla put her phone away. Did the two men not trust each other? A sense of foreboding was growing inside her. Despite what Deakins had said to her, she knew she was right about Bromsgrove. What that man was hiding could make or break this case. It was the ramifications that bothered her.

If a potential Minister of Justice was hiding information about this case, then the truth could be explosive.

But at least now Johnson couldn't stop her from questioning Bromsgrove again. She now had proof that Crichton and the MP were in contact close to his death.

She rang Johnson, but it went to answerphone. She left a message, asking permission to bring Bromsgrove in for questioning. Harry pulled up outside the address in East Croydon. It was an apartment complex, one of the metal and glass newfangled ones with a sliding gate. Harry had to get off the car and press the buzzer to speak to Crichton's brother before they could be allowed in. Arla noted the new car park, and the clean elevator as they went upstairs to the fifth floor. The two brothers lived in distinctly different surroundings.

Robert Crichton was holding the door open as they arrived. He ushered them inside after shaking hands. He was older than Chris, and Arla knew from the files that his age was sixty-three. The apartment had works of art stuck on the wall. The cream marble floor glistened. Expensive antique objects lined the shelves. Arla wondered where the older Crichton had made his money.

She heard a sniffing sound and looked towards the white leather sofa. Robert Crichton sat hunched forward, a tissue around his nose. He sniffed again, and looked at them with red-rimmed eyes.

"I can't believe my brother's dead," he said.

Arla sat down opposite him. Harry sauntered to the windows and looked down at the street.

"Were you close to him?"

Robert nodded, wiping his nose. "I'm sorry. I just didn't expect him to go so soon. And like this."

Arla gave him a minute to compose himself. "Did your brother say anything recently? Was he worried?"

Robert shook his head. "He had no concerns. He was a wealthy man. All this," he spread his hands, "came from him. He bought me the apartment as well. Very generous man, he was."

Harry was listening, standing behind the sofa. Arla looked up and their eyes met. Harry said, "These are original works of art, right? Must be a few quid."

Robert nodded. "We used to buy them in auctions. He had a thing for twentieth-century modernists."

"Did he buy this apartment as well?"

"Yes."

Arla's mind was running hoops. Just to check, she asked, "Did your brother have any other properties?"

He seemed surprised. "Yes, he did. He was a property developer in fact. But he sold off most of his assets. This apartment and where he lived were the only two he had left. No mortgage on them, obviously."

"Where else did he have properties?"

"All over London. I don't know details unfortunately. He had business partners, but I never knew them."

"Was he married?"

A strange look passed Robert's face. He looked downwards and seemed evasive. He got up and took out some tissue from a box of Kleenex. He sat and blew his nose.

"He used to be," he said. "She left him eventually."

Something in his manner was amiss. The earlier warmth and sincerity had faded, and Arla detected a coldness.

"What was her name?"

"Katherine. Katherine Mendonca. She was… a foreigner."

"A foreigner?"

"Her family came from Portugal, I think."

"Didn't you like her?" She went for the direct approach.

Robert looked away again before replying. "Not really, if you don't mind me saying. She was married before, with children. She left them, and she was well… on the streets, sort of."

"How on the streets?"

"My brother never spoke about it, but she was a drug addict. Might have been a prostitute as well, I don't know. She left her family and was hooked on drugs when my brother met her somewhere. He was besotted with her. I told him she would leave him one day, and I was right in the end."

"When did they break up?"

"A long time back." He thought for a while. "Late-90s, I would say."

Arla asked a few more questions, but she had found enough already. Before she left she asked if Robert had a photo of Katherine Mendonca. He shook his head. "No, I don't, sorry."

Arla chewed on her lower lip, wondering if she should ask the next question. Then she realised that she had nothing to lose. "Mr Crichton, a woman called Charlene Atkinson was killed recently. We think her death and your brother's might be related."

Robert Crichton's face went rigid. He swallowed hard and stared at Arla. Then he dropped his eyes and walked away a few steps towards the window. Harry and Arla exchanged a quick glance.

Arla pressed forward. "Mr Crichton? Do you know anyone called Charlene Atkins?"

Robert Crichton had recovered. He looked from Arla to Harry and shook his head slowly. "No."

"Are you sure?" Arla frowned.

"Yes."

"You seemed a bit bothered when I mentioned Charlene Atkins' name."

"No, I misheard you. I was thinking of someone else."

Arla's eyes never left Robert's. He met her gaze and stared back impassively. In the end, she nodded. "If you can think of anything, please give us a call."

Arla thanked him, and they left the apartment. When they were outside, Harry said, "What the hell was that? He looked like he'd seen a ghost when you mentioned Charlene's name."

"I know." Arla's head was bowed and she was deep in thought. "He's lying. He knows something about Charlene."

"And he's trying to hide it." Harry shook out a cigarette and offered one to Arla, who refused. He lit up and said, "Shall we bring him in?"

Arla paused. "No. Do some checks on him, make sure we know if he gets a ticket to leave the country. For now, just watch him."

Her mind was wound up in knots. *Who were you, Charlene?*

Harry smoked while she rang Johnson. It went to answerphone again, and she left a message for the second time. She hoped she wasn't being ignored. As far as she knew, Johnson was in the office today.

She said to Harry, "The team will need some help in going through the phone data, and pinpointing who bought that video recorder. Why don't you head down to give them a hand?"

"Where will you go?"

Arla winked. "Somewhere."

Harry stared back at her, unamused. "Don't do it, you'll only regret it."

"Like you know what I want to do."

"You want to see that MP again."

Damn him. He knew her too well, and the look on her face must have given her away. But she didn't want to admit it. If Harry knew the truth, he would have to lie about it when asked. She would never knowingly put any of her team in trouble. That went for Harry, too.

"Go back to the station and help them. I need someone to lead while I'm gone."

Harry shook his head once again then walked off towards the nearby East Croydon station, which had direct links to Central London.

*****

Robert Crichton watched from his window as the two detectives walked down the road. The woman was talking, gesturing with her hands while the man listened. Robert passed a hand over his eyes. He made sure the Detectives weren't coming back, then sat down heavily on the sofa. Memories were pressing against his head, bombarding against his skull like cannonballs. He could only think of Katherine's face, once happy and smiling, then drowned in the sadness of her terrible life. He thought of his brother, and he hung his head and cursed to himself. Maybe he should have done more while he had the chance. But now, it had all gone to waste.

And the woman called Charlene was dead. He couldn't believe it, and grief speared his heart, forcing tears from his eyes. Yes, he should have done more. He might have been able to save her, even if she hadn't wanted him. He would carry that reget to his grave.

He knew her death would not be coincidental to his brother's. *They knew.* And one by one, all of them would be eliminated. Robert shivered, a cold fear spreading through him. He got up and started to pace, seized with a restless energy.

He had to do something. But what exactly?

CHAPTER 55

Arla swung the car around and headed in the other direction across the tramlines. The snow had stopped and was turning into grey slush under car tyres. Traffic merged into a mishmash of blue and black as she tried to connect the images that ran through her mind. The dead face of Vincent Bruhn. Still so young, and one who had suffered so much in his brief life. At least the other victims had lived longer. That was no consolation, but she felt for Vincent more. She knew the patterns of non-accidental injury. The injuries of child abuse. Poor Vincent.

A resolve grew inside her. She would find this killer, no matter what it took. Before he struck again. She felt she was getting closer: slowly, the cloud of secrecy was lifting.

She noticed the car after a while. A black Mercedes. She had seen it a few times, as it changed lanes a few cars back. Now it was right behind her. Traffic began to lessen as she left the gridlock of Mitcham Lane, and took a left, heading up north from the south of London's outskirts. The black Mercedes followed. She tried to see the driver but couldn't make out his face, hidden by a hooded top.

Suddenly, Arla realised where she had seen the car before. It was very similar to the car that had picked up Tara. Same model and make, same black tinted windows. Although she hadn't taken down the registration that night, she memorised it now.

One eye on the Merc, she took a sharp left, aiming to use the backroads to skip the traffic towards Battersea. The car followed and accelerated to almost rear-end her. Arla still couldn't make out the face of the driver. She speeded up as the road was empty now, and so did the Mercedes.

In the blink of an eye, the powerful car changed lanes, and sped past her. Arla shouted and braked as the Mercedes almost rammed her, pushing her towards the edge. She swerved, tyres kicking up dirt from the kerb, and slammed on the brakes as the Merc's red tail lights glowed brightly. She couldn't avoid the BMW's front grill smashing into the rear bumper of the Merc. Her neck snapped forward, and pain surged through her forehead as it hit the steering wheel. There was a tearing sound of metal, a loud revving of engines, and the Merc took off at high speed, its tyres leaving black marks on asphalt.

Shaken, Arla watched the Merc speed off. She debated whether to give chase. All of a sudden, she wished Harry was present. He would be in hot pursuit already. She felt dizzy from the pain in her head. The blast of a horn made her jump, making her pain blossom anew. A truck had come up behind her, and gears clashed as it jolted to a stop. Arla heard someone yelling. She wiped her forehead, her eyebrows smeared with sweat. She pulled the window down and started to drive. She pulled into a service station and switched the engine off. Her hands were shaking as they came off the steering wheel. She stood up and got out of the car.

The front fender was a mess, bent in the middle. Both the headlights were smashed, and the front end of the bonnet had a dip on it. She put her hands on the side and leaned against the car. A cold fear spread inside her. She hadn't seen Tara since their last argument. Had she been in the car? But Arla hadn't seen a passenger, or anyone in the back seat.

Arla took her radio out from the car and rang control to give them the car's registration number.

Then she picked up the phone and called the care home. Loretta answered and told her she hadn't seen Tara that morning. Arla made a point of catching up with the teenager later tonight. She got back in the car, filled her up with fuel, and drove straight to Bromsgrove's office. She called Johnson again, only to get the same response. She jerked to a stop outside the office and looked at herself in the rear-view mirror.

She had a bruise across her forehead, a nice shade of purple and red smack in the middle.

Arla touched her foehead as her phone rang. Lisa's excited voice came over the phone.

"Boss, I have some interesting news about Bromsgrove."

Arla forgot her woes at once. "Go on."

"You know he has all these companies? Well, one of them, called Mandarin Holdings, made a transfer, many years ago, to St Martin's Estates."

Arla fought to clear the confsion in her mind, then remembred. "Chris Crichton's company. Are you sure its not a different St Martin's Estates? Must be many companies with that name."

"I cross checked with Crichton's company filings. His company did receive a cash payment of two hundred and seventy five thousand pounds from Mandarin Holdings."

Excitement clutched inside Arla. She gripped the phone tighter. "This is important. Can you take this information to DCS Johnson, and send it to me as an email as well?"

"Of course, guv."

"Lisa, hold on. Do you have dates of the transfer?"

"Yes. 23rd July 1997."

"Great." Arla hung up.

Something struck her mind. She opened her phone and searched her emails for the details of 243 Clapham Common Road. Her mouth opened in shock. She hunched forward, staring at her feet.

The building had been sold on 5th September 1997, to St Martins Estate for exactly two hundred and seventy-five thousand pounds.

CHAPTER 56

Arla got out and headed inside the MP's office. This time, she had tried to follow due process. It couldn't be her fault if her boss wasn't bothered about getting in touch with her. She sent a text to Johnson before she went in, letting him know of her intentions.

The receptionist looked up at her, and she flashed her badge.

"Where is Mr Bromsgrove?"

"In a meeting with his const... Miss, you can't go in there." The receptionist scrambled from behind the counter as Arla pushed open the double doors. She got into the hallway, with the receptionist hot on her heels. Arla stopped and faced the woman.

"Tell Mr Bromsgrove DCI Baker is here, with new information about Chris Crichton. If he doesn't come out, I *will* go in, and he will not like the consequences." Arla glared at the receptionist, who took a step back at the force of her comments.

"Now!" Arla said, pointing to the door of his office. The lady swallowed and knocked on the door. She had a quick word, then shut the door and waited. After a while, Bromsgrove's sweaty, red face made an appearance. His blue suit and blue tie were clean pressed. He stared at Arla with disbelief. He shut the door behind him and strode towards her, a snarl on his face.

Before he could open his mouth, Arla had opened her phone, and pressed on the file Lisa had sent her. She turned the volume on loud. The receptionist scurried past them to the double doors. It was quiet in the hallway, save the sound of their laboured breathing. Crichton's voice filled the silence, and Arla watched as Bromsgrove frowned then blanched white as he recognised the voice. When the message finished, Arla switched the phone off.

"Chris Crichton called you a week before he died. What was it about?" Arla asked.

The snarl was back on Bromsgrove's face. Red mottled patches were spreading across his cheeks. He reached out and plucked the phone out of Arla's hands and smashed it down on the carpet floor. The phone bounced off and hit the wall, coming to rest against an alcove.

"You," Bromsgrove said, raising a chubby finger in Arla's face. His voice seethed with hatred. "I told you to stay away, but you couldn't help it, could you?"

In a calm voice, Arla said, "You have quite the reach, Mr Bromsgrove. Your influence reaches one of the Deputy Asisstant Commissioner's of the London Metropolitan Police Force. Who's next? The Prime Minister?"

Mr Bromsgrove bared his teeth. "You don't know what you're dealing with here."

"Try me."

He put his hands on his waist, panting, looking like he was going to explode. "Get out of here. If this isn't the last I see of you…"

Arla stepped forward. "Then what? You'll ask your friends at the top to end my career?" She didn't want to say it, but every vein in her body was pulsing with anger. Never in her career had she come across a man so obnoxious. "You need to come to the station to give a statement."

"Fuck off."

"If you are resisting, then I can arrest you."

Mr Bromsgrove's face fell open. "Arrest me? On what grounds?"

"Withholding information about a homicide. Being a suspect in the same case. Do you realise, Mr Bromsgrove, that any other member of the public would have come to the station a while ago to give a statement?"

Bromsgrove glared at her, his red face heaving. Arla decided to bring out her trump card. She had intended to save all of this till he was in the station. But now she knew he wouldn't come of his own accord. She would have to arrest him, and if she did so, Arla knew the consequences would be grave.

"Mr Bromsgrove, one of your companies, Mandarin Holdings, made a transfer of 275,000 Pounds to Chris Crichton's company, St Martin's Holdings, on the 23rd July 1998. Is that correct?"

A deep, jagged frown twisted Bromsgrove's face. He took a step towards Arla then changed his mind and stepped back.

He delved into his pockets and came out with a phone. He walked off, spoke to someone, and came back with a satisfied smile on his face. Arla's phone rang a second later.

She answered it. She wasn't surprised to hear Johnson's voice.

"Get back to the station right now," Johnson said, biting the words out between his teeth. "And I mean right now. That is an order, DCI Baker."

CHAPTER 57

When Arla entered Clapham Police Station, she was stopped by the duty sergeant at the desk. She recognised him: Sergeant Brody. Arla turned impatient eyes on him, and the man seemed to shrink back.

"What is it?" she asked. She knew her voice was harsh, but she didn't have time for pleasantries.

"The DCS is not in his office. He has gone to Lambeth HQ and told you to be there tomorrow at 8am for a meeting."

Arla felt her intestines constrict, and a cold sweat at the back of her neck. A wave of nausea swept through her. She held herself rigid and upright, staring back at the man. Lambeth HQ was the regional command and control centre for South-East London. Johnson wouldn't have called her there for another dressing-down. With a sense of dread, she recalled Deakins' threat of a tribunal. Surely she would get more notice before they called her to a tribunal?

"Alright, thanks." Arla walked down the corridor into the detective's open-plan office room. She headed for her office at the back. Harry's desk was outside her office and two heads were hunched over his, staring at a screen. Harry caught her eye.

"Are you alright?" He had obviously heard about the black Mercedes chasing her.

"Head hurts a bit, but I'll live. Any news on the owner?"

"It's a rental car, and whoever rented it paid in cash. Gave a name of John Smith, and a fake address."

"Sounds like a fake name too," Arla fumed.

Lisa stuck her neck in from the side door. "Boss, you really need to see this."

Arla joined Lisa and Toby flanking Harry. He pointed at the screen. There was a list of numbers on it. "This is Vincent Bruhn's call data. Guess who all these numbers belong to?"

"Tell me."

"Steven Wade. The man who identified Charlene."

"And the man who was seen going onto the Common just before Vincent," Arla murmured, almost to herself. Her current woes lifted from her like a cloud. Excitement clutched her guts. This was a real breakthrough.

Lisa asked, "Shall we call him in?"

Arla shook her head. "No. I think the station spooks him. He'll clam up again. Do you have his work address?"

Lisa nodded. "Don't you think he did it, boss?"

Arla stroked her cheek. "Not sure. Just not sure. Let's go and speak to him." She wiggled her eyebrows at Harry.

Harry's tunred his lips down. "My poor BMW. I liked her so much. Let me get a new car from the pool, and I'll see you at the back."

Arla rolled her eyes, exasperated.

He literally ran out of the office. Toby shrugged; Arla and Lisa shook their heads. Toby walked off to his desk, leaving the two women alone.

"Who needs men, eh?" Lisa asked.

"Like a fish needs a bicycle," Arla said, quoting an old saying. Her eyes twinkled. "Having said that, I think our Rob is interested in you."

"Oh. I see." Lisa's voice was flat. The expression on her face stopped Arla. They stared at each other for a few seconds, then Lisa said, "I'm not into men, guv."

"I just opened my mouth and put my foot in it, didn't I?"

Lisa shrugged. "You weren't to know. For the record, I have a partner, and we're getting engaged."

"She's a lucky woman."

"Thanks." Lisa grinned. "I'll bring her to the Xmas do this year. She wants to show off her ring."

Lisa's bright, beaming face reminded Arla of the emptiness of her own life. A cold wind blew across her heart. Would she ever know happiness like Lisa had? She smiled at the detective sergeant.

"I'll be in the office. Call me when Harry comes back."

She slumped in her chair and cradled her head in her hand. Men had come and gone from her life like ships in the night. She had two meaningful relationships in the thirty-six years that she had lived. It wasn't a trust or commitment issue. It was fear. She didn't want to start a family that would end up being like hers. Oppressive and violent. She pressed harder on her forehead, pushing the thoughts back into the dungeon. That's where they belonged – chained and bound, a part of her soul she didn't want, and couldn't forget.

Harry knocked on the door, and she looked up. Without a word, she brushed past him, heading for the car park. Harry let silence reign as he drove. They parked near the tube station, and took the tube to Regent Street, where Steven Wade worked in the HMV shop.

"Alistair Brown," Harry said.

"What about him?" Arla sighed.

"There're two with that name who have video production shops. One is recent, and the other more interesting. In Richmond. Been in business since the 70s. Sole proprietor, website says used to make movies."

"Hmm."

Harry said, "You need to get that forehead looked at. It's bruising up."

"I'll live."

They walked on past the crowd and traffic. Harry left her alone, knowing she was in a mood. People streamed in and out of the large HMV store. They walked in and asked one of the floor assistants where Steven was. He pointed to the counter. Across the snaking queues, a line of men and women were manning the long counter. Arla spotted Steven at the far end. He didn't see them until they were right in front of him. He looked up and went white as a sheet. He smoothed his hair back, recovering, looking around self-consciously.

"Wh... What are you doing here?"

Arla leaned over the counter. "Can we go somewhere to have a chat?"

"I've told you everything I know."

"No you haven't. There's a lot you are hiding, and we know, Steven. It's all going to come out, and it's going to look very bad for you. So I'm giving you a chance here. Let's go for a talk."

Steven licked his lips and his eyes darted around the shop. "Like I said…"

Harry said, "This is your last chance, Steven. Or we have to take you to the station."

The girl working next to Steven began to take an interest. She wore large hoop earrings and dyed long, black hair. Steven lowered his voice. "Please don't make a scene."

Arla said, "That's up to you, Steven."

He considered for a while then nodded, looking exasperated. "I have a break now. Give me five minutes."

They waited while another girl appeared to take Steven's place. They followed Steven to the back of the store and through the door. They stepped outside into the street. Cigarette butts littered the floor. Opposite, a large square was open, ringed with food shops. Steven crossed the street and sat on one of the benches. It wasn't lunchtime yet and the square was almost empty. Traffic rolled on Regent Street, the sounds muted by the buildings.

Steven had put his coat on, but he still shivered. He bunched his fists. "What do you want to know?"

Arla said, "We know that you knew Vincent. He called you several times the day he died and almost daily before that." Arla stopped, remembering how Steven had reacted when he was shown Vincent's photo. It made sense now, but he could have been acting. She watched his expression closely. Serial killers had large personalities, bloated egos. They liked to think they could act their way out of trouble. Was Steven the man she had been looking for all this time?

Arla said, "We found his phone. In a day's time, we will be listening to the calls. All will be revealed."

They were silent for a while. Steven stared downwards, cheeks hollow, face pale. He shook his head. "You don't understand," he whispered.

"Understand what?"

"I can't, I can't. Not because of that, but because…" His voice trailed off. Harry and Arla exchanged a look.

"You're not making much sense, Steven."

He stood up suddenly. "I'm sorry, but you've wasted your time. I have to get back to work."

Arla blocked his path swiftly, and Harry took up position behind him. "Steven Wade, I am arresting you on suspicion of murder. You have the right to remain silent…"

Steven stumbled back, his face ashen. He bumped into Harry and recoiled. He sank back in the bench and gripped his head with both hands. "Alright, alright!" His face was contorted with pain. "Oh God. Oh God." His body began to shake, and his fingers became claws on his head. He began to sob.

Arla shuffled closer to him. She touched his arm: he didn't notice. But a mist was clearing in her mind, and a picture was emerging. She knew this wasn't acting. This was genuine grief.

They gave him some time. When he looked up with red, bloated eyes and a streaming nose, Arla handed him a tissue. He accepted it with thanks.

Then he said what Arla now knew. "Vincent Bruhn and I were lovers. He was the kindest, most gentle man I knew." He succumbed to a fresh bout of tears.

After a pause, Arla said, "That night on the Common, you were going to meet him, weren't you?"

Steven recovered and wiped his nose. "We hadn't known each other long. We met online, and over the last three months started getting closer. He was going to move from Nottingham and look for a job in London. He was from here originally." A strange look passed his face.

"Carry on."

"Vincent was a troubled man. He had a difficult childhood and lived in care homes." He looked up at her, sadness covering his face. "He was abused."

"I know," Arla said softly.

"But it didn't make him bitter or abusive. Happens to many people, you know, but not to Vincent. He was becoming my soulmate."

Steven covered his face in his hands.

"I'm so sorry," Arla said. Her voice choked up for some reason, although Steven's pain was not hers. Yet she felt for his loss, because she had suffered at the hands of the same cruel, senseless fate. She cleared her throat and felt Harry's hand on her shoulder, light, comforting. She looked up at him and nodded. He kept his hand there for a little longer, then removed it.

Arla asked, "You were keeping your relationship under wraps." It was a statement, not a question.

"Yes," Steven replied. "My parents…they…" Steven raised his arms and flopped them down on his legs. "What the heck. I haven't come out yet."

A lot about his past behaviour now made sense to Arla. The need for secrecy, the shock. And she felt a deep remorse for the young man. He had nowhere to turn, and the only friend he had was gone, dead in a horrible fashion.

"We will find who did this, Steven. I promise you that."

"That's good. But it won't bring him back."

"No," Arla said, looking vacantly ahead, an old, familiar weight at the back of her throat. "Once they go, they don't come back."

"Boss," Harry said gently.

Steven said, "You know, he was trying to find something. A document or paper. He said it was important."

Arla turned to him. "How do you mean, important?"

Steven shook his head. "I don't know. He wasn't very open about it. I could see it bothered him, so I left it. I was going to ask him soon, though. He came to London more frequently to find this document. He used to meet with a guy in Fleet Street."

"A journalist?"

"Yes. I don't know his name or who he was. Vincent wouldn't tell me either. He kept it quiet." A light sparked in his eyes, and he turned to Arla. "You don't think someone killed him for that, do you?"

"Could be." Arla was frowning heavily. "Can we put all this in a statement from you?"

He shrugged. "Can't see why not."

"Steven, have you told anyone else about this document?"

He shook his head. "Why do you ask?"

"Because I want you to keep this secret for now. Don't tell anyone. By the way, you don't really have a girlfriend, do you?"

Steven looked shamefaced. "I'm sorry. She works with me, and she's helped me out in the past." He consulted his hands again and sighed deeply.

"If nothing else, this shit has taught me I can't live my life like this. Living a lie."

Arla stood up. "We will be in touch, Steven. Please be careful."

He faced her, eyes searching his face. "Am I in danger?" There was no fear in his voice anymore. If anything, he seemed relieved, yet sad.

"To be honest, I don't know. The more we dig into Vincent's phone, the more we will find out."

They said goodbyes and left.

*****

The dark-haired man stood hidden behind the awning of a shop, a newspaper over his face. He lowered it to see DCI Baker and DI Mehta walking away. He had followed them from Clapham Common tube station. As they got closer to the HMV shop, he had known who they were going to see. He had kicked himself and cursed. He wanted to get there first and deal with Steven Wade. Now he had lost that opportunity. He didn't hear their conversation, but he was sure he was mentioned.

He was angry with himself. He had given that fool Vincent too much information. Secrecy was never guaranteed. Luckily, he had used a false name with Vincent. His identity would remain a secret, hopefully. But he needed to find out how much Steven knew. And then he had to deal with it.

He folded the paper under his arms and followed Steven as he walked back to the HMV shop.

CHAPTER 58

"Document?" Harry asked as they brushed past the hordes of shoppers on the main street.

"It could be a motive," Arla said. "Did Nottingham PD get back to us about the search of Vincent's house?"

"Not yet." They joined the torrent of humanity pouring down the stairs to the subway and stopped talking.

When they got back to the station, the whole team was present. Arla wanted to see the results of the cross-check of Crichton and Vincent's call data. If Charlene had a phone, they hadn't found it as yet.

"Here." Rob pointed a short, hairy finger at the numbers he had circled on the relevant pages. "Crichton called this number several times before his death – the pay-as-you-go number. Vincent called this number, too, as you can see here."

"Are we any closer to finding the owner of that phone?"

Rob shook his head. "CCTV images are inconclusive. It's a busy shop, and it could have been anyone. The person who bought it paid by cash, so there's no record of their name."

Arla said, "What is the last known location of the phone?"

Lisa spoke up. "That's the funny thing. A mast in Lambeth picked up its signal a week ago. Nothing after that."

"Today is the 31st, so the last use of the phone was on the 24th. Is that correct?"

Rob checked once again and spoke with his eyes glued on the screen. "That's right. 24th was the last time that phone was used."

Arla looked at them. "What happened on the 24th?"

Lisa nodded slowly. "The first victim died."

"Correct. We found the body on the 25th. Both Crichton and Vincent have called that number. Did the person respond?"

Rob looked at his notes. "Call durations are less than one minute on the 24th, so they could all be answerphones, or hang-ups. But there are three occasions before that when Vincent connected to that number. This was in October."

They looked at each other, suddenly excited. Both Vincent and Crichton had called this number before their deaths. After the 24th, the number stopped responding. Could this be the number of Charlene, the first victim?

"Let's not get ahead of ourselves," Arla said. "It could just be coincidence that the number is not replying after the 24th. What I would like to do is get hold of the phone."

"Lambeth is a big place, guv," Harry observed. Arla was about to respond when she saw Sergeant Brody enter the office. He had a grim look on his face. He walked right up to them and planted himself in front of the group.

"Apologies for the interruption, guv."

"What is it?" Arla asked.

"DCS wants to see you now in Lambeth. He just called. The meeting has been moved forward."

Only Harry knew about her last visit with Bromsgrove. The rest of the team looked on, confused.

"Right now?" she asked.

"Yes guv," Brody said, his tone apologetic. "That's what they told me to tell you."

"I can drive you," Harry said.

"No need," Brody said. "There's a car waiting for you at the back. What shall I say?"

Arla steeled herself. "Tell them I'm on my way."

She met eyes with her team, and by the looks on their faces, she realised they all knew what it was about.

"Good luck," Harry said softly. Arla nodded at them and strode out.

Sergeant Brody led her down the back to the parking lot. A deep-blue Range Rover was purring in front of the gates, and Arla stepped inside. Apart from the driver and herself, the car was empty. The driver did not speak. They drove the short distance to Oval, where the Lambeth HQ was situated.

The premises consisted of a number of brown-brick buildings, each with the blue and white London Met logo. She was taken to the middle building, where the desk constable checked her in. She followed him up to the elevators, and they both stepped in. They got to the third floor, and walked down the deep carpeted, white walled corridor.

A polite knock on the door was answered immediately. The desk constable left, and Arla faced Johnson, holding the door open for her. She saw a bigger than average-sized, plain office, with a large mahogany table in the middle. The table had a green leather top, and a laptop open in front of each of the three chairs. DAC Deakins was seated to the right, but she didn't recognise the uniformed woman in the middle.

"Come in," Johnson said in a neutral voice. Deakins didn't rise, but the woman in the middle stood up. She was in her late-forties, with short-cut, blonde hair and a pretty face, despite the hard, thin lines of her mouth and nose.

"I am Assistant Commissioner Joanne Murphy, in charge of professionalism," she said in a light voice. Arla shook the hand, feeling the firm grip. She held on for slightly longer than necessary, awed at being in the presence of an Assistant Commissioner.

Johnson took his seat to the AC's right, and all four of them sat down. Murphy opened the conversation with a surprising comment.

"Have you been seeing the psychiatrist, Dr Seddon?"

Arla faltered. She had missed the last two meetings. Dr Seddon had called her, but she hadn't been able to reply during working hours. She swallowed.

"No, I haven't had time for the last two sessions."

Deakins took over. His voice was scathing. "At our last meeting, I informed you to seek permission before seeing Mr Bromsgrove. You ignored my advice completely."

"No, sir." Arla kept her voice stable. "We are pursuing a new lead that involves Mr Bromsgrove with our third victim deeply. I called DCS Johnson several times on his phone and didn't hear back from him. In the end, I sent him a text."

Johnson spoke, and she levelled her eyes with him. "I was in a meeting,

DCI Baker. You should have waited till you spoke to me."

"You weren't in a meeting when Mr Bromsgrove called you up, were you? In fact, you answered him immediately."

Johnson clenched his jaws. His eyes looked daggers at Arla. "It was just an opportune time. I had just come out of a meeting, and was about to call you, in fact. But what I heard instead was that you were there already, disobeying a direct order."

"DCI Baker." Arla gazed at AC Murphy, her erect posture dwarfed by the two tall men seated on either side of her. "Why did you disobey the order?"

"Ma'am, Bromsgrove needs to give a statement to explain his connection to the victim. But whenever I try to get information from him, he is evasive and rude. We have a fast-moving investigation, and despite new evidence, this man refuses to help."

"You didn't answer my question."

Arla felt frustrated. She wanted to vent but knew this wasn't the right time or place. At the same time, she was tired of this whole game. "I am the SIO in this case, Ma'am. Yet I have no authority over a crucial suspect in this case. Today, I tried to contact DCS Johnson. But when I couldn't, I had to act."

Deakins said, "You threatened to arrest Mr Bromsgrove. Is that true?"

"If he was anyone else, he would have been arrested by now. I don't have to tell you that, sir."

That shut Deakins up for the moment. Johnson said softly, "How many more times, DCI Baker?"

She was about to retort, but Deakins raised a hand to silence Arla. "There is something relating to this case that has come to our attention."

After a pause he said, "You visit the Cedarbrook Care Home for middle-age children. Is that correct?"

Arla felt a premonition of danger at the sudden change of subject. She frowned. "Why do you ask?"

"Is it true that the first victim – known as Charlene Atkins – tried to contact you on your phone?"

Arla opened her mouth to say something but no words came. Her throat was suddenly dry. That was what Tara had told her. But how did they know?

She hadn't looked back on her call list to see if there was an unknown number. It suddenly struck her that if she did find a number on her phone, she should cross-check it with all the numbers from the phones of the two victims.

"I was told that she might have done, yes."

"And there are CCTV images of her coming to the station, asking to see you?"

"Yes. But I didn't get to meet her. We only realised it when we did a search on our systems with facial recognition software."

"And yet you did not feel it relevant to report this?"

"It was common knowledge, sir. And I wasn't aware that she had come to see me."

Deakins asked, "Did you know Charlene Atkins?"

"No, of course not." Arla's voice was indignant.

"Did you know any of the other victims?"

Arla shook her head. "Am I a suspect now, sir?"

"No one is saying that, DCI Baker. But you must admit, it is strange that you attended a care home that Charlene Atkins frequented, but you never met her. She called you apparently, and then also came to see you, but you don't know about that either."

Arla looked at all three of them in turn. "I did not know this woman. She used a fake identity. However, I believe we are close to finding out who she really was."

Deakins said patiently, "There are CCTV images of you running after a teenage girl outside this care home. What was that about?"

"Am I being monitored now?" Arla's voice was incredulous.

Johnson said, "Can you answer the question please?"

Arla said, "The teenage girl's name is Tara. I was concerned that she was getting mixed up with a gang. I was trying to stop that from happening."

Johnson stared back at her with a stony face. Then he turned to his colleagues and raised his eyebrows.

Arla had enough. Johnson was clearly trying to ingratiate himself with his superiors. She hardened her voice. "Why are you trying to protect Richard Bromsgrove?"

The gasp of surprise was almost audible. Arla stared back at all three of them defiantly. If she wasn't allowed to do her job, they might as well tell her.

In the silence, Arla spoke. "That is what this is about, isn't it? Deflecting suspicion to me so he gets less heat."

Deakins' jawline was firm. "We have legitimate concerns about you. Despite your impressive career record, you are a maverick. These complaints"—he lifted the sheaf of papers from the IPCC—"are proof."

Arla stood up, her chest heaving. She couldn't tolerate this grilling any longer. She knew what she had done, and what the consequences would be. But enough was enough.

"Will that be all?"

Deakins shook his head again, and the three senior officers exchanged a look. Joanne Murphy said, "DCI Baker, my role is to uphold the professionalism of officers of all ranks. I am disappointed by your attitude."

"And I am disappointed by a potential miscarriage of justice. Just because a suspect happens to be the next *Minister* of Justice."

Arla turned to leave but Murphy's voice followed her. "Stop!" She obeyed and turned around.

"As of today, you are relieved from your post as DCI. You are suspended until further notice. You will remain on full pay for the duration of your suspension. Do you understand?"

Arla felt like she had been punched in the gut. It was what she had expected, but even then, a wave of nausea rose inside her. Her chest felt hollow, and a pressure grew behind her eyes, at the back of her throat. The light in the room flickered and fluttered, and she blinked, trying to focus. Deakins' voice followed from far away.

"Surrender your Warrant Card and badge."

Arla unhooked her card and badge, walked to the table, and looked them all in the eye. Only Johnson looked away, an uncomfortable expression on his face. She put her badge on the table, turned and walked out of the room unsteadily.

CHAPTER 59

Bright, watery sunlight spilled into the corridor as Arla walked out. She shut the door behind her. The soft click was deafening, an eruption that travelled up her hand, elbow, shoulders, and reverberated in her head.

She blinked, feeling dizzy again. Part of her mind was moving furiously, trying to fathom what had just happened. But most of it was heavy, like it was waterlogged. She stumbled into the corridor, and completely missed the woman who almost bumped into her, holding a folder to her bosom. Arla apologised and moved away.

She walked to the exit, a need to get away burning inside her. The elevator was rammed with people. She took the stairs, and a welcome solitude greeted her. She went down two flights, her low heels clicking on the cement. A headache was starting at the back of her skull. She rubbed her scalp, but it grew, like hammer blows on her occiput. She held onto the railing and sank down on the stairs, feeling the cold cement on her buttocks as she sat. She cradled her head in her hands. The dizziness persisted, but her eyes stopped shaking after a while. She got up, trembling, and walked down the rest of the stairs.

What was she going to do now? Go back to the station to get her stuff? *Sod it,* she thought. She walked away from the complex of buildings, and the barrier at the gates lifted as a car came through. She walked out of the pedestrian access as the guards stared at her. She walked on the road until she came near Oval tube station.

Taking lungfuls of cold air, she lifted her face up to the sky. It was a brilliant early December blue, a guilt-free, wind-washed, pure expanse. But it gave her no relief. An iron fist curled around her throat, making it difficult for her to breathe. She cleared her throat and felt the headache return.

The tightness in her throat made her cough, and she bent at the waist in a fit of coughing. She coughed until a trail of spit came out of her mouth, and she was almost kneeling on the pavement. She wiped the trail of mucus from her nose and mouth and straightened herself. Commuters gave her strange looks as she boarded the train. As the train burrowed deeper underground, her chest grew tighter, and she succumbed to coughing again.

By the time Tooting Broadway station came around, her throat was raw, and her chest was heaving. Every side of her head was pounding from the headache. She clung onto the black rubber of the escalator's side rail as it rose up. She knew what she needed. The pub opposite the station. She stumbled in, the old Irish labourers and West Indian workers looking up as she swayed at the entrance.

Arla ordered a rum and Coke at the bar and drank it quickly. She downed another, feeling the smooth stuff ease the burn in her throat. Her apartment was close, four streets away. She had four drinks, finishing them quickly. A pleasant numbness spread to her fingertips, dulling the pain.

The junction was busy when she got out of the pub, and she tried her best to walk. The coughing remained, joined by a feeling of nausea.

The sickness rose from the pits of her stomach, as somehow she managed to find her way back. The cold sunlight glinted daggers in her eyes. She scrambled with the key and trampled over the pile of post on the floor. Bile was rising, choking her throat. She tried to run up the stairs but slipped and fell. A moan escaped her lips. On all fours, she climbed up the last few stairs, and crashed inside her apartment. Leaving the door open, she ran to the bathroom and heaved over the toilet.

She sank back against the wall, head spinning, a bitter taste on her tongue. The headache was now like a steam train in her head, threatening to burst out. In the kitchen, she rummaged in the drawers until she found some aspirin. And a bottle of wine in the fridge. It was almost 6pm on her watch. She staggered down the hall and slammed the front door shut.

She shrugged off her coat, and her eyes fell on the photo. She couldn't stop thinking of Nicole all of a sudden, or the tears that suddenly spilled out of her eyes. She opened the drawer and took out the purple amethyst earring, with small golden ringlets arranged in a circle around the stone, and pressed it against her cheek. The cold stone felt sharp. She pressed it until it hurt, then closed her fingers around it. This was her last gift from Nicole. Both of them had a matching pair. Nicole was wearing it the night she left.

The coughing started as soon as she took a sip of wine, almost choking her again. She waited for a while, then sipped some more of the wine. Her forehead felt hot, sweat plastering hair across it.

She thought of her father. Old and bitter, with no friends.

A rain cloud of memories settled on her mind.

Timothy Baker had always been a quiet, reserved man. Maybe the burden of raising two girls as a single parent, helped by his mother, had weighed on him more than she had realised. Arla had never known her mother. Gran Moon, as Nicole and herself had called their grandmother, was the only female parent they had known.

Her father told them their mother had left when they were young. He didn't know if she was alive or how to contact her. For some reason, neither of them believed him. As they grew older, their questions had grown too. What had she looked like? He must have a photo?

He always denied or headed out to the pub when their questions got too much. Gran Moon, the only person the girls trusted, shrugged her shoulders. She didn't know either. When Gran hushed them to sleep at night, Arla used to reach up and twirl Gran's silvery hair.

"Who is my mummy, Gran?"

CHAPTER 60

The old woman used to stroke her cheeks and kiss her. Arla had always been the sensible one. She was feisty, but not as much as Nicole. Her sister had a penchant for trouble and spent more time off school and out of home than anywhere else. Arla was Gran's favourite.

And when she asked Gran about her mother, she could tell by the shadow that fell across Gran's eyes that she was lying.

"Your mummy's gone, sweetheart. Up into the sky, with God. Rest in peace," Gran used to whisper. Then she switched the light off and tiptoed out of the room before Arla could ask anything else.

Then the unthinkable happened. When Arla was eleven, and Nicole fourteen, Gran Moon died. Her father withdrew into his shell, and hit the bottle hard. Whatever semblance of normality their make-believe family had, vanished almost overnight. She remembered her father coming back home at night, drunk and shouting. It became a routine. She lay in bed, pillow over her head, listening to his shouts. Then the footsteps coming upstairs... Nicole got the worst of it, because she answered back. She was angry, like her father was, and she wanted answers, but there weren't any. There was nowhere to go.

The Pinot Grigio's faintly acidic, sour taste filled Arla's mouth. She swallowed in gulps, finishing half the bottle before putting it down with a thud on the counter. She gasped, staring down, her fingers suddenly itching for a cigarette. If Harry was here she could ask for one. Instead, her fingers curled around the top of the bottle again. She put it down after two gulps this time and slid down the kitchen counter to the floor.

That floating sensation, when the pain hit her, hurt her, but it's dull, not pointy and sharp, not drawing fresh blood. Scars she didn't mind. She was covered in them already.

She could hear Nicole and her father swearing at each other as she cowered underneath her blanket. Then the sound of someone being hit, and the door slamming. Glass smashing on the ground. More screams.

Arla remembered the morning after Nicole disappeared. Arla got up and fixed her own breakfast. Her father left early for work, despite staying out the night drinking. Work was his salvation, he had told her in one of his rare sober moments. She prayed for salvation herself, although after Gran Moon died, she never went to church on Sundays anymore. But alone, Arla did pray for Nicole to come back.

It never happened. Instead, the social services came the day after Nicole disappeared, just like Nicole had said they would.

Her father was comatose, snoring on the sofa when the two social service keyworkers turned up. Arla let them in, and they asked her questions, then woke up her dad.

Nicole was gone. Like their mum, she never came back.

Next day, one of the same social workers turned up to see Arla in school. She wrote down everything Arla said, then called the school nurse. They told her to take her clothes off. She had a bruise on her ribs, her back, and two more on her legs. He hadn't meant to push her, Arla said, and he had only done it because he was drunk and trying to open the door. It was true, she told them. Her dad never came into her room at night. He had hit Nicole too, but he had never touched them in *that* way.

He drank, shouted to himself, and then passed out. She had learnt to stay in her room or hide in the cupboard when she was scared.

The next day, the same social workers returned to her home, with a police car. The policemen came inside. Neighbours stood outside their doors, watching. Arla felt ashamed, and hid in her room.

She remembered her father sobbing uncontrollably. It was all a blur. It was best if she lived somewhere else, the social worker said.

"What if my sister comes back?" Arla had asked.

"Your sister has not been found," they said.

"What about my father?"

"He needs help," they said.

Still, Arla had been one of the lucky ones. Her stint at the care home didn't last long. What she saw inside made her skin crawl. The girls went out in groups and came back shit-faced. She never understood where they got the money from. The teachers knew they couldn't stop the older girls. Some even got pregnant, then left. No one bothered with schoolwork, and they made fun of Arla, with her nose in her books. Books were the only thing that made Arla forget about life.

But she couldn't forget about Nicole. In that horrible care home, as girls crept around in the darkness, lifting windows and jumping out, she wondered if her sister had been one of those girls. Her heart used to break then. She wanted to help Nicole. Maybe if she could see her again, they could look after each other.

How, she didn't know. She was only twelve. But she would find a way. If only she could see Nicole again, things would be alright. Nicole had been her best friend. She had taught Arla how to tie her hair into braids, how to do a smooth ponytail with no hair sticking up. She had showed Arla how to keep her hands still when she put nail polish on.

Her fingers curled around the bottle again, and when she lifted it to her lips, she swallowed her saline tears and mucus. Angrily, she swiped at her nose, and rubbed her eyes on her sleeve. She took a long swig, then smashed the bottle down.

In Esher, a leafy suburb of Surrey, a couple became her foster parents. Jill and Austin Meacher. Arla remembered the first time she saw them. They looked so... normal. Husband and wife, standing next to each other. The fact that she could live with them was interesting, but she didn't hold out much hope. Her burning ambition, even then, was to find Nicole. It was a desperation. Only *she* could help Nicole. And between them, they could make their dad better as well. He could stop drinking, and maybe they could live together again.

She told this to Jill, and that she would only live with them if they accepted Nicole as well. When Nicole came back, of course. She would come back, Arla was sure of it.

Most foster children move from one home to another. Arla stayed in the Meacher home for the next eight years of her life and went to university. Jill and Austin had never had children of their own. Arla took up a bedroom in their house and filled an empty space in their hearts.

They came to her graduation. She remembered holding Jill, both of them crying. When she stopped, Austin pointed out a man who was sitting one row behind them.

Timothy Baker looked a lot older, and he had glasses. But it was her dad. Arla wanted him to come over, to give her a hug. But he did nothing. He sat there, looking at her from behind his glasses. He had tears in his eyes, too; he wiped them, then shuffled away, a bent and broken man. That was the last Arla saw of her father until she graduated and joined the police force.

She lifted the bottle again, only to find it was empty. She tossed it to one side. It rolled on the floor and came to a rest against the cabinet. She lurched to her feet. The headache was now numbed with alcohol. Her vision was blurred, like she had spinning around inside a washing machine.

She stumbled to the bedroom. From the mantelpiece, she took the framed photo of the three of them. Of her, standing between Nicole and her dad. Nicole had her hand draped over Arla's shoulder.

She kissed Nicole's face on the cold glass, and fell into the bed, curling up like a discarded foetus. The purple amethyst earring was still in her fist.

CHAPTER 61

From a distance, a sound creeping at the edges of her consciousness. It grew louder, more insistent. Dilated airwaves burst upon her tympanic membrane repeatedly until suddenly she was awake, sitting up in the bed with a start.

That was a bad move. Her head rocked around, splitting into a hundred fragments. She held it together with her hands, wishing the sound would stop. She recognised the source. It was the front door, and it was being banged so hard she could hear the walls of the apartment shaking. Someone was shouting her name.

She was still fully dressed. The earring fell from her hand as she stood. She bent down to pick it up – another mistake. Her brain almost fell into the fireplace. She groaned and, putting the earring in her pocket, stumbled to the door.

"Who is it?" she shouted back, wincing at the noise. It was daylight, but she didn't know the time. It was also cold as hell, her skin pimpling in the frigid air.

The banging stopped. "Harry," said Harry's voice from behind the door.

She looked through the spyglass for good measure then opened the door. She turned and went back to the bedroom, flopping down on the bed. The curtains were drawn, keeping the room dark. Harry switched on the light, and she groaned, curling a hand over her eyes.

"Jesus," said Harry softly. She heard him go out, then come back again. Strong arms cradled her neck, then lifted her up, resting her against raised pillows. Arla didn't have the strength to resist.

"Here. Drink this."

With an effort, she opened her eyes. A glass of water was being held out to her. Harry had a day's worth of stubble and a serious expression. It almost didn't suit him. She wanted to refuse but then saw the look on his face. She took the glass while Harry went up to the window and pulled the curtains aside. A tepid light crept inside, not bothering her headache. She drank as much as she could before she felt sick again. She lay back down.

"I heard," he said. "Then I got your messages."

Arla replied after a while, without opening her eyes. "I messaged you?"

"When?"

"At four in the morning."

"I did?"

"Yes."

She cringed at the thought. What else had she done last night?

Harry said, "Don't worry. Nothing rude. A bit odd, to be honest. Your three texts all said the same thing. Find her."

She stiffened, hoping Harry wouldn't notice it. "Who is in charge of the case now?" A feeble attempt at changing the topic.

"Don't worry about that now." Harry's voice was gentle. He hesitated, and she could sense it without looking. "Who did you want me to find?"

Arla didn't reply. Harry said, "Charlene Atkins?"

She got up, the whole room twisting on its axis like a ship in a storm. When she came back from the loo, Harry was standing against the window, looking down at the street three floors below.

"What did they say?" he asked.

"Not much. My professionalism is not up to scratch." She checked the time. It was 7.30am. She had slept for almost twelve hours.

"They gave you grief about Bromsgrove."

"It's what I expected," Arla said in a weary voice. "Who's the new SIO?"

Harry shook his head. "No one knows. For now, I am heading the investigation and reporting to Johnson."

Arla's lips twitched. "Do I have to take orders from you now?"

"Only if you don't behave," Harry said without smiling. He sighed. "Arla, I…"

She sat down on the bed. Partly because she didn't want to hear it. But then she didn't know what he wanted to say. Maybe that had always been the problem between them, unspoken desires that remained hidden, forming a barrier. Or maybe she was just full of shit, dying of a hangover.

"I don't know what's going on with you. I mean, I know you're intense, but this case seems to have taken over your life. You don't sleep-

"Harry." Her voice rang out harsher than she had intended, and she immediately felt sorry. "It's OK. I'm alright," she followed in a hollow voice. "Tell me what's happening with the case."

"You sure you want to talk about that now?"

Actually, she didn't. She couldn't even move from the bed. Harry said, "How about I get us both some breakfast. Bacon and egg sandwich?"

The thought of food made her tummy rumble and she wondered how long she had been without food. She nodded, and Harry went out the door. In half an hour, he was back with a takeout fry up. Arla smelled the toasted bread, bacon and eggs and realised how ravenous she was.

They sat down at the dining table and tucked in. Arla felt life slowly flowing back into her limbs. She gazed at Harry over the steam from her cup of coffee.

"Now tell me about the case."

Harry slurped his tea and said, "Crichton's brother's apartment was bought by a company. We are pulling up the company records to see what else he owned."

Something stirred at the back of her mind at the mention of Crichton's name. She went to the living room and got her jacket. In her purse she had kept the ripped photo – of Crichton standing in front of a terraced house.

She ran her finger along the jagged edge, feeling the old paper flake and crumble, wondering who the missing person was.

She said, "His brother said his wife was called Katherine something, right?"

"Yes. Katherine Mendonca."

"What did you dig up on her?"

"Portuguese immigrant. Entered this country in the 70s, then held odd jobs. Seems she didn't work most of the time. From her National Insurance and tax records that's all we got. No council tax bills in her name, so not sure where she lived. Didn't join the electoral vote anywhere, so not on the register."

"Dead or alive?"

"Portuguese authorities came back to us last night. Her passport was never seen again. So no word of her."

Arla frowned. Thinking was making her headache worse, but this could be important. "She could know a lot about Crichton. That might make her a target as well. Are we sure she hasn't been eliminated already?"

Harry shook his head slowly. "Nothing in the death register in her name since she entered England."

"And yet, she was Chris Crichton's wife for how long?"

Harry took out his pocket notebook. "Five years. Then they divorced, according to his brother."

Arla went to the bathroom. God, she was a mess. Her hair was now sticky, tangled into knots. She splashed water on her face, taking the remnants of last night's make-up off. She cringed when she thought Harry had seen her like this.

Harry was turning his phone off when she came back to the kitchen. He was leaning against one of the cabinets. "That was Nottingham. They're going into Vincent Bruhn's home tomorrow. I thought it would be good if I could join them."

Arla nodded. She took a few rapid sips of her coffee. "Nice place, Nottingham." She studied Harry.

He narrowed his eyes. "No."

"Come on."

"You've just been suspended, for crying out loud!"

"Doesn't mean I can't travel. I need a break. Might go and see Sherwood Forest."

Harry grimaced. "What are you, Robin Hood of the London Met? No way, José."

She put her cup down on the counter. "Think about this. I go up on my own and just happen to be in the neighbourhood when the SOC guys are finishing up. What harm can it do?"

Harry was silent, watching her. She said, "It's not like Johnson's spoken to them about me. This is an internal matter."

He craned his long neck upwards and twisted his head, making a clicking sound.

"Gross," Arla frowned.

CHAPTER 62

Harry lingered at the door as he was leaving. "Remember the video recorder owner?"

"Alistair Brown? You narrowed him down to some guy in Richmond."

"Yes, him. I called him up. He was acting funny. Didn't want to come down to the station. Then I realised who he was."

"Who?"

"A retired MP. He was a Minister in the 80s, in fact."

Something constricted at the back of Arla's mind. Another MP. "Did he have any links with Bromsgrove?"

"I don't know. Unlikely, as they are from different generations."

"So you're going to meet him, right?"

"Later today."

Harry left, leaving Arla thinking. That video recorder belonged to Alistair Brown, but Charlen Atkins had acquired it, somehow.

There weren't any tapes in it, but it could still have fingerprints and DNA. It was frustrating to think that she couldn't interrogate Brown herself. She considered turning up at his studio but quickly discarded the idea. She would only be making Harry's job harder.

Although she was hung-over, physically she felt better than yesterday. But her mind was in a shadow of its own. Policing had been her life. Without it, she was nothing. She made a decision. She got dressed and went outside, heading for the station. Before she got there, a headline in the *Daily Mirror* grabbed her. She looked closer and her eyes widened. On the bottom half of the front page ran the headline:

Disgraced cop taken off serial killer murder case.

There was even a photo of her, a small, round insert, which thankfully showed very little of her face. She snatched the paper up and read it quickly. The article was a summary of the case and her punching the paedophile after he got free. There was no mention of suspects, or of Bromsgrove's name. *Typical,* she thought. Then she remembered the reporter who had come up to her on the Common. He, too, had known of her past. She paid for the newspaper, anger now seething inside her.

This was a witch-hunt. They were out to hound her, make her a laughing stock. Well, they had picked on the wrong woman. But she would have to play her cards close to her chest. Could she trust Harry? She had worked with him for more than five years. What she knew of him was comforting. She did need some friends.

Newspaper in hand, Arla got off at Clapham Common tube station, and began to walk towards the church. The tall watchtower was visible from a distance, its white, triangular pedestal suddenly bright, catching the sun's glow.

She was walking towards the bandstand, the scene of the first crime, when she stopped. Across the street laden with heavy traffic, she could see the row of terraced mansions on Clapham Common Road. She could also see the derelict building, number 243. It features were clearer in the sunlight.

Her attention was drawn to the spire that rose from the centre of the broken tiles of the roof.

Something about it was familiar, like she had seen it recently. She frowned, staring, then suddenly the realisation hit her like a steam train. She dug her hands inside her coat pocket and found what she wanted.

The photo of Chris Crichton standing in front of the building. The terraced house behind him was partially obstructed by his body. But she could now see the familiar shape of the upper windows. And between them, rising like a twisted chimney, a spire. She compared it several times. It was the same.

Her brain was whirring and clicking all of a sudden. A pathway was opening up, lines were getting connected by firing synapses.

The photo was taken in front of this building.

Arla walked up to the bandstand then walked back towards the boundary of the Common with the A3. She stopped and turned to look at the spectre of the church looming behind her. She traced a straight line from the bandstand to the church, and another to where she was standing. She was near the spot where Vincent was found.

It was a triangle. A body at the bandstand, another where she stood, and the final point... The church.

And each body had been marked with a black triangle. Arla's pulse was surging, and a dread was sinking into the pits of her stomach.

Arla looked at the church, a sudden realisation suffocating her. If she was dealing with a psychopath, then their minds moved in symmetry. They liked order. And this was the perfect example. A triangle of bodies.

That didn't explain Crichton, but he could have been an outlier. It must have been essential to silence him.

In the triangle where she stood now, only one person was left. The vicar.

Arla sprinted for the church.

CHAPTER 63

The harsh December wind tore at her lungs, and her feet sank in the soft grass. Rivulets of sweat ran down her face as he reached the concrete awning. She paused against one of the stone columns, panting. Her phone rang, and she snatched it up.

"Harry, its me."

"Hi. What's up?" Harry asked sharply.

She struggled to control her breathing. "I'm going inside the church to speak to the vicar. How soon can you get here?"

"At the office, so in ten. What's going on?"

"Just get here, quick."

Arla hung up and entered the church. The pews were empty, and the nave was filled with the sweet aroma of burning candles. At the pulpit, she saw a small hooded figure. The nun. Arla approached and the nun looked up. She came down from the pulpit.

"Can I help you?" Her spine was bent at the waist, and her face was wrinkled with age. But her voice was firm. She looked Arla up and down with careful eyes.

"Is Sean Decker around? It's, uh, it's Detective Chief Inspector Arla Baker from Clapham Police Station."

"I have to check his office. Stay here please."

Arla fidgeted while she waited. She heard the door open and saw the figure of Sean Decker appear through it. She breathed a sigh of relief and walked towards the black-robed figure.

"Inspector Baker," the vicar said, his green eyes steady on her. "How pleasant to see you here again."

Arla ignored the irony. They had got off on the wrong foot the last time, and she wasn't here to settle old scores.

"Father Decker..."

"Sean, please."

"Sean, have you seen anything suspicious around here recently?"

His brows creased. "How do you mean?"

"I believe you could be in danger. The killer is operating around here, and his last stop might be the church." Arla explained her thoughts about the triangle. The vicar's face hardened then became concerned.

"This is just your hypothesis, right?"

"He leaves the mark of a triangle on all his bodies. We didn't find it on the old man, but only because the body was badly decomposed. The two bodies on the Common had it."

If Sean Decker was bothered, he didn't show it. "I see. Hence you are concerned about my safety."

"Yes."

"I fear no one but God, Inspector Baker."

"That may be so, Sean. But this man is deranged. He could act at any time, and both you and Sister Meredith would be in danger."

The vicar was unmoved. "There is no mortal danger that worries me, Inspector."

Arla fought her impatience. A thought struck her. "When you spoke to Charlene, did she ever mention Vincent Bruhn? He's our second victim."

He frowned and paused. "No."

"Did you ever meet Vincent?"

His voice was stiff, and his face hardened. "No. Will that be all, Inspector?"

A sense of futility swept through Arla, along with increased suspicion. Sean Decker was acting in similar fashion to when she had asked him about Charlene. Steven Wade and Vincent had been lovers. It was not beyond the realms of reason that Vincent had visited Steven in church.

What was the vicar hiding?

*****

The Keeper stood underneath a tree, hidden from any observer. Behind him, a bank of bushes rose up to shoulder height. He only had to lean forward in order to hide himself. He had followed the Inspector from her home to the Common. He had seen the lanky officer leave her home, and envy had seized him. How dare he! She was marked now. For himself. The triangle would soon be upon her. The trinity of faith, lust and sin. He made the triangle in the air as he watched, breath clouding his eyes.

On the tube Arla had barely noticed him, dressed as he was in casual clothes. She seemed preoccupied. He didn't blame her, given the news that had hit the papers. He wished he could feel sorry for her, but feelings were a blank to the Keeper. Feelings were a curiosity, something he could examine, like a specimen in a cage. He knew what they were, and how they worked even, but he couldn't feel them. This made him feel better about himself. He was superior. Pain, guilt, sadness, these were for weaker beings. A sense of rabid exultation filled him, firing his veins. His mouth opened, and he closed his eyes and breathed out.

She had surprised him by running off to the church. He had been too far away to hear what she said on the phone, but it was clear she was excited. And she was looking at the old house. The house where it all began.

He thought of her with her clothes stripped off. Arousal hardened his organ. The time had come for the female inspector. He had waited long enough. The trinity would soon be complete.

CHAPTER 64

Arla almost bumped into Harry when she came outside. He looked frantic. She looked at him sceptically.

"Easy, tiger," Arla said.

Harry was out of breath. "What was the urgency?"

Arla told him about the location of the bodies, shaped in a triangle. He nodded slowly. "Matches the triangles in the body."

"We need to look into cold cases now. Look for isolated murders, but where the bodies could have been left in a geographical triangle."

"Same MO, right?"

"MOs can change, as you know. Depends what sort of sick mood the killer is in."

"I will look at that later," Harry said. "Guess what I found about the derelict house?"

Arla looked at him expectantly. Harry's eyes were glinting. "There was a PCN issued against it, back in 2000. An unknown person had called to report a crime. That's where it gets weird." PCN – Police Crime Notice.

"How?"

"There is no record of what this crime was. I have looked through old files and didn't find a thing. The PCN was recorded, but no other details."

"So, no one knows what the crime was?"

Harry shook his head. Arla said, "Why didn't this come up on our systems when we checked the property?"

"It was in the Special Branch records. I had to get Johnson to ring up for it."

Arla was deep in thought. She had been right, there was something secretive about the derelict house. It clearly had a history, one that had eluded her time and time again. Special Branch and MI5 records were not readily available to police officers. They were treated as intelligence files, and Arla wondered why this police call in 2000 had been transferred to Special Branch.

Apart from the sense of foreboding, a deep disturbace was rearing up inside her. She had no logical reason to think this could be connected to Nicole. But Nicole had disappeared on this road, close to these houses. Arla needed to get inside, she knew that much.

Then Harry said something which took her breath away. "The folder had another comment on it. The building was once used as a care home. It had a name. Sunrise Care Home."

Arla felt her knees buckle. They were close to a park bench and they sat down. Her voice was strained when she spoke. "A care home?"

So close to where Nicole disappeared? This couldn't be a coincidence, could it?
"Yes."

Arla cradled her head in her hands. Her jaws flexed. Ten years of training as a detective took over. She needed to plan this step by step. She couldn't just barge in there, like she had done last time, even with a warrant. She needed to get a SOC team in there and search the place top to bottom.

She considered Harry's position in all of this.

Arla said, "You know that this will now be flagged up?"

"You mean the database will be alerted I searched for a cold case. That's normal. So what?"

There was a deep frown on Arla's face. "Think about this case, Harry. A potential Minister of Justice is involved, right? And I bet my bottom dollar this care home, which is now the derelict house, is connected." She paused. "We just have to be careful, that's all I'm sayin."

Harry said softly, "I can watch my back, guv. Don't you worry."

Arla collected her thoughts. "When are you going to Nottingham?"

He looked at her guardedly. "In two hours' time. Heading to King's Cross soon."

"Let's head that way then." Arla smiled sweetly, but he turned his face away with a frown.

She got her tickets at the busy counter of London's main train station and walked out onto the huge concourse. A white spider's web of beams spread out like branches of a tree, joining the ceiling. It was packed, but she caught sight of Harry waiting for her. He turned, and she followed him to the station.

Nottingham took three hours to get to, and she dozed off, head against the cold window. Harry was sitting at the other end of the cabin. He shook her by the shoulder when they arrived. She awoke with a start. Her sleep had been deep and dreamless, and it had left her groggy. She followed him outside. For once, it wasn't raining. The slanting ray of the afternoon sun fell on her face, and she turned her head to it. There was no warmth, but it felt good to have some light on her face.

Harry hailed a cab at the station, and they took it to the address near Nottingham University Hospitals City campus. The terraced house was in a residential street three blocks away from the sprawling city complex. There was a white tent outside the house, and roadblocks had been placed at the ends of the road, manned by uniformed officers. Harry showed his ID, and they walked through.

SOC officers had finished their work and packed up for the day. Another uniform let them in. They put on shoe covers and gloves. Arla pointed to the sterile mats that had been placed on the floor and the staircase going up. It was a narrow, thin house, with the staircase not far from the opposite wall. Across the constricted hallway, a kitchen opened up. Before that, a lounge, and then dining room. Arla stepped into the kitchen, noting the simple décor. She opened the cabinets, checked inside the oven, and the now empty fridge. Frustration reared inside her. SOC would have taken most evidence away to the station.

Harry stepped out from the lounge, and they checked the dining room. Apart from table and chair, and a show cabinet with glass shelves, there was nothing. The shelves were empty. A door at the end led out into the garden. Arla pointed to the garden shed. Mats had not been laid on the grass, or the stone slabs that formed a path to the small shed. She couldn't see footprints either. That meant SOC hadn't been as yet.

Arla stepped on the ground slabs and reached the shed. It had one window, and the door was locked.

"Great." Arla hefted the heavy padlock in her hands. She felt for a hairpin. She had picked an old lock in the past with a hairpin, but this one was newer.

"Move," Harry said behind her. "I can't let you do anything. You should know that."

"You're just enjoying giving me orders." Then she looked down and saw the jangle of keys on Harry's hands. She grinned. Good old Harry. He tried several, then the lock clicked. Harry carefully removed the padlock and put it into a plastic bag. The door creaked open. A smell of dust and damp hit their nostrils. Harry stepped in, feeling the walls for a switch. A light sprang to life.

Arla looked around her. A hand-pushed lawnmower stood in one corner. On the wooden shelves there was a toolbox with instruments inside. She examined each one, including a small hammer.. At the base of the shelves, she saw a small box, like one kept in clubs for petty cash. She knelt on the floor and opened it.

She found newspaper clippings, cut out with scissors. Her heart beat faster. She lifted them up to the light and stood. Two of the clippings showed Richard Bromsgrove when he visited Nottingham for a party conference. The rest were of Charlene Atkins' recent murder.

She gave them to Harry then bent back down. At the bottom, under the clippings lay a small piece of paper. One edge of it was torn off. She frowned and picked it up. It was a photo of a young woman, and with some effort, she made out someone's arm around her shoulder. The photo had been ripped down the middle. Arla squinted, the woman looked familiar.

A sudden explosion detonated inside her brain. She felt dizzy. She stood up quickly and felt inside her purse. She retrieved the photo of Crichton in front of the derelict building in Clapham. With trembling fingers, she brought the two torn edges together. It was a perfect fit.

Harry was leaning over her shoulder. She heard him swear softly.

Arla could feel her eyes bulge out. The woman was a younger version of Charlene Atkins. Chris Crichton and Charlene stood close together, beaming out of the photo. They had their arms around each other and were obviously a couple. The building stood behind them.

"The first and last victim, together, in the same photo," Harry whispered.

Arla said, "They were in a relationship. Could she be the wife that Robert Crichton, the brother, told us about?"

"What was her name again?"

"Katherine Mendonca."

Her eyes flickered and contracted. There was something here, but she couldn't put her hand to it. If this was the wife, then Charlene Atkins' real name was Katherine Mendonca.

Arla was trying to the untwist the spaghetti junction in her mind. "We can show Crichton's brother this photo. Then we have her ID."

She opened the door and stepped outside in the cold, sunny air. The back of the house was visible. "But the real question is, why did Vincent have the photo?"

"The other half was in Crichton's old album. Could Vincent have known Crichton?"

Arla said, "Or did Crichton rip off Katherine's photo and keep one half? And Vincent picked up the other."

Harry had stuck his hands deep inside his pockets, and he loomed next to her, breathing through his lips.

"Vincent had been in care homes, right?" Harry nodded.

"Did we find out which ones?"

"Yes, we have a list, but I haven't looked at it yet."

The realisation came to them both at the same time. Arla became animated. "Vincent could have stayed at Sunrise Care. The one that Chris Crichton owned."

Harry pulled out his phone and, one hand in pocket, barked instructions down the line. Harry listend for a while then hung up. His face was flushed.

"Yes, Vincent lived there for 2 years. He left when it shut down."

Excitement clutched inside Arla's guts. Now they were getting somewhere. "Call back base and get hold of Robert Crichton's phone number. Then take a photo of this"—she held up Charlene Atkins and Chris Crichton's torn photo—"and send it to him. See if he can ID Charlene as Katherine Mendonca."

She paced around in the garden as Harry did the needful. He marched up to her eventually, his eyes shining. Without a word, he held up the phone to her eyes. There was a text message from Robert Crichton.

Yes, that's her. Katherine Mendonca.

CHAPTER 65

It was almost 17.00 by the time they were on the train back. The countryside outside was covered in a cloak of darkness, and all Arla could see was the lights of the compartment reflected back on the window pane. The strands of the case were slowly coming together. She wished she could be back at the office but knew that was impossible. Her phone beeped, and she saw a message from Dr Seddon.

How are you? I heard about the suspension. Come and see me. No appointment needed.

She texted him back. *Thank you. At London Bridge?*

Yes. Are you OK?

Coping.

Where are you?

On a train, coming back from Nottingham.

Remember what we talked about. Don't project. Take it easy.

I know.

Maybe a rest is just what you need.

She didn't reply to that. She needed to get on with the case, not sit at home. Not that it was her case any more. But she knew things were finally moving, the mask was slipping from the faces covered in whispers, secrets and blood. *Typical,* Arla fumed. Suspended when she was getting closer to the truth.

Harry appeared, and she put her phone away. He sat down beside her heavily. "Rob just called back. Apart from the Sunrise Care Home, Vincent had also spent some time at another home around the corner. Cedarbrook."

Cedarbrook Care Home.

Arla was leaning forward, a pressure in her forehead trying to force its way out. She held her head in both hands.

Harry frowned, and put his hand on her back. Then he understood. His eyes widened. "Of course, that's the care home you go to. Where Charlene Atkins used to visit as well." He sat back in the seat, thinking.

Arla raised her head. The dizziness and headache were returning, with bruised memories she couldn't hold back. She didn't answer Harry.

Softly, like he was afraid of the answer, he said, "Why do you go there, Arla?"

She couldn't look at him. She remained silent, staring out the window.

After a while, he got up and walked away. She let him go. He walked back to his seat at the end of the compartment. She whispered to herself then got up. As the train shimmied its way down the steel lines, she held on and lowered herself next to Harry. He seemed surprised. She still couldn't look at his face.

After a while she said, "My sister, Nicole, left home one night and never came back. My father was an alcoholic, so I was taken to a foster home. I never heard from Nicole again."

Harry's voice was gentle. "And your mother died, right?"

Arla nodded. That much Harry knew.

They were both silent. Only a few people sprinkled around in the compartment, either dozing or reading. Harry knew better than to interrupt her.

"I filed the case with the police. Social services said girls like her run away all the time. Some come back. Some don't." Arla closed her eyes, and her head sank down. Was this wise? What happened when the wall came down? An evil ocean of despair awaited her, its dark waves unfurling like a serpent's fangs. She could feel it. But she couldn't stop now.

"I went from one police station to another. I blew up old photos of Nicole and put them on lamp-posts. I even wrote to the Mayor, the local MP and the Police Commissioner. I was thirteen years old."

She was thankful for Harry's silence. She pressed on. "That's why I joined the police. I never understood why they couldn't find her. An alive, flesh and blood girl." Arla looked away.

She didn't know how much time had passed. She felt Harry stir next to her. "Is that the girl you look for on the missing persons database?" he asked gently.

She had forgotten that her computer at work might be used by someone else. It had only been two days. Still, she was glad it was just Harry. She nodded, letting out a shaky breath.

"I'm sorry," he whispered. She felt his big hand close over hers. She didn't draw it away. He gave it a squeeze then let go.

She said, "I could never find her. I dug up the old files. I interviewed them at the care home so many times I almost became a member of staff. I knocked on every door on that street. No one had seen her. No one knew.

"You know what's worse?" she said suddenly. "It's the not knowing. If I knew she was dead, I could deal with it and move on. But part of me thinks she's still alive, somewhere..." Arla's face was like a ghost's, skin stretched tight, white, gaunt eyes staring out of hollow sockets.

"I'll help you," Harry said. "Don't do this on your own."

She swallowed and came back from her daydream. She glanced at him. "Thanks but I've been doing it on my own all these years. I doubt anyone can help." She raised her head stiffly. "I need to sit alone."

"OK."

Harry hesitated when he got up. "Who else knows?"

"Johnson. No one else." The thought now filled her with bitterness. In the early days, Johnson had helped her with the enquiries. That was how they had become colleagues. Then he had climbed the ranks and become more of a bureaucrat than a policeman.

She cradled herself on her seat, staring out of the opaque window. Her own face reflected back, a sight she couldn't tolerate. She closed her eyes. She had done it. The wall was dismantled. Then why didn't she feel released? She felt lost now, in the grip of a deep, grim grief she bore like a tumour inside her. The train plunged on, and she let the black waves carry her away.

CHAPTER 66

The Keeper stood behind a pillar in Kings Cross station. The throng of passengers streamed out of the train that had just returned from Nottingham. He held a newspaper in his hands, and he wore his suit. Underneath the suit, he wore a black lycra running outfit. A ski mask was in the backpack slung over his shoulders, along with his hunter's knife. But to any of the hundreds of passengers streaming out of the trains that had just docked, he looked like another office worker waiting for someone who had just arrived at the station.

Then the Keeper saw the tall Detective, and his female partner right next to him. DCI Arla Baker. His heart thudded in expectation, breath warm with adrenaline. A predator's smile crossed his lips.

She was here. Tonight, there would be no escape.

*****

Harry was behind Arla as they came off the station. They stood close together at the taxi rank, watching the cars pull over, loved ones hugging and chatting. Headlights blinked on and off. Despite the busy traffic, Arla felt the need to wrap herself in a cloak of invisibility. A cab approached them finally.

She said, "I'm going home. I'll see you tomorrow."

"Will you be alright?"

"Yes." She was heading for the car, when she turned back and stood on her tiptoes and pecked him on the cheek. Without saying a word, she turned and dived inside the taxi. She glanced at his face through the window. It was a mixture of wonder and regret.

Arla took out her notebook as the minicab hurtled through the endless rows of cars. She wrote down the names of all the suspects in the case. She put questions marks next to Sean Decker and Vincent Wade. Two men she needed to delve into more. She made an arrow on Steven's name and wrote "Document" in large capital letters.

Vincent Bruhn was the victim of a sick mind, but the document could be a reason as well. Or the identity of the person who had the document. She thought back to the newspaper clippings in Vincent's shed. He had kept track of Bromsgrove when he visited Nottingham. Was Vincent planning on seeing him then?

Sean Decker was always defensive when she met him. Could she surprise him by turning up at this time? It was past 20.00. Regardless of what he knew, his life could still be at risk. She made her mind up. She ordered the taxi to drop her off at the Common.

The night was cold and still, and a stream of fog lay stretched across the street lights like a lazy cloud. Arla stood at the railings, looking at the white façade of the church in the mid-distance. She turned around, and across the road lay the derelict building. An ominous presence, always. She turned and walked through the gates inside the Common. The sounds of traffic faded, replaced by the soft clicks of her shoes. Trees reared inky shadows, bare, starving branches reaching down to her like arms. She hurried along the path, her eyes darting from side to side, alert to any sound. The sky was invisible, moonless.

A black shape darted out from the right and she stopped, gasping in fright. It crossed the path in front of her, streaking away. A cat or a fox. She breathed easy. The church wasn't far away now, its lights shining brighter. The cold was covering her face with a mask of numbness. She should have carried a hat.

It took her a while to hear it, but she did eventually. A sound behind her. She stopped walking and listened, her heart beating loud enough to drown any other sound. She turned her head to look behind. Nothing.

She started to walk, and the sound started again. Like a soft padding, creeping up to her. Fear pulsed inside her. Arla stopped, and slowly turned around. Her mouth went dry, and an ice-cold fear seized her spine in a crushing grip. In the darkness, she could make out the shadow of a figure. It was standing very still, watching her. It came closer, and Arla took a step back.

"Who... Who are you?" Arla stuttered.

The height and broad shoulders signified a man. He said nothing. He was dressed in black from head to toe, in what looked like black Lycra. A ski mask hid his face. Arla turned and ran. She felt the man getting closer, and her legs moved like pistons, but she had the wrong shoes on. A scream escaped her lips as he crashed into her, toppling her sideways into the muddy grass. Her face splashed into the cold, wet earth, and she tasted bitterness in her mouth. She tried to spit it out, but her throat closed as she started coughing. She bent an elbow and rammed it into his ribs. His grip was immensely strong, squeezing air out of her lungs. He didn't show any signs of feeling Arla's blow. He grabbed her hair, pulled it back, and Arla cried in pain and wriggled viciously, trying to dislodge him. A blow rocked the side of her face as she felt his wrist slam into her left cheek. An orange glow of pain exploded in her brain, and her head rolled forward, numb. But she still moved, bending at the waist. The mud had made his grip slippery, and she twisted around, rolling onto her back. She lifted her knee and hit him in the groin, and was rewarded with the sound of a grunt. His iron grip loosened, and she tried to squeeze out from under him. With both hands, she gripped his knee and shoved it upwards with all her strength.

The move must have surprised him. His left leg went up, and his right knee slipped on the wet earth. He came off Arla, falling backwards. Arla drew both her legs back and kicked with all her might. She didn't make a good connection, but she still hit him on the shoulder as he tried to get back up. She scrambled, her shoes vying for purchase on the treacherous ground. She got to her feet, slipped and fell to her knees, then got up again.

Panting, she ran as hard as she could, heading for the church. If she could get back on the pathway, she could run faster. Her lungs were on fire, eyes streaming, head pounding. A heavy weight propelled into her from behind, tackling her like a rugby player, arms gripping her midriff. With a scream, Arla went down, arms flailing.

This time, he would not make a mistake. A vicious blow hammered against the side of her head, then another, rocking her from side to side like a rag doll. Her face was shoved deep into the mud, and she choked, unable to breathe. He pulled her up by the neck, swore at her, then punched her across the chin, sending her sprawling back onto the mud.

Stars and shadows played across Arla's eyes. The pain was so strong it blanked out everything else. She could feel herself being pulled up by the scruff of the neck and dragged along the ground. Her vest collar chafed her neck, and she gagged. A guttural, animal sound came from her neck, but her attacker was oblivious. Through watering eyes, she realised he was dragging towards the lights of the church.

It hit her suddenly. He was going to complete the triangle. At the church. She was the final victim. Panic surged through Arla's body. She had to do something before he got closer to the church. She called for him, but he ignored her. His strength was incredible, he was pulling her along with one hand. Arla gasped, lights fading from her eyes. She craned her neck and saw his hand just above her head. Somehow, she made her dead arms move. They came up and grabbed his forearm. She lifted herself, twisted her neck, and her teeth sank into his upper hand. It happened fast, before he could react. All he felt was the sharp pain as Arla bit into his hand and held onto it for dear life.

He screamed in agony and let go, but Arla didn't. She clamped down until she felt the metallic taste of blood, and then rolled away as fast as she could. She was on the ground, and he kicked her in the ribs. She ignored the stab of pain. He was on the ground, holding his hands. The awful ski mask looked up at her.

"You bitch," he said in a low voice. He got up and lunged for her again. He was too quick for her. He got her down, and climbed on her back, his thighs pressing remorselessly on her chest. Arla was face-down, and she felt his fingers encircle her neck. She gagged and tried to shout, but only a whimper emerged. Her hands clawed at her neck, but this time, he wasn't letting go. The fingers pressed tighter, and she felt blood engorge her face. It was impossible to breathe. Darkness swam before her eyes, and lights dimmed. Arla wondered if she was dying. The lights became softer, merging into a black space in her head. Her face rested on mud and broken leaves, and she felt the last breath leaving her chest in a long, slow draw.

As she faded into unconsciousness, she heard a sound. It came again, and this time it was louder. Then there was a light, getting brighter. The fingers on her neck became loose. Arla drew in a deep breath and coughed. Mud and grit caked her lips.

She heard the shout again. "Hey, you!" A man's voice. A flashlight's bright beam danced over her face. A weight lifted off her back, and suddenly she could breathe again, filling her lungs. She coughed, spluttered and raised her head, too weak to move. She saw a black shape run away from her, melting into the trees.

Someone was crouching next to her. A hand went behind her head, and she was gently rolled onto her back. Then strong arms lifted her slowly, to a sitting position. She leaned against a body, feeling its warmth. She saw the blue dial of a phone appear in front of her, and she heard a voice call for a taxi.

The pounding haze in her brain was starting to lift. Weakly, she turned, trying to see who had rescued her.

"Are you alright?" a man's voice said. Arla could only nod weakly.

"Who are you?" In reply, the man shone the flashlight on his face. Arla stared at him for a second, finding his face familiar. Then she recognised and gasped in surprise.

It was Robert Crichton, Chris Crichton's older brother. Whose apartment she had visited in Croydon. But why was he here? Fear was still pusling in her veins. He reached out for her.

"No!" Arla shouted, trying to stand up.

"Hey, hey," Robert said in a soothing voice. "I'm not going to hurt you. Look, do you want to call the police? Here." He gave her his phone and stepped away from her.

Fighting a wave of pain and nausea, Arla lifted herself to standing. She held his phone in her hand and dialled 999. Before she pressed the dial button, she paused. Robert was standing at a respectable distance, watching her.

"Why have you been following me?" Arla asked, her thumb on the green button.

"I wanted to make sure you were safe."

"But why?"

"I think we need to talk."

CHAPTER 67

Robert took off his coat and wrapped it around Arla.

"Do you need a hospital?" he asked as they got closer to the street lights. Arla shook her head.

"Bruised and battered, but nothing that needs stitches."

The taxi arrived, and Arla was glad of the warmth inside. She was still wary of Robert. Inside the cab, she felt for her phone. She sent a text to Harry, who called back immediately. She spoke to him, eyeing Robert. He was looking out of the window.

"I'm coming down, Arla," Harry said. "This information relates to the case, and I have a right to know."

She couldn't deny that.

When she told Robert, he merely shrugged. "I knew your partner would come."

It didn't take long to get to Tooting Broadway. As they walked into her apartment, Arla couldn't make her mind up about what to do with Robert. In the end, her exhausted brain went for the easiest decision. If Robert wanted to harm her, why had he saved her? And even if he had ulterior motives, he was an older man, and Arla could overpower him if needed.

Arla left Robert in the sitting room and got showered and changed. Red welts and bruises covered her chest, face and neck. She felt the angry marks on her neck as she stared at the mirror. The pain was still intense. A nice shade of purple covered both swollen eyes. She looked like a freak. Well, this was no time to worry about appearances. She stepped out of the vapour-filled shower and put clothes on, wincing as she did so.

Robert was still sitting on the sofa, staring at his phone. He looked up as she walked in. His eyes were tired, sunk deep in their hollows. His unshaven jowls sagged downwards. He looked harmless, but, she couldn't trust him completely. She felt relieved that Harry had insisted on coming.

Robert said, "He did a good job on you."

Arla sat down opposite him. "Don't worry about me. Start talking."

Robert stared at the carpet for a while. Arla watched him curiously. Eventually he lifted his eyes, and she was surprised to see a smile on his face. It was tinged with sadness and regret, reflected in his morose eyes.

He spoke in a very quiet voice.

"I knew Katherine Mendonca."

Arla nodded. "She was your sister in law."

"Not for very long. My brother and Katherine got divorced after a few months of being together."

Arla thought of the photo of the couple in front of the care home, now ripped in two.

"Only a few months?"

"Chris, my brother, put Katherine in charge of the Sunrise Care Home. He was busy with his other properties. My brother didn't know what his friends, Bromsgrove and the others, were doing there. But Katherine found out. She called the police down there, but the people who frequented that place...they were too powerful. Well connected."

Realisation was dawning inside Arla's mind. "That's why the police raid was never reported."

"That's right. But the place got shut down as a result. Katherine felt terrible. She distanced herself from my brother, and that's when she and I got close. She was threatened at the time, and she got scared. She separated from Chris and changed her name to Charlene Atkins.

She confided in me, and we became..." The grief on her Robert Crichton's face was immense, like a mountain of granite was pressing down on him.

Arla gave him time. She got up and took out two glasses, splashing dark rum, neat, into both of them. She handed a glass to Robert.

"Thanks." Robert took a sip, grimaced, then took another, longer this time. He gazed vacantly at the wall, like he could see through it into the past.

"We were lovers for many years. But her conscience never let her rest. She harboured terrible secrets about this place. A lot of kids were abused there.

She managed to save some of the children. Vincent Bruhn was one of them."

His next words shook Arla to the core of her being.

"She got to know Nicole Baker when she came to the care home. I am sorry to say that she was being abused there. In the beginning, Katherine didn't know about it. When she did realise, she tried to put a stop to it."

Arla stared at him. "How did you know she was my sister?"

"Because Nicole told Katherine about her family. About you and how she had to go back for you."

"But why was she there?"

Robert lowered his eyes and looked to the floor. He put his drink down on the table. "She was using the place, I mean, she was *being* used for…"

Arla couldn't stop gazing at Robert, and he did everything possible to keep his eyes from hers. Arla clenched her jaws, anger suddenly spasming through her in a raging current.

"She was selling herself? For money?"

Robert coughed. "Like I said, Katherine put a stop to it."

The black weight was lodged against Arla's throat, and she felt tense. "Nicole…what happened to her?"

Robert shook his head ruefully. "I'm sorry. Katherine couldn't find out what happened to Nicole. She just disappeared one night. No one saw her again."

Just like she vanished from my life. Arla rubbed her hands on her jeans.

Robert nodded. "Katherine told Chris as well, but he didn't believe her. That was the final straw. She called the police and split up with Chris. Soon after that, she stared to get the death threats."

Dead dreams and repressed memories floated, moaned around inside Arla's head like old ghosts. She hadn't known the truth all her life, and now…could she believe him? It all made sense, but….

Arla swallowed and asked Robert, "How do I know you're speaking the truth?"

"Katherine gave me something that belonged to your sister. An earring. Nicole had two sets, and always wore one. Katherine discovered the other set when she was cleaning out Nicole's stuff."

Emotions were a cloud inside Arla's soul, suffusing her words with teardrops. She had trouble speaking. "What sort of earring?"

Robert reached inside his coat pocket and took out a small jewellery box. It was cheap, with torn felt lining the inside. He opened the box and handed the earrings to Arla.

It was a set of purple amethyst stone earring, with gold ringlets arranged around it in a circle.

Arla took the box and held it close to her eyes. It was the exact replica of the earrings that she had. Nicole's last gift to her.

The dam burst inside Arla. Twenty years of hurt, and a lifetime of regret broke the stone walls of her heart and flooded out of her eyes.

Arla collapsed on the sofa, fists clenched, head down as warm tears rolled down her cheeks. A pent up grief for a sister she would never see again. Whatever little hope she had left was now extinguished.

But even as the river rushed over her, wide and deep, she knew the story was far from complete.

She staggered up to kitchen counter and grabbed some tissue, wiping her face. She turned to Robert, whose eyebrows were creased in pain, his eyes sad and earnest.

In a broken voice, Arla asked, "How did my sister die?"

CHAPTER 68

"I am sorry, Arla," the broken old man whispered. He stared at the floor, and said, "No one knows what happened to Nicole."

Arla digested this in silence. A conviction was growing inside her. What ever happened to her sister, the clues would be inside the derelict building. The former Sunrise Care Home.

She said, "For all these years, Katherine kept this to herself. Why would she bring it out now?"

Robert was silent for a while, and he seemed uncomfortable. Arla repeated her question.

"Well, she used to help out at Cedarbrook Care Home and the church. She stopped going to the church when she saw Sean Decker as the vicar. She used to see him at the old care home. It brought back bad memories. Then she saw you at the Cedarbrook care home. I guess you look similar to your sister. She didn't know who you were till she got your name and rang the police station."

Arla couldn't breathe. "That's why she came to the station...to see me."

"Yes. She couldn't bear the thought of facing you without being able to tell you what happened to Nicole. So, she faced them."

Arla looked at Robert. "She faced them because she wanted answers?"

"The guilt as well. I watched it eat her alive. She always felt she should have done more for those kids."

"She helped Vincent."

"And she tried to help Nicole. But there were a lot she couldn't." After a pause, Robert said, "She could also blackmail them. I'm not sure if she had a videotape from the care home. But even if she didn't, she could just go to the press to tell her story. That alone, at the time of a by election, would create a media storm."

Arla shook her head in frustration. "That's why they silenced her."

There was a knock at the door, and she went to answer. It was Harry. His face blanched when he saw her. "Oh my God."

Arla didn't resist when he put his arm around her shoulder. Right now, she needed a hug. It didn't matter who it came from, but it was nice that it came from Harry. He drew her in without a word, and she put her arms around his midriff.

"Bad, huh?" he murmured after a while.

"Like you wouldn't belive." She broke off from him, and they walked inside the living room. Arla explained to Harry about Robert, who was still sitting in the same spot.

"He told me everything, Harry," Arla said, once she finished explaining. But questions were still bubbling inside her mind.

She asked Robert, "Who killed Katherine?" The thought of it now made her blood boil, and a sense of futility screamed inside her. Regardless of what Robert was saying, Arla suspected Katherine would've known what happened to Nicole. Or she would have a very good idea.

If only I had known. If only.

Robert shrugged. "I don't know. It could be any of them, I suppose. I know the names of the men Katherine gave me, that's all."

Harry took out his pad. "Can I have them please, just for the record." Robert reeled off the names they knew already: Bromsgrove, Decker, Brown and Percival.

Arla ran a hand through the tangled knot of her hair. "The killer could be any one of them. But the one who tried to kill me was fast, athletic. And of those four…" She looked up at Harry.

Harry said, "Only Sean Decker fits the bill. He's in shape."

Arla nodded, remembering the lifeless, cold stare from Sean Decker's green eyes. A shudder ran through her and then anger. Did Decker kill Katherine?

Robert's confessions had left her in no man's land. The periphery of the jigsaw was taking shape but there was a big hole in the middle.

What happened to Nicole?

Arla opened the box and looked at the earrings again. She took it to her bedroom and put hers next to it. They were exactly the same. It still didn't prove Nicole had given these to Katherine, but the likelihood of this being mere coincidence was very small, Arla knew.

The derelict house. The place was literally calling out to her. She felt it in her bones, a cold, gruesome longing.

She wouldn't know till she went.

She clenched her fists and turned to the two men.

"Harry, can you head to Alistair Brown's house, tonight?"

"What's the rush? Can't it wait till tomorrow?"

"Someone tried to kill me tonight. I reckon the net's closing in. I have a feeling by the time you get to Alistair Brown it might be too late. He could be dead by tomorrow, and the tape gone."

Harry stood, recognising the urgency. "What do you want to do?"

Arla thought quickly. "You head up there. The minute you find something, call me. Robert, please go back home. We can call you if we need anything."

Robert looked uncertain. "Are you sure I can't help?"

"You are best off at home, safe and secure. Harry will give you a lift back." Her voice softened. "And thank you for saving my life tonight."

CHAPTER 69

Tara was standing quietly under the tree when the Mercedes pulled up, idling at the kerb. Loud bass music drummed from inside. A window lowered, and smoke rolled out of dark interior. Tara stepped forward and got inside. He had a hood on today, so she couldn't see his face properly. They drove in silence. She smelled the strong odour of cannabis and took the lit joint from his extended hand. She pulled on it, and the acrid taste made her cough. She rolled the window down quickly. He didn't say anything. After another puff, which she managed to keep in, she gave the joint back to him. She breathed out, exhaling smoke.

She glanced at his hands. His left hand had a deep gash in it. She could see bandage around it.

"What happened?" she asked.

"None of your business," he said. His voice had an edge to it. His head jerked around, checking the mirrors, like he was afraid of being followed. It made Tara paranoid.

"What's going on?" she said. Her head felt light, and her limbs more relaxed. The joint was strong, skunk laced with chemicals. Far more potent than ordinary cannabis.

"Shut up," he snarled. The car went around a bend and screeched to a stop on a side street. He got out and opened her door. He grabbed her hand and pulled her out.

"Hey!" Tara protested. He pushed her against the car and got his face close to hers. She could smell the skunk on his breath. She turned her face away, but he grabbed her and forced her to face him.

"Today is the final test. You pass this, and I make you a partner. Fifty-fifty. You want that?"

"Yes, I do," Tara said, fighting not to show her fear. She hated it when he was like this. A crazed animal. She had to agree to what he said, or he would get violent. She had no choice but to put up with his moods. She had saved up a couple of hundred quid now. She needed at least a grand to take a train and get away from there.

"What do I have to do?" she asked.

"I'll tell you. Just come with me." They walked to the end of the street, and Tara recognised the sprawling Common opposite. They didn't cross the road. They walked down the main avenue of nice houses until they came to one that was derelict. He reached inside his pocket and took out a bunch of keys. Tara stared at the building arching over her. It gave her the creeps. Massive cobweb curtains hung from every corner. The windows were boarded up. The place had a nasty, rotting smell and it made her nose curl up.

"What are we doing here?"

He finally managed to open the door. He pulled her in and shut the door softly, locking it. It was pitch black inside, but he seemed to know his way. He pulled her along by the hand. Tara's eyes were getting used to the dark. Shapes loomed in the darkness, unmoving, silent. They stepped in through a doorway, and she could see a light shining below her. There was a staircase, and he started to descend. Fear crept into her heart.

"Tell me…"

He reached behind and slapped her across the face. "I said, shut up, you stupid bitch. I hear another word from you, it'll be the last one."

Despite the fear, anger flared inside her. "You can't treat me like that."

He grabbed her hair and pushed her down the stairs. Tara screamed and fought, but he pushed her against the rough wall, and slid her down the stairs. They landed in a hallway, where a yellow bulb was burning inside a room. He pulled her in that direction. Tara kicked at him, but he sidestepped, and hit her across the head. Pain exploded inside her skull, making her dizzy. She felt herself being hurled inside a dark room, and a door slammed shut.

*****

The four men met inside the building in Westminster. Alistair Brown, the older statesman, stared at the other three men. He said, "How did it get so bad?"

Sean Decker cleared his throat. "The female copper came to see me again. She's sorted out the triangle." He glared at Alistair Brown. "Now what?"

Brown clenched his jaws. "I'm going to see him. What have you got, Richard?"

Richard looked at his phone. "Someone just checked the police records on the property. We have alerts on it, anytime someone accesses the database."

"Great," Alistair fumed. "Just bloody great."

Tim Percival was watching them. He spoke at length. "I thought you had this, Richard. What was the point of putting you forward for this ministerial crap if you can't pull levers?"

"I *did* pull levers," Richard growled. "Got that bitch suspended. How was I to know she'd carry on, despite giving her badge up?"

Alistair said, "Calm down. Sean and I are heading back to the church. If someone is checking records at this time of the night, I have a feeling something bad is going to happen. We can't wait till tomorrow."

Sean Decker nodded. "We need to guard it."

There was a hint of panic in Richard's voice. "Be careful. We can't have a bloodbath on our hands."

Alistair Brown shook his head. "I'm afraid it's too late for that." His voice was grim. The two men left, leaving Richard and Tim staring at each other.

*****

The Holy Communion Church stood like a shining white beacon in the night's close shroud. Brown and Decker parked in the rear car park and entered through one of the back doors. This exit was guarded by a tall, stout oak door that dated back centuries. It was used by the wealthy patrons of the church in the old days, the ones who could afford the front pews. Decker flicked a switch inside and recoiled in fear. A black shape was standing in the middle of the ancient corridor that led up to the living quarters.

The Keeper raised his head slowly and removed the black shroud he had covered himself in. He smiled at the two men. "Did I scare you?"

Brown stepped in front of Decker. "Let me handle this," he whispered. In a louder voice he said, "You should be guarding the house. Why are you here?"

"I have been at the house. It's all fine. I also have a reward stashed in there now. For my pleasure later on."

Brown paled visibly. He stepped forward. "We spoke about this. With the last three people, we killed them because we had to. Now, the police have their attention focused on us. We can't risk any more…"

The Keeper raised his hand and pointed his finger at Brown. "Your methods. That's what I used. Tell me that is not the right way."

Brown spread his hands. "It is. But there is a time and place. There is a chance that the police might be there even tonight. Who have you got there?"

The Keeper told him.

Brown shook his head. "No way. Let her go immediately. Take her back if you have to. You can do what you want with her later. But for now, we play safe."

The Keeper came forward and stood with his face a few inches from the two men's. Both watched him with worried eyes. The Keeper liked that. He didn't understand what it meant, but experience had taught him it signified fear. And he liked exploiting fear in others.

"Play safe?" he mimicked. Then he smiled. "Safe for who? You taught me to be bold, even when you seduced me, remember?"

Brown put his hands up as if the memories were unpalatable to him. "Please, not now."

"I think now is the best time. After all, I was like her once. You took me under your wing. Gave me lessons. I learnt a lot from you. Now it's this girl's turn. She can be my protégé."

Decker gripped his forehead, and Brown's face turned ashen. "What are you talking about?"

The Keeper raised himself to his full height. Arrogance radiated from him, and he felt limitless, ethereal, like he was floating. Damn right he was the Keeper. Brown might have been his teacher, but he was old now. Useless. He had the power now, and he felt dizzy with it.

"I need someone to pass on my skills. Just like you did with me."

Brown licked his lips. His voice croaked. "You were the right type. Don't you get that? This girl is not the same." His voice changed, and he pleaded.

"Listen, just let it go, at least for tonight."

The Keeper hunched closer, and Brown put an arm on his shoulder.

Brown didn't see the flash of the dagger under the shroud. The sudden, brutal shock as the tip of the blade sliced through his clothes made his eyes bulge in pain, and his mouth opened in a silent scream. Brown looked down disbelievingly at the hilt of the knife protruding from his abdomen. Guttural sounds came from his throat. With a flourish, the Keeper drew the blade out. Blood pulsed from the open wound. Brown staggered back, his face congested and purple, holding his bleeding stomach with both hands.

Decker turned and ran for the door behind him. He wasn't fast enough. The Keeper slid on the floor and tackled his feet. Decker went sprawling. The Keeper jumped on top of him, sitting on his chest.

"No, please, no," Decker begged, his face bone-white, sweat pouring down his forehead. "I'll give you anything you want."

The Keeper raised his eyebrows then frowned. "Why do all of you say that?"

He didn't give Decker a chance to reply. The knife plunged down on Decker's neck, ripping through his trachea, cutting through the interior jugular vein and carotid artery. Blood pulsed in a high arc, smattering the Keeper's face with crimson drops.

He got up and walked over to Brown. He said, "We could have gone on to make many conquests. But you got scared as the stakes rose." He shook his head. "Shame."

He grabbed both men by the collar and pulled them down the corridor. A broad smear of red brushed on the floor, marking their passage. The Keeper entered the nave of the church through the small door. He deposited both bodies on the pulpit. Brown was making small sounds from his mouth, barely audible.

The Keeper knelt before the cross and closed his eyes. His lips murmured in near silence. Then he stood up, and without a second glance at the two bodies, he walked back. As he was nearing the door, the sound of a lock opening stopped him. The shrivelled face of Sister Meredith appeared as she walked along the corridor and stopped abruptly. Her eyes widened with fear when she saw him.

"Who… Who are you?" she quivered.

The Keeper smiled and walked towards her.

CHAPTER 70

Harry turned the engine off, and the street sank back into silence. He looked at the blue dial on his dashboard. 22.30. It was late, and the cold was creeping in through every gap of the BMW, making his hands cold. Or maybe his freezing hands had something to do getting inside Alistair Brown's house. Harry knew he wasn't allowed to do this. But like Arla had said, Brown's life might be in danger. Or he could be a very dangerous man himself. There was no time to get a search warrant. Harry had to do this now.

He got out of the car, and the looming trees of the leafy street in Richmond towered over him. The opulent houses were set back from the road with white picket fences and well-tended front lawns. Security lights flashed on him as he walked past several of them. Richmond was known to be the home of the rich and famous. Harry wondered if some of them were looking out of their windows, wondering who the hell he was.

He got to Alistair Brown's house. There were no security lights. The front was overgrown with weeds, and the handsome, detached Edwardian house was pitch-black dark. No one home. Harry pressed the buzzer. After ten minutes, and four more presses, nothing happened. He walked around to the back. The garden was immense: he could make it out by the light on the back garden of the neighbours. The back entrance was a folded patio door. It was locked. There was a side door as well, with glass panels. That, too, was locked.

Harry took out the collection of keys from his pocket. He fiddled with them, and the fourth key got him lucky. He turned the handle softly, wary of an alarm. No sound came from inside the house. Gingerly, he stepped in. He felt for the flashlight in his pocket. He shut the door and realised he was in a kitchen. The furniture was dated, and the kitchen had a closed smell about it, like the windows hadn't been open in a while. Floorboards creaked under his foot.

He prayed no one was in the house. If they were sleeping, he was going to give them one hell of a surprise. He crept out softly, and found himself in the dining room. He kept the torchlight down, but on the walls, he could see framed pictures of Old Masters, art that had survived for centuries. Alistair Brown must have earned a pretty penny once in his life.

Across the landing, he found three doors. The last of them was not a drawing room like the other two. It was a study, with a table and bookshelves. Harry left the room and tested the stairs. Trying to minimise the creaking, and turning the flashlight off, he went up the stairs slowly. Nothing but inky darkness greeted him. He listened hard. No sounds at all. It was almost unnerving to be in such a large house that was utterly silent. He knew now the place was empty, unless there was someone in the attic. He checked the bedrooms and three bathrooms upstairs. The en suite master bedroom was easily the size of his entire two-bedroom apartment.

He went down the stairs and entered the study at the back. He shut the door and checked for windows. There were none. He swung his light around. On the floor he found an old TV, the type which had an opening at the bottom for a videotape. The table top was empty. He rummaged around in the drawers. Old bills and papers, nothing of any value to him right now.

On the bookshelves, he read the titles. History and classics of literature. Jack Reacher and other action thrillers. He found some crime novels as well. On the bottom shelf, the light fell on a stack of books arranged neatly. Their hardback spines shone in the light. Harry looked around the room further. More books and newspapers stacked on the floors. He felt frustrated. He was looking for something related to the video recorder. Maybe some tapes? So far, he had found nothing. And yet, a sixth sense told him, it was this room that he needed to search in.

He went around the corners, knocking on walls. No hollows, all solid. There was a painting, which he lifted in vain hope. Nothing. He looked at the floor and ripped up the carpet from the ends of the skirting board. He couldn't take off the whole carpet, but the corners of the floor revealed nothing but intact floorboards.

He gritted his teeth and went back to the bookshelf. He ran his flashlight down the titles. Brown obviously enjoyed reading. The long bookshelf took up one whole wall. He got to the bottom shelf near the table, and his eyes fell on the hardcover collection. As they were hardcover, they were better preserved. On an impulse, he picked one up.

It didn't come off the shelf.

Harry crouched and shone the light inside. The books were all... He ran his hand over them, and suddenly his mouth went dry. The stack of books were all one piece. He pushed the whole stack, and it moved back on well-oiled hinges. There was a clicking sound, and the books vanished into a compartment. Inside, his light picked up two videotapes. His pulse quickened. Could these be the videos Brown had recorded?

He took them out and brushed the dust off them. He plugged in the TV, and it worked. He inserted the videotape. There was static, jagged lines, then a grainy image appeared. A teenage girl lay on a sofa. Her vest had been ripped at the front. She appeared to be drowsy or sleeping. Then the figure of a man appeared, and Harry's hair stood on end. A cold, clammy fear scratched at the back of his throat, making him sick. The man was naked. With deliberate, slow steps, he approached the girl.

Harry felt like he had been hit in the gut by a sledgehammer. After a few seconds of watching, he bent down and pressed fast-forward. The old VHS tape whirred slowly, and when he stopped the grainy footage started again. He averted his face, revolted. A rumble of nausea appeared deep inside his gut. He got up, and crashed out of the room, not caring if he made a noise. He ran out of the back, into the garden, and vomited on the grass.

CHAPTER 71

Arla's arms were folded across the table, and her head was cradled on her elbows. She was fast asleep, mouth slightly open. The phone startled her by its loud ring. Irritated, she grabbed it and reduced the sound. It was five to midnight. Harry was calling. She raised her exhausted, swollen head. It felt full of lead, and more than anything else, she wanted to close her eyes.

But Harry wouldn't be calling if he hadn't heard something. She forced her painful eyes open.

"Listen to this," Harry's voice was calm, no trace of tiredness. It made her sit up as well.

"I went inside Alistair Brown's house. He used to be an MP." He paused. "I found the videotapes." Harry's voice had dropped very low.

"What's the matter, Harry?"

He told her. She listened, her mouth open in shock, a pressure pounding in her forehead. They were silent for a long time when Harry finished, listening to each other breathing.

"Arla, are you there?"

"Have you got the tapes, Harry?"

"Yes. I bagged them and left them at the station."

"I need to see them."

"Arla, you know I can't let you do that. There's an active investigation going on." He dropped his voice and became apologetic. "I'm sorry."

Arla was breathing fast, each breath painful. "That video could have been taken in the Sunrise Care Home. Where my sister used to go. Where she was probably abused."

Harry said nothing, and she could tell he was thinking the same thing.

"Oh God," he said eventually. "You don't think that video could have your sister..." his voice trailed off.

"I don't know till I see it." Her voice broke at the end. Could she even see it? Would she cope after she had seen it?

Harry's voice was firm. "Arla." She liked the calm way he spoke her name. "I can't let you do that. Not right now, anyway. Look, with this tape, we can arrest Alistair Brown, and maybe Bromsgrove as well."

"If we live tonight, that is. I have a bad feeling about tonight. Is Robert safe?"

"Yes. I dropped him off and made sure he locked his door." He paused for a while. "This is a big can of worms."

"Only opens from the inside, Harry." Arla said.

He sighed at the other end. Arla thought for a while.

"If you won't let me do look at the tape-"

"I can't, the tapes are in the station already…"

"Then I'm heading down to the derelict house, Harry. Number 243. See you tomorrow." She hung up as he started to protest.

She dressed quickly in a black polo neck and black jeans and tied her hair in a tight ponytail. She put on hiking boots that would grip on wet ground and fingerless gloves. She put her Swiss Army knife in her jeans and stuck a small, five-inch kitchen knife down her sock, after wrapping a mass of cling film around its blade. On her front belt line, she stuck her flashlight, its handle a weapon in its own right.

She took a last look around the apartment, then locked the door and went down the stairs.

CHAPTER 72

When she got off the tube, it was twenty minutes past midnight, and a light drizzle had started. She crossed the empty road and jogged her way to the derelict building. She tried to push the thoughts away from her head. A sixth sense was drawing her towards the place like a magnet: something about it always had, ever since she first laid eyes on it. Whatever she found today, she would have to deal with it. She needed to focus.

As she got close, she saw a tall figure standing outside. She relaxed when she could make out Harry's form. He seemed stiff, too, until he recognised her.

"You dressed as Lara Croft, Tomb Raider?" he asked.

"I'll raid you if you don't watch it."

They crept in through the creaking gate. The large oak door was shut and wouldn't budge when they pushed and prodded. Arla went to the left, Harry right. She found it first. A passage, leading down the side of the house. She whispered his name, and he joined her. She took the lead, stepping into the wet ground stones. The entire edifice was sunk in darkness: not a glimmer of light showed from anywhere. Arla's eyes were now used to the dark. The rain whispered against the secretive bricks, a sibilant murmur of voices that seemed to rise up from the ground. They passed a doorway, and she stopped. The door was locked, but there was a window next to it. She nudged Harry, who casually reached forward and fiddled with the window pane. It was stuck to the sill, but a few hard pulls dislodged it with a crack.

Arla sank to the ground, pulling Harry with her. In the silence, that sound would travel. They stayed down for a minute, then she moved. Harry gave her a lift, and she put her hands on the windowsill and scrambled inside. The flashlight was between her teeth. As her eyes got used to the dark inside, she could make out a basin and commode. A bathroom. She flattened herself against the door and opened it a fraction. The loud creak it made would have given her away, but she didn't have a choice.

She opened the door wider and slipped through quickly, sliding down to the floor. She could feel a very threadbare carpet. She was in a hallway, in what she reckoned was the ground floor. A sweeping staircase went upstairs, and a smaller one led down. A pair of double doors led to the front of the house, and another to the back. She turned the flashlight on, covering the mouth, pointing the beam to the ground.

She let Harry in, opening the rusty sliding lock on the door with some difficulty. His feet creaked on the floorboards, and they both stopped, listening. It was as quiet as a grave, and Arla couldn't imagine someone was here, unless they had walked into a trap. Which was always a possibility.

She pointed down with her hand, and Harry lifted a thumb. Softly, she padded out, testing each floorboard with her feet. Harry took up position where she had been, watching both the entrances.

Arla got to the smaller staircase, which was still wide enough to allow two men. She tested each stair as she went down. The beam of the flashlight was still guarded by her hand over it.

She was in a basement. That much she could tell by the bare concrete walls. But it was big. Two corridors branched off in either direction, and she could make out closed doors. She turned right, and followed the corridor down. She thought about checking the doors, but first she needed to do a recce. After five minutes, she felt a change in the air. The old smell still remained, mixed with an odd, nauseating smell, like that of dead rodents. But the air became cooler, more damp. And softer. She looked down and saw the concrete had given way to black, sodden earth. She lifted her foot, and it came away squelching.

Heart hammering against her ribs, Arla crept forward into the strange chamber. It was a dead end, and the smell was now almost overpowering. She turned the beam around. Four walls. Against one wall, she saw an assortment of spades. She frowned. This wasn't a gardening shed. A thick feeling appeared at the base of her throat, making swallowing difficult. She trained the beam along the ground at the corners.

On the right, at the far end, she saw a mound, then a small depression.

Like earth had been dug up, and not levelled back. She walked up to the mound and put her right foot on it. It was firm. Sweat tricked down her forehead. Her guts were like iron. She took a deep breath, then turned the light down into the depression.

It was uneven ground, and she could see where the spade had been used to level it. She turned and walked to the other side, about ten feet away. She lifted up a spade. The wooden handle was cold, and the iron rusty. She carried it back to the depression. She put the flashlight down on the ground. It cast an eerie glow against the wall.

Arla clenched her teeth and dug the spade into the ground. It took a few goes, but she managed to get it in, and then loosened some earth. She did it again, and again. Sweat poured down her face and heat caked her body. Suddenly, the spade hit something. She felt a chink and stopped. She grabbed the flashlight and shone it down.

She down on her knees and used her hands to brush away the wet earth. Then her eyes bulged, and fear cascaded through her like a blue-white electric bolt, rooting her to the spot. She dropped the light, and clamped her hand over her mouth, falling backwards.

CHAPTER 73

Harry strained his ears to the maximum, head bent. He could hear some soft thuds from below, then they stopped. He wondered what to do. It made more strategic sense for him to stay there in case someone came in. But if Arla was being attacked downstairs... He decided.

He stood up from kneeling, his joints clicking. He was about to move towards the staircase when he saw a shape emerge from it. He relaxed. That must be Arla. He kept his flashlight turned off. The shape stopped coming up the stairs. It had spotted him.

Then he heard a soft whisper. "Harry?"

"Yes," he whispered back.

"Move back," the shape said.

Harry wondered what Arla had seen down there. He shuffled back along the wall. The shape came up into the hallway and stayed bent double. As it got close to Harry, it straightened suddenly, and Harry felt a sickening blow plough into his solar plexus. He bent over, breathless with pain. He didn't have time to react. A mass rushed towards him, hard and metallic. It exploded against his skull, smashing his head against the wall with brutal force. Blood sprouted from his temple, and he slid to the ground, unconscious.

*****

Arla's chest heaved up and down rapidly. The air was cool, but dank and smelly. Nausea had knotted her intestines, and she felt a bitter taste at the back of her mouth. She raised herself and felt for her flashlight. With trembling fingers, she pointed it downwards. The bones of a hand were raised up from the ground, devoid of flesh. It stayed there, hanging mid-air, as if the entire skeleton would suddenly pry itself from the ground and stand up. Gritting her teeth, Arla dug the spade around the sides, heaving up more earth.

The shoulder and ribs came into view. The arm was flexed at the elbow, and she gently lowered it down, fighting the fear that was heaving inside her like a volcano. She pushed the spade further up and excavated around the head. As the spine-chilling, hollow eye sockets appeared, she gasped in fright. Arla was no stranger to dead bodies. But only once had she seen a skeleton in a crime scene.

She steeled herself and dug around. More of the skull appeared, its teeth bared in a macabre, ghastly grin. She stopped and flashed the light beam. Half of the head was showing. As she moved the beam, a glint of something caught her eye. She went back to it. She took out her Swiss Army knife and scraped below the skull. Tiny insects scattered away. She hit something metallic again. Left arm pointing the light, she loosened more of the earth.

It was a round, metallic object, caked in dirt. She picked it up with the knife, and then used her hand to get rid of the dirt. Then she put it down and shone the light on it.

Suddenly, Arla couldn't breathe.

Past and present collided in a fearsome crash, a maelstrom of memories, regrets and sorrow that swept her up in a tidal wave. It carried her to the farthest corner of her soul and smashed her against it. She shattered like a sheet of glass hit by a speeding truck. A cry escaped her lips. She involuted, caved in, disappeared into a black hole at the centre of her being.

The object on the floor was a purple amethyst earring, with gold ringlets arranged in a circle around the central stone.

CHAPTER 74

A searing pain, like a spear, was stabbing into her chest. She brushed away the tears and picked up the earring from the ground. There was no doubt in her mind. It was an exact replica of the earring that Nicole had given her.

Of course, it could all be coincidence. The remains in front of her could be someone else's, and they could have the same earring. But Arla didn't believe in coincidences, and she knew who she had just seen.

She heard the sound before she felt the movement. A soft graze along the ground, like a rat scurrying on the floor. As she turned, the blinding glare of a flashlight struck her like lightning. She tried to stand up but fell back against the wall and lifted her hands up against her eyes.

"So, you found her at last," a gentle voice said. Arla felt a block of ice slide down her spine as she heard the voice. It was familiar.

Through her fingers, she could make out nothing but the intense dazzle of the beam, turning night into day. The voice came from behind the light again. "Your friend upstairs won't be coming down anytime soon."

Harry. Fear pulsed through her. She clenched her teeth. "What have you done to him?"

"Oh, just made sure he's sleeping."

"If anything happens to him..."

The man laughed, and again Arla felt her spine chill into an icicle. Where had she heard that voice before?

"Are you wearing a ski mask this time?" Arla challenged.

The man stopped, then his voice became wistful. "Oh, Arla, if you only knew how much I have wanted to reveal myself to you."

Arla's mouth opened in shock. A space opened beneath her feet, and she felt she was falling through it, an endless black chasm. It wasn't possible. The figure stepped forward, and in the half light, Arla could now see his face.

It was Mark Seddon, the psychiatrist.

He said, "But then again, you know me already, don't you?"

Arla shook her head, unable to speak.

"With you," Mark said, "the trinity will be complete. Just like the last three, who dared to expose us. Well, tried anyway."

Arla was thinking fast. She had to keep him talking. Time had flown, and she wouldn't be surprised if it was two in the morning. Light was a long way away, and if Harry was down, she had no other help.

She said, "You killed all three of them. Charlene, Victor and Chris."

"That's right."

"They found each other, then threatened to expose you. Didn't they?"

"We do have our thinking cap on tonight, don't we?"

Ignoring him, and the way her skin crawled every time he spoke, Arla continued. "You have a ring of child abusers, paedophiles, who abuse children in care homes. You have been doing it for years. No one knows because your members are an exclusive club. Powerful politicians, civil servants, I reckon even senior law enforcement people. That's why Charlene was ignored when she reported the care home to the police."

"You think so?"

"I know it. The game is up, Mark. We have a videotape which shows everything."

Mark was silent, his features hidden in the shadows. Only a portion of his face was illuminated, his body in darkness.

"Crichton's boss is on this as well, isn't he? Did Crichton make the list? Is that why he had to be killed?"

"He knew too much," the man said softly.

Arla asked the question she could not escape. She had to grind the words out between her teeth. "Who killed my sister?"

"You'll never know the truth, Arla," the man said softly. "Don't move."

"Tell me!"

Mark remained motionless. Then it occurred to her. "If Alistair Brown liked taping himself, was it he who…"

Mark's voice became revenrential. "He used to be my master." He changed tone quickly and gave a short laugh. "But the trinity is complete now, and the master has handed it over to me, his discipile. He is gone."

Arla took that as a yes. It was Brown who had killed Nicole. Rage and frustration raised a tsunami inside her, and she kicked out, hitting some loose stones, raising dust. Mark's last words suddenly came back to her. She frowned.

"What do you mean, he's gone?"

"Both him and Sean Decker have gone to meet their maker. I made sure they had."

Arla had been trying to get closer to the spade. She stopped. In a pained voice, she asked, "What?"

"They're dead, Arla. I am now the Keeper, as I always have been. But now, no one speaks above me. I make my own destiny."

Arla had no way of knowing if he spoke the truth, but his calm, matter of fact manner chilled her to the bone.

"Why are you doing this... Mark?"

Mark Seddon smiled and turned the flashlight briefly towards his face. Lit from below, the psychiatrist's face was marked with shadows, looking ghostly.

"We needed each other. I knew that from the start."

"I never needed you," Arla said, stepping forward towards the light.

"Stop!" Mark raised his voice.

"You tried to kill me once. You failed. What makes you think you can succeed this time?" Her voice was loud and mocking.

"Oh, this time, it won't just be you." His voice was confident, and a cold fist of fear sank in her intestines.

"What do you mean?"

CHAPTER 75

His body jerked in response, and he turned the flashlight to the ceiling. The light reflected and lit up the basement chamber. Arla's eyes widened. Held against his chest, was a barely awake Tara, head rolling forward. He pulled on her neck with his elbow, and Tara moaned, her eyes opening.

Arla's chest constricted, expelling air. Mark lifted his right hand, showing her the knife. The long, jagged blade was close to Tara's eyes.

"Let her go," Arla said. "Please." She stepped forward. He moved back, and his feet hit the spades resting on the wall. He didn't have anywhere to go.

"Stop!" he shouted again. "Or she dies before you."

Arla calculated her chances. She still had the small kitchen knife in her sock. Getting it would be a problem, but Mark was also limited in his movements. He held Tara on the right, and with his left hand he grasped the flashlight. There were about five feet between them. He had to let go of either the light or Tara, if Arla attacked.

It was now or never.

"Please," she said, "please." She sank to the floor, covering her face with her hands. Her voice quivered. "I can't take this anymore." The light beam followed her. Arla was resting on one knee, the other folded but toes on the floor. She made a sound like crying, while holding her face.

In a gruff voice, Mark said, "What are you-"

Before he could finish, Arla sprang off the floor, using the leverage her feet had on the ground. She aimed for his right and slammed into Tara, who had seen her coming. Arla grabbed for the right hand holding the knife, pinning it against his chest. That meant she trapped Tara as well, but the teenager had ducked her head already, and her right leg kicked Mark backwards.

He stumbled against the wall, and Tara squeezed free. The flashlight fell from his hands, and the basement was suddenly plunged into darkness.

"Run, Tara!" Arla screamed. Both her hands were pressing on Mark's right hand, but his left hand was free. She felt a stinging blow land to the side of her skull, and an orange-yellow fireball of pain exploded in her eyes. She still pressed on his hand and grappled for the knife. He grabbed her ponytail and bent her hair backwards. She lifted her knee and drove it into his groin. He grunted, and she lifted her right arm to punch him in the face. She pushed his head back, but he rebounded and spun her around. It was her turn to slam against the wall, breath leaving her chest in a cold shock. But her right hand was still encircled around his wrist.

She saw a shadow heading for her, and she ducked, and he screamed as his left fist hit the wall. Arla pushed her feet against the wall and bundled into him. Together, they reeled across the floor. His feet hit the mound of earth, and he toppled backwards, Arla on top of him. The knife nicked her forehead. She felt the sharp tip draw blood.

They crashed on the ground, inches away from the skeleton. Arla was on top. She sat up on his chest, but he reached out an arm and grabbed her neck. She broke free, but in the tussle, her right hand came off the knife. He stabbed, but she had rolled backwards already. She heard him get to his feet. It was pitch black, but she could make out his shape moving around.

She lay very still, controlling her breathing. She reached one hand inside her sock and took out the small knife. He was gasping, and she sensed by his movements he was looking for the flashlight. If he found it, it would be over. His knife was larger, and he was practised in using it.

He came forward towards her, groping blindly. She could hear the knife swishing in the air.

"Come on, Arla," he slurred in a taunting voice. "Don't be shy."

Well, arsehole, you asked for it.

She could make out by the knife's arc it had moved away from her. She lunged like a leopard, catapulting herself into him, knife outstretched. She smashed into his midriff. The six-inch blade pierced through his shirt and buried itself to its hilt between his lower ribs.

He screamed in agony and tried to bring his knife around. But Arla had the advantage of surprise. She withdrew the blade and stabbed him again. She heard him roar with pain and fury, as he collapsed. But she was attached to him still, and his knife came plunging down on her back. She tried to roll off him, and the blade slashed through her polo neck and ripped into the side of her right shoulder. It was a glancing blow, but enough to cause a shearing, vicious pain, the blade cutting into her muscles.

Arla grunted and moved away. Despite the stab wounds, he was light on his feet. He was up quickly, and she felt a stunning blow to the middle of her chest as he kicked her. She recoiled on the ground, and he kicked her again to the head. Her head shook and vibrated in blistering pain, and a flash of light appeared in her eyes. Blows rained down on her, kicks to her head, ribs and legs. She curled herself into a ball, covering her head with her hands.

Suddenly the place brightened with light. The blows stopped. Arla groaned softly and opened her eyes. Every bone in her body was racked with pain, but she could see. His shoes were in front of her, and as she watched, he stepped backwards. He covered his eyes against the light.

Arla scrambled back quickly. Her hands touched something metallic on the floor. It was the spade. She picked it up, wincing as the heavy object hurt her arm.

Tara was holding the light, panting heavily, her face a mask of fright. Mark Seddon was bathed in a white glow. He clutched his chest, and Arla could see blood pouring out between his fingers. She must have hit an artery and punctured his lung.

They stood still for a second or two. Tara and Arla kept stepping backwards. Arla clutched the spade tightly in her hand. With a bellow of rage, Mark Seddon flew at them, knife raised high in the air. He rushed forward, and his fleet slipped on the slick of blood on the floor. He fell forward, sprawling on the ground.

Tara had moved back, but Arla stepped up. She raised the spade as high as she could, and brought it slamming down on Mark's head. The shock of the blow sent jolting vibrations up her arm, and shock waves of pain into her injured right shoulder. Mark made a horrible gurgling sound like something was stuck in his throat. He lifted his head, put his palms flat on the ground, trying to get up. Arla brought the heavy spade down again, the metal hitting the side of Mark's head with a resounding thwack.

"Is this what you used to dig my sister's grave?" she screamed, but her voice was a broken whimper.

Rage pulsed inside her. She lifted the spade again and, this time, changed her grip to bring it down sideways. The slicing metal cut into his head, and the blood sprouted from the scalp. Arla hit him repeatedly, until the spade fell from her exhausted hands. Blood ran down her shoulder wound, dripping down her fingers.

She collapsed on the floor, tears running from her eyes, mucus streaming from her nose and mouth. The rage drained from her system, leaving her deflated. An inconsolable, incalculable grief shrouded her, and sobs wracked her body. Next to her, Mark Seddon's body lay motionless, a rivulet of blood streaming down the congealed mat of his hair.

That was the last thing she saw before her eyes closed and the lights dimmed.

*****

Voices. Strobing, probing lights. Exclamations. Movement. She was moving, dragged, then sat against the wall. Her head rolled back, but someone cradled her neck. From a distance, someone was talking to her. It was a dream.

Her body shook, and the pain came alive. She cried out and tried to move away. That hurt even more. Why was she always in pain? It made her open her eyes. Only they got stuck halfway. Sweat and grit caked her lashes, and the swollen lids were lethargic. But the voices became stronger, and the light brighter.

"Arla?" She recognised the soft voice, and a hand shook her again, gently this time. It was Harry. Through dimmed eyes, she could make out his head was covered in a bandage. She glanced around her. Arla opened her eyes. She felt a soft body next to her and found Tara gaping, relief on her face as. Tears had drawn lines down the teenager's cheeks. Arla reached out, and Tara gripped her hand. They held each other.

A woman wearing a green uniform was bent over Mark's figure on the floor.

Like a supersonic train in a tunnel, it came back to Arla. She shrieked, kicked out with her legs, and recoiled against the wall.

"Hey, hey," Harry's voice was soothing.

Behind them, the basement was a hive of activity. Harry got up, directing white-suited SOC and uniformed officers. Presently, he came back. He sat next to her and ran his hand down her cheek. She clenched her teeth, forcing the tears back into her eyes. Harry moved away, and a man in a green uniform crouched next to her. With a pair of scissors, he cut away the cloth around her shoulders. He squeezed it gently, and Arla cried out again.

"We can suture this here, ma'am. Can you tolerate an injection? Local anaesthetic. It will numb the area, and we can stitch it up."

Arla nodded. The paramedics got busy on her shoulder. They were right about the injection being painful. She could feel the bloody needle slice deep into her muscles. But then she couldn't feel her shoulder at all as they cut and stitched. When the bandage was on, Harry helped her to her feet. Tara still held her other hand, like she was afraid to let go.

Arla stared at the white bandage that looped around Harry's head, and the bright-red blob of blood that stained it.

"Are you OK?" They were the first words she had spoken since she had come to.

"I'm fine. We need to take you to a hospital," Harry said.

Arla glanced to where Nicole's remains lay excavated. SOC officers were taking photos. They had rigged up a tripod, and it was bright. "I can't leave her here," she said, pointing.

"Bandy's here. He will take her to the morgue."

Their eyes met. Harry pointed to the bandage on her shoulder, and the sling her right arm was in. "You need to have some xrays, apparently."

"I'll survive." Arla smiled weakly. "Did you raise the alarm?"

"Tara called the police from a payphone outside," Harry said. Arla squeezed Tara's hand in gratitude. The teenager smiled back.

CHAPTER 76

Detective Superintendent Johnson faced Arla and Harry in his office. They were all sitting, but Arla could read the agitation on his face.

"Oh Jesus," he said, wiping his forehead. He opened his drawer and took out a brown envelope. He slid it across the table to Arla. She accepted it, wincing as her right shoulder hurt whenever she moved. The sling had been refashioned in the hospital, and she could barely move her right arm now.

Harry helped her to open the envelope. Her warrant card and badge were inside. The raised gold badge was embedded in a black leather surface, its soft back flattened and worn with use.

Arla tried not to grin as she clipped her badge back on her belt.

Johnson cleared his throat. "DCI Baker, you are reinstated in your post. You are to resume your full duties as soon as you are able." He looked away, then his eyes flitted from hers to Harry's. "And I belive the department owes you an apology. You were right about Richard Bromsgrove."

Johnson's voice dropped. "Preliminary forensic tests are complete from the body you discovered at the crime scene in 264 Clapham Common Road. The dental records came back, as did the skeletal survey."

Arla knew what the results were already, as Bandy had called her. But she waited nonetheless. Johnson said, "The dental records are of Nicole Baker DOB 16/4/1982. No fractures were noted in the skeletal survey."

"That lays it to rest, I guess," Arla said. "But I want her and Katherine's bodies buried next to each other."

Johnson shrugged. "Robert Crichton is the only next of kin for Katherine. And he doesn't mind."

"I also want the remains to be analysed by a forensic anthropologist."

"Yes, I saw you put in the official request for CAHID in Glasgow University already. I can't see that being an issue either." He hesistated. "But are you sure…"

284

"Yes, I am," Arla said flatly. "If she has any evidence of torture or subtle fractures, I want to know. I've always wanted to know, for the last twenty years."

For a while there was silence, each of them the points of a triangle in whose centre lay the final truth. All of it, finally there.

Johnson shifted his big bulk on the chair. He tapped a piece of paper on the table, whose copy Arla held in her hand. "Are you going to do it now?"

Arla waved the arrest warrant. "You mean this? Yes, of course."

Johnson pursed his lips and nodded. They all stood up. Johnson extended his hand, and Arla shook it. They held each other's eyes.

"Thank you, Arla. I know how much finding Nicole meant to you. I am sorry."

Arla couldn't hold his gaze. She looked away, feeling overwhelmed.

Would she ever be alright? Her heart was broken, and all the pieces would never come together. She would carry on like this, fractured but healing, one of the many walking wounded on the streets of this lonely city. That was life.

She said to Johnson, "That's quite alright, sir."

*****

Harry drove the black BMW, now repaired to its former glory. Two squad cars drove behind them. They pulled up outside the white Edwardian semi-detached house in the leafy suburb of Petersham, near Richmond. Two uniformed officers followed Arla and Harry as they walked down the gravel pathway and up the stairs. Arla rang the bell and waited.

After a while, an attractive woman in her late-forties opened the door. She was dressed in jogging bottoms and a pink full-sleeve top. Behind her, Arla could see the flushed, anxious face of Richard Bromsgrove.

"Can I help you?" the woman asked.

"It's about your husband, ma'am." The woman turned to look behind. His face now red, Bromsgrove stepped forward.

Arla said, "Richard Bromsgrove, I am arresting you on suspicion of being a key member of a paedophile ring that sexually abused children over decades. You are also arrested on charge of murder and of being an accomplice to murder."

She carried on. "You do not have to say anything. But, it may harm your defence if you do not mention when questioned something which you later rely on in court. Anything you do say may be given in evidence."

Mrs Bromsgrove's face went deathly white, and she stared at her husband with unseeing eyes.

*****

The last mourners had gone, apart from Harry, who stood discreetly to one side, under a tree. Katherine Mendonca and Nicole Baker had been laid to rest side by side in Balham Graveyard. It was cold, but luckily the sun was out, and it was dry. Large, white sailboats of clouds moved lazily across a blue sky. Arla sat next to Robert Crichton. Both of them stared at the two graves in front of them.

"What was Katherine like?" Arla asked in a small voice.

Robert said, "Bright, bubbly. She could fill up a room. But she had a dark side too."

He didn't speak for a while, then said softly, "I loved her once."

Arla turned to face him. His voice matched Arla's in quietness, as if he was afraid of disturbing the long departed.

Robert asked, "How about your sister? Nicole, I mean."

Images, still bright in her mind, floated across the blue sky. "Nicole was everything to me. My protector, carer, friend." Arla couldn't say any more. She wore the purple earrings today and reached up to touch them once. Fleetingly, a memory came back, of Nicole holding the earring against her left ear. Arla blinked.

"I'm so sorry," Robert said.

Arla patted his hand. There was no need for words anymore. She didn't know what she felt herself. Maybe one day she would understand. Or maybe she wouldn't.

Robert said, "I hope you forgave me for not telling you everything that night you came to my apartment. I didn't think it was the right time."

"Don't worry. You came through for us in the end. Just glad we are still here."

"Me, too," he said.

Arla sat still, wondering about her life. The past was here, resting in its grave. A closure she had craved her whole life. Tears prickled the back of her eyes. She would never get back what she had lost. Her dreams had died. She would carry the memories like stars in an inky sky, always there when she looked up at night. She would stare at them in silence, and always wonder if it could have been different.

She rubbed her eyes and squeezed Robert's hand. She glanced at Harry, and by the way he was fidgeting, she could tell he was dying for a smoke. He wouldn't smoke in a cemetery, she knew that. She could lean against him as he smoked and feel his never-ending arm drape across her shoulder like a shroud.

She stood up and went to him.

THE END

FROM THE AUTHOR

If you've read this far, I'm hoping you enjoyed this book. I am a self-published author, and I don't have the marketing budget that big publishing houses possess. But I do have you, the person who read this book.

If you could please leave a review on Amazon, Kobo, Nook or Ibooks, it would make my day. Reviews take two minutes of your time, but inform other readers forever.

Many thanks
ML Rose.

WANT TO READ MORE?

THE SECOND BOOK OF THE ARLA BAKER SERIES – THE NIGHT KEEPER - IS OUT NOW ON PRE ORDER!

JUST VISIT AMAZON, KOBO, NOOK, IBOOKS AND SEARCH UNDER ARLA BAKER SERIES.

ACKNOWLEDGEMENT

Writing a book is a solitary task. But before publication, the book goes through several revisions. I have to thank my editor Jessica, at Red Adept Publishing, for her helpful and incisive comments.

My team of beta readers spotted so many typos, and other issues, then wrote to me about them. Particular thanks to Andy Hall, Colin Spencer, Cindy Grow, Robin Campbell, SueDinicola, Ken Lingenfelter, Joan Barczsz, Annette Smith.

To my wife and family, for giving me the time to write.

To Kim, Tanja and the team at Deranged Designers for the covers and images.

Couldn't do it without all of you. There are others, you know who you are. If I have forgotten any names, the fault is mine alone.

Many thanks
ML Rose.

Made in the USA
Middletown, DE
07 August 2023

36322860R00175